"This Southwestern cozy comes with a spicy, Tex-Mex flair. Its delightful characters and clever mystery will have you stomping your boots for more."

—Mary Ellen Hughes, national bestselling
author of *License to Dill*

"Adler's debut sizzles with West Texas flavor and a mystery as satisfying as a plate of fresh tamales. Slip on a pair of cowboy boots, pour yourself a margarita, and kick back to enjoy this Texas-sized delight."

—Annie Knox, national bestselling author of
the Pet Boutique Mysteries

"Rebecca Adler's *Here Today, Gone Tamale* is a much needed addition to the cozy mystery genre. Terrifically tantalizing . . . and as addictive as a bowl of chips and salsa. Settle in for a mystery fiesta you won't soon forget."

—Melissa Bourbon, national bestselling author of
the Magical Dressmaking Mysteries

"What a tasty idea for a new series! In *Here Today, Gone Tamale*, Rebecca Adler merges the warm and vibrant West Texas town of Broken Boot with a clever murder mystery that kept me guessing until the exciting finale. Josie is an engaging hero who must solve the mystery while helping her delightfully quirky family and balancing trays of steaming tamales!"

—Kathy Aarons, national bestselling author of
the Chocolate Covered Mysteries

Here Today,
Gone Tamale

Rebecca Adler

BERKLEY PRIME CRIME, NEW YORK

An imprint of Penguin Random House LLC
375 Hudson Street, New York, New York 10014

HERE TODAY, GONE TAMALE

A Berkley Prime Crime Book / published by arrangement with the author

BERKLEY® PRIME CRIME and the PRIME CRIME design are trademarks of
Penguin Random House LLC.
For more information, visit penguin.com.

ISBN: 978-0-425-27591-7

PUBLISHING HISTORY
Berkley Prime Crime mass-market edition / December 2015

PRINTED IN THE UNITED STATES OF AMERICA

10 9 8 7 6 5 4 3 2 1

Cover illustration by Ben Perini.
Cover Photo: *Limestone background* © by P. Chinnapong/Shutterstock.
Cover design by Judith Lagerman.
Interior text design by Laura K. Corless.

Penguin
Random
House

For my parents and my sons,
James, Seth, and Pierce,
with love

Acknowledgments

I was truly blessed to have the love and support of my friends and family during the writing of this book: Harold Carnley, JoAnn Woodall, Carl Woodall, Chris Carnley, Cathy Hubili, Ryan Woodall, Michelle Woodall, De Springer, Joli Garguilo, Carissa Brown, and Diane Lincoln. Thanks to Pat French and B.L. Brady for their friendship, prayers, exquisite meals, and hospitality. Did I mention the meals? Thanks to Nancy Connally for the tour of Weatherford and the insight on what it's like to be a journalist. And to Sergio Soriano, one of the best storytellers I know, who made the trek to Marfa a delight.

Big thanks to the Cowtown Critiquers—Jen FitzGerald, Clover Autrey, Chrissy Szarek, and Michelle Welsh—for their critiques, brainstorming sessions, and unwavering friendship. Thanks to the members of North Texas RWA for never failing to inspire. And to the mystery and suspense writers who shared with me their expertise and love of the genre: Linda Castillo, Angi Morgan, Melissa Bourbon Ramirez, and Wendy Lyn Watson.

A special shout-out to Molly Cannon, whose humorous stories of Southern romance never fail to amuse and whose friendship led me to this series. And to my former editor, Andie Avila, who entrusted me with this story so dear to her heart. I hope I did you proud. My deepest gratitude to my fearless agent, Kim Lionetti; my editor, Rebecca Brewer; and the excellent staff at Berkley Prime Crime and Penguin Random House who turned this story into a much better book.

Acknowledgments

In the midst of a hectic life filled with demanding deadlines, I find the solitary business of writing both a balm to my soul and a thorn in my side. It soothes, challenges, and often kicks my butt. Without the support of my family, friends, and fellow writers I would still be on chapter one.

Chapter 1

"Josie!" Aunt Linda's high-pitched drawl soared like a heat-seeking missile up the wooden stairs from our restaurant below, through my quaint living room, and into my sweet but tiny bedroom.

There are three things Aunt Linda and Uncle Eddie have in common with tamales: they're unpretentious, comforting, and fattening when consumed in excess.

"Be right there," I bellowed.

"I'll believe it when I see it, monkey."

I groaned, but it was all for show. Long gone were the days of hiding beneath the warm cocoon of my quilts. I was no longer that grieving twelve-year-old orphan, yanked from the concrete glamor of Dallas and plopped into the dust bowl of the West Texas desert. Back then, Aunt Linda forced me to partake in what she knew best, the banality of folding napkins and the comfort of tamales. Now I craved the nostalgic aromas and chaotic chatter that would soothe my eviscerated heart and humiliated pride.

And it was time to boogie downstairs to set up for tonight's festivities before the stink of self-pity started oozing from my pores. I scrunched up my nose at my reflection. "You may not be a waitress, but you can toss plates with the best of them."

My dog, Lenny, barked from the doorway in disbelief, his bright button eyes and long, silky coat trembling with excitement.

"Little man, watch and see." With a sigh, I smoothed the red bandana at my neck and yanked up the neckline of my peasant blouse so as not to inspire a lecture on modesty from the matriarch of our clan, Aunt Linda's mother-in-law, Senora Mari. I tightened my ponytail and turned to my four-legged confidante. "Where is your bandana?"

"Yip." Wagging his shaggy, miniscule tail a million times a minute, Lenny trotted to his doggie bed. The bed's designer had gone to a lot of trouble to create a sophisticated bed for beloved canine companions, and I'm sure in her mind it was a thing of beauty. Unfortunately, it reminded me of a crunchy taco with a golden outside and a brown lumpy cushion. It even emitted the faint fragrance of meaty dog bones and beefsteak with just a hint of flea powder. Lenny nosed around under the cushion until he found his own neckwear, wet from drool.

"You are the smartest Chihuahua in all Broken Boot," I said, tying his bandana so as not to pull his long black-and-white coat. I scratched behind his ears. "Yes, sirree."

I know what you're thinking: *Another Latina with a Chihuahua.*

Ah, but I am Irish, and Lenny is a Jewish Chihuahua, or so his previous owner told me. And how many of those do you come across?

My Irish-American father, Galen Thomas Callahan, had planned on naming me Joseph, but after my petite mother survived the rigors of her first, and last, childbirth, he was devastated to find that a girl's name was needed. It was Aunt Linda's new husband, the young Eddie Martinez, who suggested *Josefina*.

Scooping Lenny into my arms, I headed downstairs into an aromatic cloud of mouthwatering possibilities.

"Don't bring that dog down here," Linda said as she stole him from me only to cradle him in her arms. "You know you don't belong at our *tamalada*," she said in a baby voice reserved for Lenny. "But you are the cutest doggie in all of Texas, so you can stay."

On Monday nights we closed to refuel after a busy weekend of takeout tamales and endless tables of fajitas and enchiladas. Lenny and I would plop on the couch, prop up our feet, and haze the cheesy TV dating shows. Or if we happened to be in the mood to eat dinner at Casa Martinez, otherwise known as the home of Aunt Linda and Uncle Eddie, we would join my family for burgers and brats while we argued over the culinary choices of the contestants on *MasterChef*.

But tonight was special. Milagro, our family's restaurant, was hosting a tamale-making party. Though a *tamalada* was typically a Christmas holiday tradition in our family, a night of sharing stories and reminiscing about the past year's events, this year, the Wild Wild West Festival committee decided to celebrate the arrival of their annual weekend shindig by gathering to make tamales. While partaking of yummy Tex-Mex and margaritas, the committee would also be contributing fodder for the festival's kickoff event, The Broken Boot Tamale Eating Contest, which raised a healthy sum each year for the Big Bend County Children's Home. Our staff could have easily made the tamales on their own, but we were more than happy to oblige the community movers and shakers who served on the committee.

"That dog should be roasted on a spit and fed to the hogs," Senora Mari said, more from habit than any actual aversion to Lenny. Shoot, we didn't even own hogs. She emerged from the restaurant kitchen with her hands on her hips, wearing her usual uniform of a peasant blouse and a red flower in her hair. She had added the apron we gave her for her seventieth birthday that read *Get It Yourself*.

"Hola, abuelita." I ran to give her a kiss on her soft, wrinkled cheek. She wasn't truly my grandmother, but she had invited me to use the endearment. If she was displeased with me, like when Lenny ran into the kitchen to sniff at her ankles and break several health code violations, I was expected to call her Senora Mari—same as her daughter-in-law, Aunt Linda.

"Don't *abuelita* me." She pointed her finger at the trembling dog. "He's not going to get under my feet and trip me up tonight."

"Of course not."

"Of course not." A slim young man with dark expressive eyes stepped from behind Senora Mari.

I tried hard not to grin at his cheekiness. "You do realize you have tonight off, right?" Our newest busboy and fill-in dishwasher, Anthony Ramirez, was a cutie pie of charming efficiency. If our newly laid plans for expansion panned out, he'd soon be promoted to waitstaff. When that happened, his pockets would overflow with tips from our female customers.

"Yes, Miss Josie." Anthony dropped his chin and gazed up at me through his inky lashes. "But with all these people coming tonight, I thought you might need an extra pair of hands."

Linda slung Lenny under her arm and gave Anthony a motherly pat on the back. "Come on." And with a patient smile she started for the office. "You can pick up your paycheck."

As they left the room, Senora Mari raised her eyebrows. "Why didn't she ask me? I could have used the help."

"You're not fooling me." I gave her a smile. "You'd rather die than have anyone help you tonight."

"Humph," she grunted, wiping down the already clean counters.

While her back was turned, I slipped into the office. Amber Rose, my favorite country band, was playing in Odessa in July, and I was in need of someone to take my shift so I could satisfy my craving for their howling blend of Southern rock and Texas blues. It would be the perfect opportunity for our newest employee to gain more experience, if Aunt Linda would agree.

My aunt was planted in her monstrous wooden swivel chair, flipping through one of the many stacks of papers on her desk. "Anthony, I promise," she said, not looking up, "if we get slammed during the festival, I'll give you some tables."

"I'm ready." He cast a glance my way. "Tell her, Miss Josie. I can handle waiting tables."

"Absolutely."

Shooting a look of exasperation my way, Aunt Linda handed Lenny back to me. "He could be the best waiter in Big Bend County, but he doesn't have seniority. And I'm not going to take a shift from Camille. She has mouths to feed."

He fisted his hand, crumpling his paycheck. "My brothers and sisters need me. They couldn't support themselves if they wanted to—they're too young."

Aunt Linda's voice rose. "I'll give you some tables when we bring in more customers.

"If we want to keep our doors open," she continued in a quiet voice, "we'd better pray for a stampede of tourists during the festival."

He looked at me in surprise, and I nodded. We'd tried to keep it quiet, but Milagro was limping along from payday to payday.

After a moment of awkward silence, Anthony relaxed his hand and smoothed out his crumpled paycheck on the edge of the desk. "Thank you, Miss Linda. You treat me fairly. I'm sorry."

My aunt pushed back her swivel chair, stood, and held out her hand. "No hard feelings?"

"No, ma'am."

I flashed a grin at Anthony. "Uh, Aunt Linda," I began in my most beguiling tone of voice, "when I go to Odessa in a few weeks—"

"Absolutely not. Everyone works the week of the Fourth."

My best smile flew out the window with my patience. "Don't worry. I'm not talking about the Fourth of July. And I have an excellent replacement standing right here." I placed my arm around Anthony's shoulders.

In a flash, a "no" formed in her eyes.

I held up a hand. "It's not as if I'm leaving tomorrow." With a nod at Anthony, I headed for the door. "You can think about it while we entertain the committee."

With me leading the way, we filed into the kitchen.

"See you tomorrow night, Senora Mari," Anthony said, slipping his paycheck into his pocket.

"Wait, wait," she called as he reached the back door. With a frown in my direction, she reached into the front of her dress and pulled out a folded bill. "Ask Dayssy to bring me a few jars of pickled okra."

Beaming, he returned to take the fifty from her hand. "How many jars do you need?"

Her brow furrowed. "Ten."

If memory served, we still had nine of the last ten jars Senora Mari had purchased from Anthony's sister.

"*Gracias*, Senora," he said with a nod and a saucy wink.

I waited until the door closed behind him. "I knew you had a heart."

"So I like pickled okra. So what?" she said, shrugging her narrow shoulders.

Lenny whined and tried to wriggle out of my arms. "Be still. You're going to supervise Uncle Eddie while he makes margaritas. Isn't that right?" I scratched him under the neck.

"*Ah, Dios!*" Senora Mari narrowed her eyes to slits, once again the tough-as-nails matriarch. "Put him in his box, we don't have time to dance over his tail all night. You want us to lose our license?"

By box, she meant crate, which I had already hidden in the storage room behind our rustic oak bar. "Say good-bye to the angry lady," I crooned into his ear.

"Yip," Lenny said.

We walked into the other room and, after a quick kiss on his delicate head, I placed him inside his spacious second home and washed my hands.

No one made tamales in our restaurant without the iron-fisted oversight of Senora Mari, otherwise known as Marisol Ramos Martinez, and tonight would be no exception. Delicious, traditional tamales were our specialty. They had a secret ingredient. Lard. We weren't foolish enough to share this secret with others, but everyone who makes real, old-school tamales knows the truth. Real tamales, at least in the Martinez family, are made with pork fat.

Much to Aunt Linda's chagrin.

After years of towing the Martinez traditional line, she taught herself to make healthy tamales with veggies, brown rice, beans, and healthy oils. At home, she even ventured into dessert and fruit tamales. Uncle Eddie and I loved her cooking, even if they didn't fill us up in quite the same way. Once, a few years back, she made the mistake of suggesting we add her healthy recipes to the restaurant menu, for health-conscious tourists. Senora Mari threatened to creep into her bedroom while she slept and pull out every hair on her head. I knew she wouldn't do it and so did my aunt, but sometimes Senora Mari would get that look in her eye, the one that made me think one day the crazy on her side of the family would bust loose. Aunt Linda must have thought so too, for she had yet to ask again, though she often made her healthy and flavorful tamales for the rest of us.

Earlier in the day, Senora Mari had supervised our kitchen staff in assembling and preparing all the precious tamale ingredients: corn masa, succulent pork and beef roasts, roasted chickens with crispy skins, onions, garlic, spices, lard, and our giant steamer, the *tamalader*. I had only to light the ivory pillar candles in the wall alcoves for ambiance and the restaurant staff would be ready to greet our guests with open arms. I sent up a prayer that Senora Mari's Saltillo tile had

completely dried from its recent mopping. The evening would
be an epic fail if the mayor slipped on the wet tile.

In the kitchen, the ladies all laughed, a rare and precious
sound. The cowbell above the front door began to clang,
twenty minutes before our guests were scheduled to arrive.
Their conversation stopped and then continued, and I realized
they trusted me to greet the first guests on my own.

At the entrance, a young couple waited. They were tall and
striking and— Oh, no, my past had come back to haunt me.

"Howdy, Josie."

My heart sank into my socks. "What are you doing here?"
He was no longer Ryan Prescott, my college boyfriend, study
partner, and French-kissing instructor, yet he was still mighty
cute in an all-American way. Years had passed, but his blond
hair was still thick and curly. Now he herded football players
over at West Texas University, and by the look of things he
still worked out as well. Guess his BS degree in physical
fitness had come in handy after all.

I hadn't seen him up close and personal since I'd made a
surprise visit home and barged into his engagement party at
Milagro three years earlier. It must be something in the water,
because Ryan never made it to the church with his adoring
dental hygienist, just as my ex-fiancé, Brooks, left me with
fuchsia pew bows and matching thank-you notes.

"Eddie said you were shorthanded and asked if I'd fill in
and tend bar."

Everyone enjoyed a margarita or a glass of wine as part of
the festivities. It made the *tamalada* more fun. Strange, Uncle
Eddie hadn't mentioned a conflict to me, but I hadn't seen
neither hide nor hair of him since breakfast.

Ryan turned to the woman by his side—the willowy, blond
woman by his side. "I think you know Hillary."

Who didn't know Broken Boot's very own beauty queen?
Start the drum roll. It was Hillary Sloan Rawlings: the former
Miss West Texas University, Miss Texas, and third runner-up
to Miss America.

She lunged into my personal space, giving me an air kiss on my cheek before I knew what hit me. "Josie! You are as cute as ever."

Engulfed in the aroma of Chanel and hair spray, I struggled to speak as memories of our college days rolled through my mind. "Why, how are *you*? I didn't know you were in town." This was not quite true, as a little bird—my aunt—had told me Hillary was teaching English and journalism at the college.

Ryan reached out to give me a hug, but after a quick glance at Hillary he dropped his arms. "Eddie told me you were home. You okay?" His face was open, his voice sincere.

Hillary's wide eyes gleamed even as her mouth formed a moue of displeasure. "What happened?" she asked, cocking her head to one side. "Things didn't work out at the *Austin Gazette*?" By this time, everyone in Broken Boot had heard about my recent layoff and messy breakup.

What was the big deal? I couldn't be the only reporter to mistake two innocent Slovakian brothers for jewelry thieves? To top things off, a week later, the man I thought I loved, the man who argued over every detail of our upcoming nuptials— from the color of the bridesmaids' dresses to the satin ribbons on the church pews—unfriended me on Facebook, changed his status to single, and flew to Australia to see the Great Barrier Reef.

"Hillary." Ryan gave her a look somewhere between surprise and disappointment.

Two years ago, Hillary and I had both applied for the coveted local news reporter position at the *Gazette*, and I won. Guess she figured she had the right to crow.

She smiled and tucked her chin. "I'm playing." She flicked her shoulder-length hair from her neck. "We go way back. Right, Josie?"

Way back to me stepping in to save the college newspaper by writing her articles in addition to my own. I wrote my butt off and barely managed to keep my scholarships and shifts at the restaurant while Hillary *managed* to make it to Atlantic City.

Ryan gave me a nod and a crooked smile. "Where should she report for duty?"

"Aunt Linda and Senora Mari are in the kitchen." I didn't remember Elaine Burnett, the committee chairperson, mentioning that Hillary was putting in an appearance, but go figure. Hillary was big news and the festival needed big publicity.

Ryan tried to lead the svelte woman through the swinging doors, but she planted her pink and turquoise cowboy boots on the floor and refused to budge. Before my eyes, her countenance changed from spite to remorse. "Josie, I want to thank you. If the *Gazette* had chosen me instead of you, I would never have finished my master's, found this fabulous position at West Texas, or met Ryan." She tilted her expensive highlights toward his shoulder, her gaze level and clear of malice.

And the Oscar goes to . . .

The football coach beamed with pride at the homecoming queen's performance. He raised his eyebrows at me, demanding reciprocation.

"You're welcome?" I shrugged. It sounded like a bunch of hooey to me, but there was Ryan, still watching me with those puppy dog eyes, hoping us girls would be fast friends. "Congratulations," I offered. "May you enjoy all the success you've earned."

"Thanks," she said. She looped her arm through his, and they strolled off to the kitchen.

Some people catch all the breaks, and the rest of us eat too many tamales.

Next to arrive was our dedicated committee leader, Elaine Burnett, owner of Elaine's Pies, where the locals dropped in for homemade desserts, including empanadas, savory pies, and a bit of gossip. She was the ultimate festival committee chairperson. Well-mannered and pleasant, she and her daughters, Melanie and Suellen, handled the *tamalada* invites and

reminder phone calls to the other committee members. Even
though she was small in stature, she possessed the Southern
knack of asking in such a way that none of them dared to
refuse. They knew, as I did, one should try to stay on Elaine's
good side for she enjoyed paddling her fingers in several local
pies, like the town council, school board, and chamber of
commerce.

"*Buenas noches*, y'all," Elaine called out as she and her
daughters entered, carrying a white sheet cake decorated with
giant blue roses and the words *Happy Tamalada*. In spite of
their confusing decision to bring cake to a tamale party,
Elaine's daughters were no slouches.

"Melanie, don't drop the dang thing," mousy-haired Suellen chided as her sister stopped abruptly to wrangle the strap
of her Coach bag onto her shoulder. Suellen ran Elaine's Pies
now that her mother had retired to play with her grandchildren
while Melanie, the source of those little blessings, displayed
her Southwest-flavored paintings at her own gallery, Where
the Sun Sets.

"Welcome," I said, holding open one of the swinging doors
to the kitchen. "Right in here."

"I don't know why we both had to come," Suellen murmured under her breath as they proceeded. "She knows I can't
stand tamales." To quote Katharine Hepburn, Elaine's oldest
was all elbows and knees. She was stretched tall and thin,
and I blamed it on working long hours at the pie shop with
little time for romantic interludes. Melanie ignored Suellen
and presented her cake for all to see. "I thought we could use
something sweet as a reward for all the hard work we're going
to put in." Elaine's youngest daughter was Texas tall and tuned
tighter than piano wire. Her hair was cut in a glossy, chic
pageboy with retro bangs, as if she'd just walked out of a
Manhattan salon.

"*¡Ay!* What's that?" Senora Mari asked, wrinkling her nose
as if she smelled a dirty diaper.

My aunt laughed. "Don't pay her any mind. It looks positively yummy. Y'all are too thoughtful." Her generous smile went a long way toward smoothing away her mother-in-law's bluntness. "Bring it right over here." Aunt Linda opened the large commercial refrigerator and indicated an empty shelf.

I prayed Lenny had gone to sleep. All it would take would be one yip and catastrophe would strike, but leaving him upstairs would have resulted in canine wailing. A banshee had nothing on the six-pound canine. How would Elaine's clan react? Would they believe that Lenny had never been near the kitchen or the food? If he made an appearance, the committee members might find it hard to believe the setup was sanitary and freak out.

With a slight hesitation, I asked. "How are those grand-kids?" Two energetic boys, with Texas-y names I could never remember. Were they Chase and Trace or Coy and Roy?

Elaine piped right up, "Wonderful! Smart as a whip, the both of 'em." With a graceful movement, she smoothed her teased, white curls with a pale, manicured hand. "The question is, how are you?" She turned to my aunt with a sympathetic shake of her head. "Linda, you must be worried sick."

"Josie's fine." My aunt drew me to her side for a quick, one-armed hug. "You're ready to skedaddle out of here, aren't you?"

Well, no. I'd only been home for three months. The slower pace of Broken Boot along with the warm acceptance of my family and neighbors all served as solace to my feelings of rejection and disappointment. Aunt Linda and Uncle Eddie didn't worry I'd get rusty out here on the edge of the Chihua-huan Desert. If they had tried to push me back into the wide world beyond Broken Boot, I would've dug in my heels. Instead they plied me with work and the mouthwatering comfort food I craved.

Like I said, my aunt and uncle can be fattening.

I smiled. "Time heals everything, so they say." No need to have a pity party in front of company.

Elaine cocked her head in a dovelike movement and pursed her lips. "No, not quite."

On the heels of her weighty pronouncement, I changed the subject. "I'm submitting to the *Bugle*." Broken Boot's humble weekly had yet to accept one of my articles. I'd tried a community piece about the Spring Break Chili Cook-off at Bubba's BBQ, but the editor said it lacked spice. With an attempt at something more intellectual, I followed with a piece on the Texas drought. He said it was too dry and never cracked a smile.

"But you have your family," she continued with a smile for Melanie and Suellen. Her sympathetic gaze turned to Aunt Linda, Senora Mari, and then me. "Family, my dear, is everything."

In the next few minutes, the rest of the committee arrived and eagerly donned white Milagro aprons. They were a friendly bunch, mostly local business owners, which led me to believe they were wholeheartedly invested in the success of this year's tourist season. There was also a pastor, school principal, and PTO president in the bunch, if I had to judge from their perfect haircuts and hearty handshakes.

Elaine must have given strict orders for one and all to appear in Wild Wild West Festival attire, for there were enough folks wearing plaid shirts, cowboy boots, and blue jeans to provide extras for the next gun-toting, two-stepping, Texas-based Western. Come to think of it, Mayor Cogburn was likely to blame. According to the *Bugle*, he'd badgered the town council on a monthly basis to pay for a huge billboard on the highway which read, *Welcome to Broken Boot, the Hollywood of Texas*.

With the air of a military drill sergeant, Senora Mari clapped her hands. "*¡Vamanos!* Let's get started."

"But we're missing at least four people," Elaine said, glancing at her watch.

The drill sergeant frowned. "We start without them." She

waved her right hand in dismissal. "Everyone washed their hands, *sí*? You listen, I give instructions."

"That's my cue to salt some glasses," Ryan whispered. He gave Hillary a peck, on the lips, and I thought Senora Mari was going to blow a gasket. Her face turned bright red, and when the coach turned to leave she stared at me with raised eyebrows.

"Let's wash up," I spun to the sink and began to lather up with the anti-bacterial soap before anyone noticed her disapproval. After washing their hands, everyone listened politely as the older woman issued explicit instructions in a no-nonsense tone. The ground masa would be carefully blended, the tasty roasted chicken pulled exactly so, and the succulent meat chopped to the correct size and texture. By the seriousness of her expression, everyone knew she didn't suffer fools easily, and they listened intently, as if their one hope of leaving in a timely manner depended on pleasing the four foot eleven tyrant before them. Only Suellen Burnett dared to roll her eyes.

"I'll make sure Ryan has everything he needs," I said, making my escape.

I found him behind the bar, slicing limes and humming a hip hop song I'd heard on the radio. "I didn't realize you were a Drake fan."

He laughed and the corners of his eyes crinkled in that way that always made me feel so clever and amusing.

"Come on, player, I'll help you set up."

"Nah, I got this," he said and gave me his crooked smile. "I've filled in plenty of times." He stared at me with his dark blue eyes and inexplicably a few tiny butterflies swirled in my stomach. I frowned, reminding my heart it was a glacier, impervious to all male charm.

Wasn't it a man who'd forced me to un-invite one hundred wedding guests?

"Make yourself at home." I had plenty of things to do, like wrap silverware, double-check condiments, or find the breaker box and flashlight in case the AC unit blew a fuse again. "Where's Uncle Eddie? Come on, spill it."

My uncle liked to watch game film with Ryan while bouncing around ideas for lineups and upcoming strategies. You could say Uncle Eddie had played more than a little football in his day. During his freshman year, the NCAA had named him Rookie of the Year in Division III football, an unprecedented honor for a West Texas University athlete.

Ryan shrugged his straight shoulders out of his navy suit coat and hung it in the storage closet. "Two Boots, where else?"

Uncle Eddie and Aunt Linda were high school sweethearts who had married young. About eighteen years ago, they took over an old barn, named it Two Boots, and transformed it into the town dance hall, where every Friday and Saturday locals and tourists danced to the tunes of some of Texas's best country and rock musicians. On Mondays, Eddie usually completed his liquor and supply orders by five o'clock. If this were a typical fall day, he would come home early and camp out in the den for his Monday Night Football fix, away from all the chatter over whose culinary masterpiece was going to take the prize.

Lenny barked for attention and I nearly jumped out of my skin. "Shush!"

"Lenster!" Ryan said in a stage whisper as he bent down to squeeze his hands between the crate bars, the better to scratch behind the excited dog's ears.

"You don't mind if he's your barback tonight?"

"He's not going to bark, is he?" Ryan rose to his full height, six feet and change. "Wouldn't he be happier upstairs where he can run around?"

"If I leave him upstairs alone, he barks until he's hoarse or we all go crazy. Down here in his kennel, he's quiet as a white-tailed deer."

Lenny yipped in agreement.

I bent down and unfolded an old throw blanket from the

back of the kennel and draped it over the entire thing so Lenny
would go to sleep. "Okay, Lenster, it's naptime for you. Don't
say I didn't warn you."

Behind the bar, Ryan washed his hands and dried them on
a clean towel. "Kennel it is."

Ignoring one last butterfly in my belly, I grabbed a stack
of bar towels from the supply closet and carried them over.
"How are things at the college?" I wanted to ask why the
hygienist had broken off their engagement, but I didn't know
where to start.

He turned around to open the mini fridge behind the bar.
"Same old, same old. Off-season training, lifting, gearing up
for two a days."

That was what I didn't miss about Ryan, all his football
talk. "Glad to hear it." I turned away. Obviously, he wasn't
waiting for me to say something about his ex-fiancée breaking
up with him. Guys didn't do that kind of thing. Exhibit A:
Hillary.

"I'm sorry that jerk left you at the altar," he murmured.

Or maybe they did. Tears threatened, but I bit the inside
of my cheek. The pain saved me from showing my weak
underbelly. "Yeah. Thanks." I racked my brain for something
that wasn't too pathetic to say. "Life sucks, right?"

He lined up the lemons and limes across the cutting board,
and then stared at me again as if he were trying to communicate telepathically. "You deserve better."

My stomach did a slow flip-flop. That guy who bought me
three corsages for our spring formal during our senior year
at UT, so I could choose my favorite, was still in there somewhere and standing right in front of me. "Don't we all?"

On a burst of energy, Aunt Linda sailed in from the kitchen.
"Any sign of the mayor and his wife? It's only fifteen minutes
to seven, but you know Senora Mari. We're off to the races."
When Linda Callahan Martinez entered a room, people took
notice. Beautiful and slender, with chestnut hair and flawless
skin, she often passed for my older and more captivating sis-

ter. Ryan started slicing and dicing like a food processor. Was he trying to impress her with his culinary skill or had he learned that her beauty came with an Irish temper?

I expected the busboy for the evening to transport the drinks from the bar to the thirsty tamale makers, but he was nowhere to be seen. Probably smoking in the alley. "I'll go find Ivan."

My aunt followed closely on my heels as we entered the kitchen. "Ryan's looking good, right?" she whispered.

I shot her a sharp glance. "You knew he was coming and didn't tell me."

She shrugged. "It's only Ryan. No big deal." A smile played about her mouth as she made a beeline for Suellen, who was struggling to pull the cooked chicken from the bone. The others appeared to have things well in hand. Hillary stood at Senora Mari's shoulder, watching as she checked the corn husks. After soaking for two hours, they would be soft and malleable, ready to embrace the flavorsome mix of corn masa and meat.

With a slam of my hand against the push bar, I stepped into the alley and was slapped upside the head by the cloying smell of greasy Dumpster. "Ivan, come on." Instead of catching a teenager throwing his cigarette butt into the weedy gravel, I caught Mayor Cogburn and his wife in a heated embrace. It was like watching cowboy Woody and his cowgirl sidekick make out. I was horrified and riveted at the same time.

The mayor released his wife with such speed that she lost her footing and only a quick hand to the wall kept her from falling on the sparkly pockets of her too-tight jeans.

"Are you all right?" I asked.

With a glance of warning at his wife, he straightened his bolo tie. "We didn't want to arrive too early," he said, polite as a poker, unaware his wife had left coral lip prints on the side of his mouth.

I had no idea what to say or where to look. Mortified, I blurted, "Great outfits."

She started to smile, but then realized her leather vest was hanging off one shoulder. If looks could kill, hers would have skewered my gizzard to the doorframe. She thrust her arm back into place. "Why don't you go inside and fold napkins or something?" With a flounce, she dug out a small mirror and inspected her makeup.

Dutch and Felicia Cogburn frequented Milagro on Friday nights. He never left without making a suggestion on how to improve our tamales, and she made sure to complain about the temperature of the air, water, coffee, and food—all too cold, so it was odd to see her so hot and bothered.

It wasn't every day I walked outside to find two people making out in our alley, especially not local dignitaries of a mature age. My face burning, I tried to keep it light. "I'm sorry if I, uh, interrupted. You're more than welcome to come inside . . . when you're ready. We started early."

He shoved his hands in his pockets, drew back his expensive shoe leather, and kicked an abandoned soda can with a loud thwack. "Nah, you didn't interrupt nothing much."

"You can say that again," Felicia muttered, withdrawing a tissue from her handbag. "We'll enter through the front door if it's all the same to you."

"You can enter here," I said with a plastic smile, "or walk all the way around." I shrugged. "Your choice."

Mrs. Mayor spoke up, "Why don't you go back inside and check on your other guests?" In other words, *get lost.*

"No problemo." They could stay outside and bark like dogs for all I cared.

None of the gossiping chatterers in the kitchen noticed me as I made my way through the fragrant aroma of onions, garlic, and eye-watering peppers and out the swinging doors into the dining room, grateful to leave the Cogburns behind me.

Chapter 2

🌶🌶🌶🌶🌶🌶🌶🌶🌶🌶🌶🌶🌶🌶🌶🌶🌶🌶🌶🌶🌶🌶🌶

Five minutes later, the cowbell clanged again, and the mayor and his wife entered hand in hand. "Evening, folks." They joined us in the kitchen, the pinnacle of marital bliss.

At their appearance, Hillary stopped texting and shoved her phone into the pocket of her ripped jeans. Funny, all it took was an appearance by the town's power couple for her to perk up and remember how to act right.

Senora Mari stepped forward with two Milagro aprons. "Glad you could make it."

With a quizzical glance, the mayor retrieved them. He placed one around his neck and one on his wife.

"Would anyone like a margarita? Or a glass of wine?" Aunt Linda asked, raising her hand. "We've got frozen or on the rocks, salt or no salt?"

A dozen hands went up.

"Josie's going to come by and take your orders so there's no need to take a break just yet."

Suellen Burnett lifted her fingers from a bowl of shredded

chicken. "I'll take a rum and coke," she said with a grimace. Surprisingly, she didn't complain about her greasy task and went right back to tossing chicken bones into a nearby pan.

The kitchen doors burst open. "I hear we're having a party!" A statuesque wild woman stood in the doorway with her arms out wide and an ear-to-ear grin on her round chubby face.

"We are, now you're here," I said, and I meant it. Now that Dixie Honeycutt, well-known artist, hellion, and pain in the establishment's backside, had arrived, things would liven up a bit.

"Aren't you going to save the rum for the pirates, hey, Suellen?" she chortled, clapping the younger woman on the back. Judging by her speech and the state of her clothing, Dixie had started her own party earlier than the rest of us.

One never knew if Dixie was going to show or not when it came to the WWF committee events, but knowing her as I did, I wouldn't put it past her to show up a bit drunk simply to shock those in charge. She wore her usual attire, hippie chic straight from Haight-Ashbury circa 1967. Like dozens of musicians and artists of her generation, she'd migrated to the stark beauty of the Chihuahuan Desert and its austere twin, the Chisos Mountains, searching for inspiration. Where others had found unforgiving heat and monotony, Dixie had shed her urban roots like a rattler shedding its skin, finding success using rocks and precious gems to create her own handcrafted jewelry.

She whipped around to greet the rest of us and tripped over her floor-length, tie-dyed skirt.

I lunged to her side. "Dixie," I said, grabbing her arm and scooping her cloth bag from the ground. "Let me help you." Whoa, someone had been tipping the grain alcohol. When you work at a dance hall, you know what whiskey smells like on someone's breath and oozing out their pores.

"Hey, go easy," she said, pulling away from me to rub her upper left arm. "I'm a bit tender right there today."

"Making a grand entrance as usual, I see," Mayor Cogburn gave her a droll smile as he rolled up his sleeves.

"Only way to fly," she said, her chest rising and falling as she tried to catch her breath. She dug under the hem of her tank top and adjusted the waistband of her skirt. Flinging her long white braid over her shoulders, she quipped, "I'm fine. Thanks for asking." Back in the early seventies you might have called Dixie a flower child, but in the past forty years or so she'd grown in girth. Demonstrated by her tie-dyed skirts, plaid shirts, and bold jewelry, terms like Hippie Momma or Earth Mother had become a better fit. She and the artists who remained in town had transformed this small ranching community into a mini Austin with a cool, relaxed vibe.

Aunt Linda placed a hand on my arm and squeezed. "Let's go ahead and take everyone's drink order." She pinned on a hundred watt smile for the rest of the committee.

"Y'all must be powerfully thirsty." With a nod and a wink in my direction, my aunt started for the back of the room.

I thought I heard the whole room breathe a sigh of relief. They'd obviously been watching the show while soaking up juicy tidbits to share with their friends and neighbors at the first opportunity. Oh, they wouldn't go so far as to pick up the phone, for the good Lord knew that would be gossiping. But if a friend or acquaintance should ask what's new over morning coffee at Elaine's Pies or a cold Coors during happy hour at Two Boots, well, that was a horse of a different color.

"Make it four margaritas without salt for me and the lovely Burnett ladies," Dixie said, making a grand sweeping gesture.

Suellen spun toward the older woman, hands clenched, not caring that bits of chicken still stuck to her fingers. "I don't want a margarita, thank you." Her words might have been polite, but her tone was somewhere between *shut up* and *let's take this outside.*

"It'll loosen you up, prissy pants." Dixie laughed and glanced around the room as if she expected the committee to join in.

Suellen's jaw fell open in horror and snapped shut in rage. "At least they make pants in my size," she said, her voice as quiet and threatening as a roll of thunder over the desert. She turned to where I stood with my jaw hanging open. "I want a shot of Jack Daniels, a shot of Jägermeister, and a shot of Dr Pepper in a tall glass with ice."

Without drawing my attention, Elaine had appeared at her daughter's side. "That's enough, little sister," she said in a gentle voice and squeezed Suellen's hand. Under her breath, she added, "Sticks and stones."

Suellen tore her gaze from the inebriated woman to her mother's disappointed face. "Oh, alright," she muttered through her teeth. "Give me a margarita."

"Whatever Dixie says goes," Melanie's sarcasm could have melted iron.

Yesterday, I'd heard from a customer that Melanie and the jewelry maker had had a huge blowout in front of Bubba's BBQ. I made a quick note on my pad. "Ohh-kay. That's four without salt. Anybody else?"

The mayor chimed in, "Two with salt."

Felicia Cogburn fidgeted with her sparkly bangles, her eyes wide and unblinking as a gecko, smiling at no one in particular.

"Diet coke, please." Of course, Hillary needed to watch her calories to prevent her head from growing any fatter. Oops. That thought wasn't very Christian. I'd better watch it or one day I might say something to Hillary that I'd live to regret.

Senora Mari stepped into the center of the room, twitching with the need to get the tamales rolling. "Back to work, *por favor*. No breaks until the drinks arrive." Among the volunteers I detected a few groans.

With a wide smile, my aunt added, "But when they arrive you can take a nice long sit down." Someone let out a whoop.

"Lord knows, I could use one of those," said Mayor Cogburn, turning from the restaurant's industrial, double-sided sink. He was drying his hands thoroughly with paper towels from the nearby dispenser, and though his comment was clearly sarcastic, his delivery was so dry it was hard to take offense or think less of him.

"You're welcome," Senora Mari hadn't caught the sarcasm. She smiled encouragement to him and the other volunteers as she circled the room, yet again, inspecting the committee's progress.

Walking toward the group, the mayor balled up his paper towels and lobbed them into the trash can. "Hurry up with them drinks, now, ya' hear?" he said in a campy Southern drawl.

Dixie barked a brittle laugh at his remark as Aunt Linda whisked her over to the sink to wash her hands.

"We wouldn't want to deprive Miss Honeycutt of anything her heart desires." Cogburn turned and gave his wife a tight-lipped smile. "Would we, sugar?"

"No, definitely not," Felicia said. The mayor's wife turned her head toward me and whispered, "Not while we're waiting for the witch to finish the auction necklace. She's two weeks late."

The laughter died in my throat. "Don't go away," I said, infusing my voice with false cheer. "I'll be right back." I broke through the swinging doors, relieved for any excuse to skedaddle away from the melodrama.

An hour later, Senora Mari had stacked the first batch of tamales in two tall steamers, and folks were feeling mellower. Alcohol had done the trick.

"Does anyone know why in the Sam Hill we don't have more traffic on our WWWF page?" I bit the inside of my cheek to keep from laughing. The mayor's abbreviation made our Wild Wild West Festival sound like a wrestling event. "It should be really rocking this close to opening day." Only a stern look from Aunt Linda kept me from rolling my eyes.

Melanie shook her head in disgust as she headed for the sink. "A website needs to be current and easy to navigate." She rinsed her hands of masa and dried them. "The festival's next week, for pity's sake. Why don't you update the fool thing?"

Hillary sidled up to where Dixie perched on a tall stool from the bar. "I love your work, I really do," she cooed, pointing to the handcrafted necklace Dixie wore. The jewelry maker had created a series of tiny horses in the Native American style, each one carved from a different rock or precious stone indigenous to the Southwest.

Tilting her head to the side, the inebriated woman swayed forward as if trying to figure out from which planet Hillary hailed. "You got a cigarette? Filtered or unfiltered, dudn't matter to me."

The beauty queen wrinkled her nose in disapproval. "No, I don't smoke those things."

Dixie cackled. "Why, Hillary, what things do you smoke?"

With lips thinned in a painful smile, Hillary pressed on. "I've been meaning to ask you." She drew in a breath. "What does your necklace for this year's auction look like? Is it turquoise or topaz?"

"Why would I tell you, Miss Goody I-Don't-Smoke-Those-Things? It's a secret, same as always, and none of your dadburn business."

Hillary turned to Mayor Cogburn and his wife. "I thought you said you were going to display the necklace online to build up anticipation for the auction."

After a quick glance at his wife, Cogburn stuck his thumbs in the belt loops of his designer jeans. "Well, you see . . . we're still debating the matter."

"You mean there's still no photo on the website? I thought the whole point was to generate publicity for the auction." Mrs. Burnett was rarely critical, which made her quiet comment hit home.

"Um . . . well . . . I haven't received any photo." Felicia Cogburn raised her hands in a helpless gesture.

"Heck to the no." Dixie slid from the stool to stand before the mayor like a rooster at a cockfight—chin raised, eyes narrowed, and plump hands fisted. "The debate is over. It's going to be a surprise just like every other year."

From the corner of the room, a voice muttered, "What a diva."

"Who said that?" Dixie swung her girth first to one side and then the other, but not one of the committee members would admit it, though several struggled not to laugh. The remark had come from the direction of the shredded chicken.

Melanie Burnett stepped up with a toss of her head, flinging her razor-cut bangs out of her eyes. "I don't see why you won't let them show it on the website now that you're famous. It's for a good cause."

Dixie had recently hit the big time by scoring a contract with Neiman Marcus. And as a result, *The Texan* magazine was writing a feature article on her turquoise and tribal style jewelry. Hoping to ride on the coattails of her newfound acclaim, the festival committee had commissioned not only a necklace for this year's auction fundraiser, but matching earrings and a bracelet, with the hope that someone would donate at least five thousand dollars to the cause.

Like a sonic boom, Dixie slammed her hand on the metal prep table by her side. "Maybe I'm sick of no-talent hacks stealing my designs." She leaned forward, exposing a bit too much of her bountiful bosom. "Are you folks worried I won't deliver the necklace in time for your precious auction?"

Jumping in to soothe the troubled waters, Cogburn said. "Now, now, don't get riled up about it." He turned to his wife. "Felicia and I aren't worried, are we, hon?"

The mayor's wife tried to smile. "Why, no."

Suellen crossed to her sister's side. "Well, I'll admit it, even if none of the rest of you will. I'm worried." She thrust her hands on her hips and lowered her chin like a bull ready to rumble. "You haven't ever delivered early. Last year we had to hold up the auction thirty minutes so you could drive over that set of his and hers rings."

"The rings *I* designed."

The room fell silent except for Senora Mari, who chose that moment to start humming an old Freddy Fender song as she pulled another pork roast from the refrigerator. I recognized the tune as one of her favorites, "Wasted Days and Wasted Nights."

With a lurch, Dixie stepped nose to nose with Suellen. "I don't see your sister stepping up to donate her work." She tapped her forehead with a long, pudgy finger. "Hmm . . . maybe that's because everyone knows the auction wouldn't make a dime if she did."

"You . . . drunk . . . cow," Melanie sputtered and stepped back. "You should be thanking me for allowing you to sell your Native American knockoffs in my gallery." Her face flamed as she looked at one committee member after another. "Without me, she'd be selling cactus on the side of the road."

"Maybe just this once you could email a picture to me, and I could post it the morning of the auction." Mrs. Mayor tipped her glass for a sip from her second margarita, though the glass was clearly empty. She volunteered down at City Hall, maintaining the city's website and festival pages, though she had no experience.

Her husband cleared his throat. "She can't send it because it isn't finished."

Dixie reached out and patted Mayor Cogburn's hand, smiling at him as if they shared a delicious secret. "I'm creating something breathtakingly beautiful. You, on the other hand, have no excuse for your shortcomings, darling." The mayor must have caught an eyeful if the twinge of pink in his cheeks was any indication.

Without warning, Dixie lurched to her feet and pointed her finger inches from Felicia's face, cackling like a witch on helium. "You're a better woman than me." She drew a deep breath. "I would have left for greener pastures years ago."

The mayor's wife gasped as if Dixie had struck her across the face. I stole a glance at her husband. The mayor was staring at the jewelry maker with enough venom to wipe out even her large frame and, indeed, the whole county. Before the cow patties could hit the fan, Aunt Linda rode to the rescue. "Why don't we all take a fifteen minute breather?"

"Speaking of *breathers*," Dixie pulled a pack of Marlboro lights from her crocheted bag.

"No, no, no," barked Senora Mari, reaching out as if to take the offensive object. "Take it outside."

"Alright, I was kidding." Dixie dropped the soft pack back into her bag with a shrug. "Geez."

During the unexpected break, I presented the long-suffering committee members with flautas, quesadillas, and generous helpings of sour cream, guacamole, and pico de gallo. They swarmed the platters like flies on popsicles, and I rushed out the door, intent on rescuing Dixie from herself.

I found my aunt standing in the hallway outside the door marked *Niñas*. "How's she doing?" I asked, carrying a fresh cup of black coffee for our inebriated guest.

Rubbing the bridge of her nose, she sighed. "She's crying over some guy who deserted her for the Coast Guard during the peace movement."

With a bang, the bathroom door sprung open and the inebriated jewelry maker spilled out. Her eyes were red, but the tears had ceased. "I need a cigarette."

"Come on, sugar," Aunt Linda soothed, taking her by the arm. "We'll take you outside where you can smoke to your heart's content."

I hurried to Dixie's other side. "The cool air will feel nice, you'll see."

"You mean it'll sober me up."

Bingo.

We lowered her to the bench just outside the back door. "Josie's going to call your nephew to come and take you home."

Though Ty Honeycutt spent several weeks out of the year on tour with his country western band, Uncle Eddie had booked him to play during the festival, which meant he was currently bunking at his aunt's place.

"Good luck with that," Dixie mumbled.

"What's his phone number?" I asked.

Dixie eventually found the number on her phone, but Ty didn't answer any of the five times I called. And forget about leaving a message, his voicemail was full. Finally, I sent him a text.

"That boy's not going to answer," she said, leaning her head back against the concrete wall behind her, "not when he's tomcatting around."

But she was wrong. The simple reply read, See you in fifteen.

I was torn. Should I wait with her outside? Or join Aunt Linda inside to help her smooth the committee's ruffled feathers.

"Give me that coffee," Dixie demanded with a hint of fun. After a long swig, she set the cup beside her and eased her head back again. "And get out of here, girl," she muttered in a drowsy voice. "He'll be here in a jiff."

"Alright," I gave her a grateful smile and opened the door, "but I'm coming back in fifteen minutes, and you'd better be gone."

The kitchen was empty when I returned, except for Milagro's petite taskmaster. "Where is everyone?"

Mixing yet another, but smaller, batch of masa, the older woman gave me a look of disgust. "Flown the coop." She sighed and added spiced chicken to the mixture. "How's Dixie?"

"Not so good."

Shaking her head, Senora Mari quickly rinsed her hands. "I'll go talk to her. You stay here in case any birds return."

No sooner had she gone than Mayor Cogburn and Mrs. Mayor entered. "Is there anything left to do?"

What was with these two? I wasn't about to tell them that they were both wearing Mrs. Mayor's coral lipstick. I'd learned that lesson earlier in the alley.

Melanie strode in, swinging the kitchen doors aside. "What's left to do?"

"Hey, you're back," I said, trying to keep things light.

With a glare that could have leveled the Alamo, Melanie gritted her teeth. "Not that I had any choice in the matter."

"Anyone want coffee or hot cocoa?" Suellen chirped as she and Ryan edged through the doors with trays of hot beverages.

Thrusting her hands on her hips, Melanie gave her sister the once-over. "Since when did you become a team player?"

Suellen giggled, flushed, and grinned from ear to ear. As she and Ryan arranged spoons, marshmallows, and other condiments, she snuck longing glances at the young coach. Another female fan in the making.

Elaine Burnett paused in the doorway to give her daughters a look of loving approval. "Oh, I knew you'd do the right thing," she said, giving Melanie a big hug. She satisfied herself by merely patting Suellen's shoulder. "You too, sweetheart."

Picking up a cup of cocoa and a spoonful of mini marshmallows, Melanie smirked. "What else could we do after you laid one of your guilt trips on us?"

A spasm of discomfort passed over Elaine's countenance, and she pressed a hand to her stomach.

"Are you all right?" Senora Mari asked as she entered from the back.

With a sigh, the committee chairwoman gave her an uncomfortable smile. "I'm fine." She hesitated. "I can't always eat spicy food, no matter how delicious."

"Mother?" Suellen's concern was apparent.

"No, I'm fine." Elaine dismissed her with a wave of her hand. "Our family lives up to its commitments." She caught the eye of her youngest. "We keep our word, and we don't feel guilty."

As Elaine and Suellen served themselves, Senora Mari took me by the arm and pulled me aside from the group. "Dixie's gone."

I reached up and smoothed her wind-ruffled hair. "Thank goodness."

Senora Mari pulled my head down closer to her mouth. "When do the rest of them leave?"

"As soon as you finish the last tamale," I said with a chuckle. We both understood who was doing the lion's share of the work. Elaine was chatting quietly with the Cogburns in one corner while her daughters checked their smartphones in the other.

Talk about commitment.

"How is your little friend?" Senora Mari asked.

"Quiet as a mouse," I answered with a wink.

"Bueno."

"Hey," Ryan called from across the room, "something's wrong with the tamales. They're soggy."

Senora Mari shot across the kitchen like a hornet from its nest and grabbed the rest of the tamale out of Ryan's hand. "It's not soggy, you idiot. You have to let it cool." With a groan, she grabbed her hair with both hands.

After retrieving Aunt Linda from the office to help calm her mother-in-law, I escaped to give Lenny a well-deserved doggie bagel.

Guests gone? Check. Tamales stored? Check. Lights off? All but the light behind the bar. "Lenny, let's hit the stairs, little man." He blinked and snuggled into my arms. Our first community *tamalada* was behind us, and we lived to tell the tale. And I had no doubt the tale would be flying around town by tomorrow's lunch. I flipped the switch, plunging the bar into darkness. The light from the upstairs landing trickled down the wooden stairs. My breath caught in my throat, I squeezed Lenny until he yipped, and I vowed for the umpteenth time to stop watching television dramas about serial killers.

"Did you and Ryan find things to talk about?" I asked, thinking of my bed and a pint of Blue Bell mint chocolate chip awaiting me upstairs.

My fierce protector growled low in his throat.

An engine revved as a car raced through the alley, spewing gravel against the back door. Goosebumps rippled up my arms, and I forced myself to laugh. The high school students in this flea-sized town desperately needed to find something to do other than drag the deserted streets.

"It's okay." I rubbed Lenny's slender back, but he kicked his legs and jumped to the stairs, yapping. "Hey, come on!" I was tired and not in the mood to explain that the big, bad car was long gone.

Without decelerating, he flew by the doors marked *Niñas* and *Niños*, and then ran through the storage room and toward the back door.

"Slow down," I muttered. It wasn't that I didn't appreciate his protective instincts but my own feet were barking from exhaustion. "Lenny, come on!" As I approached, I realized something was caught between the door and the frame. Lenny, the wee watchdog, had it in his teeth, tugging and growling.

"Whatcha got?" I knelt to gently remove the cottony fabric from his mouth and the door swung open. Beyond the swirling storm of moths above my head, the alley yawned empty but redolent with the spicy remains of the evening's delicacies. The office supply across the graveled road was cloaked in darkness due to the owner's habit of procrastinating when it came to replacing his burned out bulbs, but four stores down the light from the resale store, Wear It Again, Sam, burned brightly.

Lenny whined, and the strange, keening sound whipped

my head in his direction. His feathery black tail jutted out from beneath a concrete bench to the left of the door that our staff used during breaks.

"Come," I ordered.

Only the tail moved, swinging rapidly to and fro.

"Lenny!"

He circled and came out nose first. In his mouth, he carried a grisly bone covered with dirt and drool.

"Let me see that." I lowered my hand to his mouth. And, of course, he turned his head away. I had no choice but to grab the slimy thing. He wasn't going to choke on a small piece of bone on my watch. "Gross." It was a discarded chicken bone, just as I suspected. "How did this get here?"

With a whine, Lenny took off again, this time for the Dumpster, the fount of fragrant garbage.

"Forget it, buster." I wasn't about to let him stink up the apartment until I found the time to give him a bath.

My six-pound wonder took off around the side of the huge metal can, with me fuming close behind. I lunged forward, determined to scoop him up, but he disappeared around the back. Unable to stop my forward momentum, I ended up in the dirt and decided to crawl to the back and surprise him.

With great stealth, I rounded the corner and froze. Instead of a saucy, long-haired Chihuahua, a body lay before me hidden in the shadows. Just as my heart began to clog "The Yellow Rose of Texas" against my chest, I breathed a sigh of relief. Dixie lay on the ground before me, eyes wide open, smiling at the sky. Drunk as a skunk and too wasted to care.

"Whoa, Nelly. You scared me to death." Why hadn't that blasted Ty taken her home?

Lenny barked a question. "I know, I know," I said to calm him while I tried to find a solution that wouldn't throw my back out.

How was I going to get her up, let alone walk her to my car? "Dixie," I said loudly and patted her hand. She didn't blink. "Time to go home." Her flesh was cool from the mountain air, reminding me of times as a child when I'd caught a trout and tried to hold the wriggling, slimy creature in my hands. I grabbed her by the hand and upper arm to help her sit up, but she was too out of it. Her smile never wavered, and her eyes remained open in a permanent study of the stars.

I backed away, scraping my knees, unearthing the truth.

Dixie Honeycutt was dead.

Chapter 3

I watched the tie-dyed fabric of her skirt rise and fall until Lenny yipped for my attention. With a sudden surge of adrenaline, my brain flew into hyperdrive. Dixie was dead. Where was my phone?

I grabbed Lenny, who immediately began wriggling like a greased pig at a county fair.

"No!" I extracted my phone from my pocket and dialed. "Dixie Honeycutt is dead," I blurted.

"911. State your emergency."

A hundred horror movie scenes flashed through my amped up brain. "This is Josie Callahan. I just found Dixie Honeycutt on the ground, and I'm pretty sure she's dead."

"What is your location?"

"I'm at Milagro, 2500 Main Street in Broken Boot."

"Have you checked her pulse?"

I bent over her body and raised two fingers, but I stopped myself when I spotted a deep furrow across her neck. Was it a heavy fold of skin or an abrasion from a necklace?

"Gently place two fingers on her wrist."

"Okay." I held my breath and did as the operator ordered.

"Ma'am, did you find it?"

I swallowed the panic clogging my throat. "I'm trying!"

"Ma'am," the operator interrupted in a firm voice, "I need you to stay calm."

I forced myself to take another deep breath. "Okay, I'm calm, but she's still dead."

"Stay where you are. An ambulance is on its way."

As I disconnected, Lenny jumped into the weedy gravel. Before I knew what he was about, he placed his two front paws on her chest and barked.

"Shush." I knelt to brush him away, and my gaze edged upwards. In the concave place below Dixie's trachea, there was an odd-shaped mark. And then I recognized what I had seen earlier in the bright light of Milagro's kitchen, the shape of a horse. I glanced around, but found no sign of the horse necklace she'd worn.

As chill bumps raced down my arms, I shoved to my feet, grabbed my canine friend, and held him close. The streetlight at the end of the alley hummed and moths danced in attendance. The three-quarter moon shone bright as a Christmas star.

And Dixie lay dead. The same, but changed forever.

I said a silent prayer of thanks that I had found her and not Aunt Linda or Senora Mari. During my college internship at the *Dallas Morning News*, I'd written obituaries for the very young, the very old, and every age in between, but I'd never actually seen a dead body. Not up close and personal. I stared, unable to blink or turn away, while her skin paled and the wind whipped her skirt around her ankles.

Gradually, I became aware of my legs quivering like cactus flowers in a windstorm, so I coerced my mind into making observations about the scene before me. It would calm me down, and I would be able to respond to any questions with clarity.

The first thing I noticed was the small dusty paw prints on Dixie's dress. "Sorry, Lenster, but you've got to go." I thrust him inside and closed the door, and he immediately began to whine and scratch.

I forced memories of Dixie's robust laugh away and concentrated on the scene before me. Someone had tossed the last of the trash and closed the Dumpster before leaving, but from where I stood, I could see that something dark and wet, probably grease, had leaked down the side of the metal container and pooled in the dirt. It wasn't how we would've disposed of kitchen grease, but I wasn't about to look a gift horse in the mouth.

Unless that wayward gift horse was a member of our staff.

While it didn't take a heart specialist to figure out Dixie likely died from a heart attack, the surrounding area would be treated as a possible crime scene until the coroner determined no foul play was involved. With nothing else to do to pass the time, I decided to take a quick, but careful, look around. I removed my shoes and, keeping well away from the body, circled around for a closer look at the pool of slime. Stopping short, to avoid ruining my socks, I confirmed it was nothing but grease by the cloying smell. I removed my cell phone from the pocket of my jeans and turned on the flashlight. Whoever tossed the trash had stepped in the mess and left a boot print in the dirt.

Perfect.

Rooting in my pocket, I found a quarter and tossed it in the mud next to the print and snapped a picture to help me prove the culprit's shoe size. The next time I was accused of taking lazy shortcuts around the state health codes, I would whip out my evidence to the contrary.

With a flash of red and blue lights, the sheriff's cruiser pulled up with two officers inside. One I knew—Sheriff Mack Wallace—but the other I couldn't make out.

"Josie, you okay?" The weathered sheriff had known me

since I was a preteen. His daughter Emma and I had played softball together up and down West Texas as part of the Chisos Mountain League.

An unknown deputy walked by his side, his khaki uniform perfectly pressed and tucked, in spite of the hour. An ebony ponytail hung below his collar, and his eyes were bits of coal, fathomless in the glow of the single bulb. Perhaps it was the fact we don't see many Native Americans on this side of the New Mexico border, but the raw angles and shadows of his face formed a mask of exotic intensity.

Holy cow.

There was a moment of silence, and then Lenny's whining and scratching morphed into angry barking.

Sheriff Wallace spoke up. "Quint Lightfoot, meet Josie Callahan."

The young deputy gave me the full impact of his expressionless stare for a moment, and then nodded. "Ma'am."

Wallace scanned the alley. "Where is she?"

"Behind the Dumpster."

As we stared down at her lifeless body, we remained silent for a spell, giving her the respect she deserved.

"How'd you find her?" Wallace asked the question, but Lightfoot removed a notepad and pen from his shirt pocket.

"Lenny, my dog, found a piece of her skirt stuck in the back door." I swallowed the sudden rise of emotion in my throat. It was as if now that I wasn't alone, my bravery was threatening to leak out like dirty oil from a busted oil pan.

Lightfoot spoke up in a quiet baritone. "What time was that?"

A sudden gust of wind tossed my hair from my face. "Eleven thirty, I think." As he made a note, tumbleweed rolled down the alley, across Dixie's body and into the parking lot beyond. My knees clanged together like two cymbals.

The sheriff took one look at my face and placed an arm around my shoulders. "Lightfoot, wait here for the ambulance and Ellis. I'm going to take Josie inside so she can be comfortable."

"Ellis?" I didn't want to leave her body with some stranger. I wanted her to sit up and argue and piss me off.

"The justice of the peace." With a firm hand, the sheriff turned me toward the door. "She's okay. Lightfoot will watch over her and find out what happened."

Over my shoulder, I saw the deputy kneel close to Dixie's body. He leaned toward her and appeared to be studying her hands.

"You mean the coroner, right? What about the ambulance?" My nerves were taut as barbed wire, and I pinched the flesh between my thumb and forefinger to keep me focused. "Where are they?"

Sheriff Wallace opened the door. "At this time of night, the local JP is called to the scene." Automatically, I stuck my foot between Lenny and the door before he could escape. "Last I heard," Wallace said, leading me gently through the kitchen, "one ambulance delivered a baby at the rest stop on Highway 90, this side of Fort Davis. They're driving the mother and child to the hospital as we speak. The other one should be here soon, God willing."

Only two ambulances served the Broken Boot area and the surrounding twenty mile radius, and new life and new death had both called at the same time.

Flipping on lights as we went, we made our way to the dining room with Lenny clipping along behind. "I'll make some coffee." Even though I had washed all the carafes an hour earlier, I had to keep my mind and hands occupied if I was to be a help to the sheriff.

"Thanks, sounds real good."

I placed Lenny on the stairs. "It's okay, go to bed."

With a short yip, he clicked his way up the steps to our apartment. He turned on the landing to give me one last sympathetic look, and then cruised out of sight.

I was grateful for the dark aromatic grounds and the common task at this uncommon hour. While the coffee brewed, we sat in a nearby booth.

"I've never seen . . ." I hid my face in my hands and refused to cry. "She was fine."

Into the quiet, broken only by the gurgling of the coffee-maker and the ticking of the UT clock on the wall, Wallace spoke. "Why was she here?" His delivery lacked sympathy or overt emotion, but it steadied my fears.

I raised my head, once again in control, and lunged for his question like a swimmer in need of a life jacket. Out poured my recounting of the *tamalada*, its purpose, who had attended, and how many tamales we had made. In other words, I blabbered.

"Was there anything unusual about Dixie this evening?"

I slid from the booth and considered the sheriff's question while I poured each of us a cup of coffee. Could I share the awkwardness of the party and her less than perfect behavior without feeling disloyal? "She . . . was drunk."

He nodded. "Did she make a stop before she arrived?" he asked, lifting his cup to his mouth.

Taking my seat, I stirred two creams and one sugar into my coffee. "I don't know, but I remember thinking she smelled of whiskey and smoke."

He tipped up his hat with his thumb and made a note. "Cigarettes?" He glanced up.

My cheeks grew warm though I was no longer a teenager. "And marijuana." I didn't realize the distinctive odor had registered in my brain until I said it aloud. College Dorm Living 101 had included how to recognize the smell of pot.

He raised his eyebrows and scribbled some more.

From outside, I heard the loud squeal of breaks and doors slamming.

"What's that?" I sloshed coffee on my hand. "Ack!" It was still hot.

Without a flicker of sympathy for me or curiosity for what-ever was going on outside, he continued. "Ambulance, I reckon."

"You sure?"

"Was she upset?"

"Uh, not at first." She had arrived in a festive mood. "Later, she was kind of sarcastic and angry."

His pencil poised above his pad, he waited.

"Nothing major happened, but she did have a disagreement with some of the committee members." I swallowed. Calling their argument a disagreement was like calling a flash flood a trickle. I hopped up and grabbed the coffee carafe and the dish full of chocolate mints by the register.

"What about?"

I topped off our coffee, dropped the mint in my cup, and gathered my chaotic thoughts. "The committee wanted to promote this year's silent auction by adding a photo of Dixie's auction jewelry to the festival website." I worried my lip be-tween my teeth.

With the patience of Job, the sheriff merely took a sip of coffee and waited.

"Dixie refused, saying someone would steal her designs if she did."

"Was that all?"

"Well, no. Some of the committee members accused her of trying to cover up the fact she hadn't actually finished making the silent auction pieces." Words escaped me.

"And?"

I sighed. I didn't want to speak ill of the dead. "Lots of folks were angry. Accusations were thrown around. Dixie tried to make it all very personal and started insulting people."

He smiled. "Sounds like her."

"She even lost her temper and slammed her hand on the metal prep table in the kitchen."

Sheriff Wallace nodded his woolly head and unwrapped a mint. "How did the committee react?"

I surprised myself by chuckling. "There was some mud-slinging, but everyone chilled out once the drinks arrived."

The sheriff tapped his pencil on the tabletop with one hand and flipped through his notes with the other. With his eyes narrowed in thought, I studied his battered face. Very Tommy Lee Jones. He wasted no words, and his fatherly manner had encouraged me to answer with care and without the rambling.

"Did you see anyone else in the alley?"

The coffee sloshed over the side of my cup again. "A coyote, that's it." A wild animal running through town in late spring was bad enough.

Without warning, Deputy Lightfoot appeared at my shoulder. I screamed like a little girl, and like lightning, Lenny pitter-pattered down the stairs, yipping as he went.

"Oh, Lordy, I'm sooo sorry."

He snatched off his hat. "You okay?"

Lenny hopped onto my lap, which gave me an excellent excuse to look down and hide my reddened cheeks. "I'm fine," I crooned to my watchdog. "Just don't do that again."

With a good-natured grin, the sheriff leaned closer. "Lives up to his name, you got to give him that."

Fearing my face was as red as a chile pepper, I snatched up my cup for a quick sip and managed to immerse my nose in my lukewarm house blend. Sputtering, I cringed as coffee droplets jumped from my nose like swimmers from the high dive on a hot summer day.

Lightfoot found a place setting from a nearby table, un-wrapped the silverware, and handed me the cloth napkin. "Was Dixie wearing a necklace tonight?" he asked in a voice so deep it jangled my nerves.

Without a doubt, I thought the sheriff was going to throttle him. Lightfoot pulled up a chair, and Wallace glared at him. "No need to speculate, deputy." He shot a glance my way. "Why don't you stay with Linda and Eddie tonight? You've been through the wringer."

"She wore a tribal necklace, one of her own designs." I

closed my eyes, filled my lungs with air, searching for the image. "Horses chiseled from different gem stones."

"And?" Lightfoot asked softly.

Sheriff Wallace's voice rose. "It's time for her to go, deputy. Your questions will keep until tomorrow."

My hand found the soft, concave spot at the base of my neck. "A large horse in the middle."

"Which stone was it?" Lightfoot asked.

An image of Dixie, leaning close to the mayor, entered my brain. "Turquoise. It was blue turquoise."

Chapter 4

I awoke the next morning, staring at a ceiling full of stars, and exhaled. I was safe. I was in my twin bed in my aunt and uncle's house. Twinkling above me were shiny bits of crystal Aunt Linda had painted into the ceiling when I was a child. If I woke from nightmares or troubling dreams I would search for the Big Dipper and the North Star until I fell asleep.

How I wished that Dixie's death had been only a bad dream. But it was real, as real as the crick in my neck from a flat pillow and the aroma of bacon and biscuits floating through the house. If I closed my lids, I would see Dixie's wide blue eyes staring up at me while her tie-dyed skirt flapped in the wind. How long could I go without closing my eyes?

Last night, the enigmatic Deputy Lightfoot had brought me to my childhood home without any further questions. By the look on his angular face, I knew he suspected foul play. Why else would he be interested in Dixie's necklace? Sheriff Wallace must have called ahead because my family stood waiting on our wide front porch in their pajamas and T-shirts. Senora Mari was pacing back and forth in her fluffy pink robe and giant elephant slippers. They threw their arms around me and hugged me hard until Lenny complained. We tried to laugh, but the sounds we made faded away on the wind as we remembered not just anyone had died, but a three-times-a-week customer and friend. We'd wiped our tears, even Uncle Eddie, and then I'd dragged myself upstairs and fell into bed.

"Josie," Aunt Linda called up the stairs bright and early, "the AC's out at Milagro. Dress accordingly." I had not wriggled an inch, but her spidey sense was working overtime.

"And don't forget your neck," Senora Mari added. As if I could forget her wacky method of staying cool in the Texas heat. I had to smile, for she was obviously treating me with unusual sympathy. During high school, she would have dropped a cold, wet washcloth in my face if I slept past nine o'clock.

After a quick shower, I found some old clothes in my closet: an atrocious broom skirt, a Corona T-shirt, and a faded, blue bandana. Nothing was going to take the place of the AC, but I knew Senora Mari would argue and nag until I tied a wet bandana around my neck, her idea of the next best thing.

"Hurry up. You can eat breakfast when we get there," Aunt Linda called, answering my question before I could ask.

Dressing for a day without air conditioning in far West Texas can be like prepping for a day in hell. The air is cool in the early morning, but it climbs to a fever pitch by ten o'clock. Imagine standing in an oven until you're broiling and your skin flakes off like the skin of a pan-seared tilapia.

Only cowboys and ranchers venture into the full afternoon sun in Broken Boot, Texas. They pick their battles out here in the Chihuahuan Desert by taking long breaks in the hottest part of the day, which comes in handy if they've stayed up too late the night before tipping longnecks at Two Boots.

A week ago, the AC at Milagro petered out during the late rush, and nine people had to sweat it out. With any luck, they convinced themselves the chile diablo was to blame.

"Josie!"

I could picture Aunt Linda now, standing at the bottom of the stairs, her image indelibly in my brain just as her energetic voice was scratched into my eardrums. She would be wearing her chestnut hair smoothed into a sleek and serviceable bun at the back of her head with a red flower pinned above her ear. Her hands would be on the hips of her Wranglers, tapping the toe of her Tony Llama boots, a wet, red bandana at her neck. Beautiful, and not to be tangled with.

"Coming!"

"I'll believe it when I see it." Moments later the garage door rose with a squealing groan. No biscuits and bacon for me.

Today the sheriff would ask me more questions, and I would be strong with my family behind me. During my shower, I'd wracked my brain. What else could I tell them?

Hungry and nervous, I slid into the passenger seat of Aunt Linda's white F150, lowered the visor, and began to apply my mascara in the mirror.

"Did you write your article for the *Bugle*?" my aunt asked in an overly optimistic tone.

She knew I'd submitted a couple of articles to the *Broken Boot Bugle*, and that they'd rejected both, saying they weren't *folksy* enough. Then last week, the editor made me an offer I longed to refuse. He wanted me to write an article about Hillary Sloan Rawlings and her new position at the university to prove I could give his readers what they wanted.

Folksy I could do, but Hillary was an unsavory morsel. At my aunt's urging, I told him I'd get right on it, as soon as we recovered from the festival.

Now if I were to cover something interesting like the Texas music scene, I'd be happier than a tornado in a trailer park. Even though Two Boots was located in a small town, it attracted the best musicians in Texas. And Texas music was no longer just for kickers and cowboys. Lots of hot guys played new country, alternative country, country western, country rock . . . you get the idea. Uncle Eddie had been playing guitar in a country rock band when he met Aunt Linda, so I came by my love of Texas music and hot musicians honestly.

I slammed the visor shut.

Most musicians were also no good, unreliable narcissists, who put their careers before their nuptials. Brooks was a slime bucket full of putrid flesh.

"Josie, don't worry about that weak, silly boy. You're strong."

I jumped in surprise and banged my knee on the dash. "Ow!" Of course, Senora Mari would be in the backseat. Where else would she be? And did I mention she's a mind reader?

"You're a Callahan," Aunt Linda proclaimed, and I laughed in spite of myself. "Callahans are sturdy stock," we said in unison. The paternal side of my family had settled in neighboring Cogburn County back in the 1800s, long before running any type of drinking and dancing establishment was considered an honorable profession.

"Did you have a good night's sleep, *abuelita*?" When she didn't correct me, I turned around in my seat and found her clutching her rosary beads, her lips moving soundlessly.

With a shudder, she opened her eyes and pierced me with a bone-snapping stare. "No. I had a visitor in my dreams."

As if someone had walked on my grave, I shuddered as well. When Marisol Ramos Martinez said she had a visitor in her dreams, she meant a person who had passed on.

"No wonder," my aunt said, "what with Dixie dying unexpectedly right there."

I rested my chin on the top of the seat between us, settling in for a spooky tale. "What did Dixie say?" I wasn't sure I believed what Senora Mari spouted from her dreams, but she set great store by them.

Taking a deep breath, she paused for dramatic effect. "*Nada*." And she nodded as if she'd bestowed a great pearl of wisdom. "Nothing."

"Do you mean she said the word *nothing* or that she didn't speak?" Aunt Linda asked with exasperation.

Without acknowledging her daughter-in-law, Senora Mari gave me a baleful stare and whispered, "She didn't speak, no words, but she poured her thoughts into my mind."

From previous experience, I knew better than to interrupt or try to lead the tortuous story.

"She was angry and sad." She closed her eyes and crossed herself. "She wants revenge."

"Revenge on whom, the cigarette manufacturers?" Aunt Linda shook her head. "Tell her to get in line."

Without looking in my aunt's direction, I pinched her leg. I wanted to hear this one, but if she continued with her skeptical remarks, Senora Mari would clam up.

"She didn't give me a name, but she told me it was no cigarette."

I wasn't about to correct my elders, even if she had said moments before that Dixie had used no words. "Did she give you a vision of how she died?"

Senora Mari pursed her lips and turned to stare out the window. A shadow of pain passed over her face. "She was so cold, so cold she couldn't breathe."

Had I mentioned Dixie's cold clammy skin to the three of them when I finally arrived home last night? No, but Senora Mari would've noticed the cool air and gusts of wind. I turned to my aunt for support. "If you die from a heart attack you probably do feel as if you can't breathe. Right?"

"Oh, sure," Aunt Linda chimed in. "You see that on television all the time. Someone dies grabbing their heart, gasping for air." She smiled reassuringly at her mother-in-law in the rearview mirror. "I bet they go hand in hand."

"That may be true, but that was not the feeling she shared." Senora Mari pulled back her shoulders and lowered her chin. "Someone stole her life, and she wants me to do something about it."

I reached over the seat and placed my hand on hers. "I'm sorry your friend is dead."

She nodded and turned to stare out the window once again.

As I started to pull away, she grabbed my hand. "You believe me, don't you?"

"Yes, I do." I believed Dixie had appeared in her dreams, and I was open-minded enough to concede there was more to life than the physical before us. But I wasn't sure Senora Mari had interpreted her dream correctly. Did being cold and out of breath mean that something nefarious had happened to Dixie? I wasn't sure.

As we drove down West Third Street, beneath a gigantic banner heralding Broken Boot's 5th Annual Wild Wild West Festival, I wondered if Dixie's death would affect the tamale-eating contest. I considered myself to be sensitive and unselfish, and my line of thinking made me feel as low as a snake's belly. But we needed the tourists to come in droves to survive the winter ahead. Our business had picked up in the past three months since Milagro made the cover of *The Texan* magazine last September, but we needed to double it to keep West Texas Savings and Loan off our backs.

"Did we make enough tamales for the contest?" I asked, trying to lighten the mood. With any luck, this year's event would draw more folks seeking good ole family fun and savory Tex-Mex. Our entire town could sure use a boost in the present economy.

"Senora Mari's making another batch today, just in case."

I swung around in my seat. "You'll need us to help you, right?" Making tamales was usually fun, but that's because it was a group activity. Sharing the work and gossiping with family made it less tedious.

The older woman shrugged. "I can do it by myself. I usually do."

"What do you mean?" Aunt Linda asked in a panic. "Where's Carlos? Is his mother okay?"

I wanted to laugh, but I bit my tongue. Senora Mari had

once again taken on the role of family martyr, which was ridiculous because she usually made tamales with the help of Carlos, our to-go cook.

Instead, I changed the subject. "How are all those tamales going to keep until Saturday?"

"We had to freeze the ones for the contest," my aunt said.

"Humph." Senora Mari disliked serving anything that wasn't fresh, but we'd finally convinced her that the tamales for the contest weren't eaten because of their freshness. They were consumed in great quantities because people wanted to win a month's worth of free tamales from our restaurant.

Turning onto Main Street, the asphalt shimmered with heat like a mirage in the desert. The LED sign at First Cogburn Bank flashed ninety degrees at ten twenty-nine in the morning. A scorcher.

A Big Bend County sheriff's cruiser had parked at the curb in front of our restaurant, and down the block, I observed the deputy with the raven hair strolling into Elaine's Pies. I had a few precious minutes to grab some breakfast and coffee before he realized we'd arrived. Could it be a coincidence? Could he merely be hungry for a savory breakfast pie? Not today.

In all my years of living in Broken Boot, I'd never heard of anyone else being found dead in the street, or the alley for that matter. The sheriff's department would be all over Dixie's death like white on rice. I had no doubt Deputy Lightfoot was preparing to tie up the loose ends by putting me through the wringer, and I had the sinking feeling he wouldn't question me in the same fatherly way as Sheriff Wallace.

As Aunt Linda drove behind the restaurant to park, our jaws fell. Yellow crime scene tape crisscrossed Milagro's back door. Half the alley, including the area around the Dumpster and Dixie's van, was blocked off with traffic cones and the same yellow tape that warned SHERIFF'S DEPARTMENT DO NOT CROSS.

"What did I tell you?" Senora Mari whispered.

I wasn't convinced. Wouldn't they mark off the scene if they were still investigating?

"People aren't murdered in this town," I chided. "You watch too many crime shows." There wasn't a CSI Broken Boot for a good reason. Who would want to watch a snooze-fest of an occasional criminal armed with a spray can?

"No, no, no! We can't close today!" My aunt slammed the car into park just as her cell rang.

We gathered our things and headed for the entrance. "Are the coolers working or not?" she almost shouted into her phone.

From the sound of things, Two Boots was having its own difficulties. I tried not to focus on the obvious, but as Uncle Eddie always said, *A dance hall without beer is like a bull without horns: there's no point.* It was a terrible joke, but we did need both locations open to ensure we had the necessary funds for the constant repairs, like the AC at Milagro and the drink coolers at our dance hall.

I caught Senora Mari ducking under the crime scene tape to eye the gravel and weeds. "There's nothing here for them to see," she murmured. "No blood, guts, nothing."

OMG. "Come out of there, you'll get us in trouble," I warned, even as every fiber of my being longed to duck behind the Dumpster to revisit the site where Dixie died. Despite my yearning, I set aside my own curiosity. Wallace and his deputies needed our support.

With a disdainful glance, Senora Mari pointed a bony finger toward the door. "I'm not the one who's going to get thrown in the pokey."

Aunt Linda had the phone pinched between her shoulder and her ear while she wriggled her arm through the gap in the tape and inserted her key. "Eddie, I don't care if you call the man in the moon. Johnson's not available."

The door swung open.

"That deputy is going to be here any minute. What do

you think you're doing?" Was I the only sane woman in our family?

From the corner of my eye, I observed Senora Mari kneeling down next to the Dumpster. I turned to scold her and caught myself just in time. She closed her eyes, crossed herself, and prayed. Her lips moved, though no sound touched my ears.

Turning back to my aunt, I found her twisted like a salted pretzel. She'd managed to slide one leg and two arms inside the tape without breaking it, but her shoulders and hips were having trouble.

"Call me back when you get a quote." She kept the phone in her hand as she pulled a Houdini, contorting the rest of body through the opening without disturbing a single yellow strip.

"I'd appreciate it if you ladies would kindly back out of the crime scene without disturbing anything."

Aunt Linda turned, Senora Mari jumped to her feet with the vigor of a teenager, and I screamed like a little girl . . . again.

Lightfoot's jaw clenched and unclenched as his hands fisted and then relaxed.

"We didn't mean any harm," I said, hoping to appeal to the brief acquaintance we'd formed the night before. "This is my aunt, Linda Martinez." I turned to her with a hint of formality. "Aunt Linda, meet Deputy Lightfoot. He and the sheriff questioned me last night."

By this time, Senora Mari had marched over to stand at his elbow. "Are you trying to arrest us?" She tilted back her head at a forty-five degree angle in a noble attempt to stare him down.

He stepped back, and she followed. He raised his hand, palm out, to prevent her from invading his space any further. "Crime scene tape is to keep you out. It's not an invitation to trespass."

"What do you mean trespass? This is our restaurant, and we're opening in two hours!" Aunt Linda screeched. Just as suddenly, her eyes flew open to the size of dinner plates and her hand flew over her mouth in embarrassment.

With a loud growl, a black and silver Harley pulled into the parking lot and came to a halt next to Dixie's van. The black T-shirted rider in the back unfastened his helmet, slung a leg over the leather seat, and leaned in to give the driver an embarrassingly thorough kiss.

"Bye, lover," his companion said, her raspy voice projecting innuendo, alcohol, and cigarettes to where the four of us stood dumbstruck. Before we could react, she secured the extra helmet, accelerated back into the street, and vroomed out of sight.

Her passenger, Ty Honeycutt, gifted us with a wide grin and a nod before removing a key from his pocket and proceeding to unlock his Aunt Dixie's van.

As he slid into the driver's seat, Lightfoot grabbed a hold of the door. "Where do you think you're going?"

"I think I'm headed to find that repo man and retrieve my Mustang." He might have been in his late twenties, but it was hard to determine. What was apparent from the slurring of his words was that he was way too relaxed for eleven o'clock in the morning.

The deputy placed a hand briefly on his holster. "Step away from the vehicle and keep your hands in sight at all times."

Tugging Senora Mari along with us, Aunt Linda and I scurried backwards until we hit the wall. We looked at each other in astonishment. I couldn't recall ever seeing an officer in Broken Boot actually draw their weapon. What had Lightfoot so excited? Was this guy's face on the newest batch of wanted posters hanging on the sheriff department's wall of shame?

The young man's hands flew up. "Hey, dude, it's cool. Chill."

"Wait!" I shouted.

Without looking back, Lightfoot barked. "What?"

"We've met before, haven't we?" I asked the young man.

"Abso-freaking-lutely, if you say so." He flung me a look of desperation. "Tell Tonto to back off."

After that racist comment, I wasn't about to say a word.

"Step away from the vehicle," Lightfoot's order rang loud and clear.

As the would-be driver stepped clear of Dixie's van, the deputy clamped his right hand to his holster.

"Whoa, man, you've got the wrong idea."

"What idea would that be?"

"Maybe you think I'm stealing this van," the young man threw his arms out wide, "but I ain't."

"Keep your hands where I can see them." Lightfoot drew his pistol.

Two hands flew up to either side of the young man's ears and froze.

"You're telling me you're the owner of this van?"

No longer grinning, the young man licked his lips and swallowed two or three times. "Okay, I ain't exactly the owner. It's my aunt's."

Lightfoot didn't give any quarter. "Show me your license."

Ty started for his back pocket.

"Easy," Lightfoot said. "Take it nice and slow."

After a thorough inspection of the proffered driver's license, the deputy holstered his sidearm. "Where were you last night?"

A shadow fell over Ty Honeycutt's face. "I was playing cards."

Driven by a surge of righteous anger, I rushed toward him. "Why didn't you pick Dixie up last night, like you promised?"

Aunt Linda called my name.

"She'd be alive today if you hadn't forgotten she existed."

Lightfoot stepped between us and gave me a hard look. "That's a bit harsh."

With a jerk, Ty turned his head away. "You're right," he

said, his voice full of unshed tears. "I killed her. I ain't ever gonna forgive myself."

In a voice devoid of emotion or inflection, Lightfoot murmured, "What do you mean you killed her?" He could have been asking what time the El Paso train arrived at the Broken Boot station.

Ty rubbed his wet eyes with his knuckles.

"She might've lived if I'd been with her. Instead she died alone in that alley like a hobo."

In spite of my self-righteous anger, I was feeling guilty myself. We'd all heard her comment that her arm was aching during the *tamalada*, but none of us had taken her complaint seriously.

I paused to form my words carefully, trying hard not to cast the first stone. "You told me you were coming to get her. What happened?"

Ty's tearful gaze begged me to understand. "They repossessed my Mustang last night around six o'clock."

"Then why did you promise to pick Dixie up?" Aunt Linda asked, placing an arm around me, reading me and my guilt as easy as the Sunday paper.

"I was winning." Ty leaned back against the side of the dented van. "Almost had enough to find that repo man and pay him off on the spot."

"Let me guess," I muttered. "You lost it all." This guy had lost all his money while Dixie lay dying, waiting on him to arrive.

Straightening his shoulders, he lifted his chin. "I did come to get her, afterwards. Ask Yancey Burrows. I borrowed his El Camino."

From my other side, Senora Mari spoke up. "You lie." She shook her finger and advanced on him.

Ty turned to Lightfoot, desperation furrowing his brow. "I swear I stopped by here, but she wasn't waiting outside on the bench like you said."

With a warning *whoop, whoop* of their sirens, two more sheriff cruisers pulled into our parking lot.

Ty shot a glance at the alley as if calculating the distance and his ability to outrun the law.

"Right this way." In two steps, Lightfoot successfully planted himself between Dixie's nephew, his intended escape route, and an arrest for obstruction of justice.

Three car doors slammed and three pairs of pressed khaki's marched over. One pair belonged to Sheriff Wallace and the other two belonged to an older deputy I didn't know and a linebacker of a female officer named Pleasant, who enjoyed her margaritas with Cuervo Gold and a side of spinach quesadillas.

"Ty Honeycutt?" Wallace demanded.

Dixie's nephew swallowed hard. "Nice to meet you, sheriff," he said, and bravely stuck out his hand.

With a hard stare designed to make a guilty man wet his pants, Wallace nodded. "I was sorry to hear about Dixie."

He and his deputies had yet to crack a smile. In fact, they were as tense as a coiled rattlesnake about to strike.

"When can I see her?" Ty knuckled a tear from his cheek.

Like the desert before a summer storm, the air crackled with electricity. Each of the deputies rested their hands on their gun holsters.

"I thought you would've already made it down to the morgue, seeing as how an officer called you this morning with the news."

"I'm trying," Ty made a wild gesture, "but your boy here thought I was trying to steal her van. I only wanted to use it to drive over there to see her."

Wallace looked a question at Lightfoot, who merely shrugged.

"For pity's sake," I began. All this *Law and Order* stuff was making me crazy. Ty Honeycutt wasn't my idea of a doting nephew, but he obviously had cared for Dixie. They needed to let him see her and do his duty. He would have to step up to get her funeral arrangements underway. "You won't have any trouble finding him in that thing." Dixie's van was bright orange with a white top, circa 1963. Who knew where she found the parts?

Senora Mari tilted her chin at the sheriff, doing her best to intimidate the much taller man. "We need to get busy." She tilted her head toward Milagro.

"She's right, Mack," my aunt said. "We have a lot to do before we open the doors for lunch."

Furrowing his brow, Wallace exchanged a glance with Lightfoot. The dark-eyed officer shook his head in response.

"I'm afraid, Linda, y'all won't be opening for lunch today." Wallace looked at each of us in turn, his glance landing on Ty. "Your aunt didn't die of natural causes."

With a grunt, Ty threw back his shoulders. "What do you mean? Anyone could see she was a walking deathtrap."

"No, son," Wallace said in the fatherly voice I remembered so well. "Dixie was murdered."

Chapter 5

Sheriff Wallace interviewed Ty Honeycutt right off the bat. Though I couldn't quite make out what he asked the young man, I could see from Ty's drooped shoulders and hangdog expression he was feeling lower than dirt over Dixie's death. I didn't have any reason to doubt his story about not finding her waiting, but I couldn't help wondering why he hadn't come inside to look for her.

All of Milagro's employees, including my family, were scattered about the restaurant in different booths, waiting to be interviewed, except for Senora Mari. After declaring she had to be questioned next, she stood making small talk with Deputy Pleasant until Ty walked despondently out the side door.

As I offered coffee and tea to everyone along with tortilla chips and salsa, I heard Senora Mari fill Wallace's ear with the details of her dream. To his credit, the sheriff hadn't cracked a smile or slowed his pencil during her recitation.

"Don't worry," Senora Mari called to the far corners of our restaurant as she rose to her feet. "I will see to it you don't starve." She started toward Carlos, our lunch cook.

With a shake of her head, Deputy Pleasant blocked the elderly woman's path. "Not until he's interviewed, senora." She softened her words with a smile. "But I sure could use some quesadillas and sweet tea."

"Don't worry," Aunt Linda said, walking over to join the sheriff at his makeshift desk. "We'll rustle you up something tasty as soon as I'm finished." The determined optimism in her voice made me cringe. I didn't envy Sheriff Wallace. He was going to have to tell this zealous businesswoman there would be no lunch service today.

The cowbell on the front door jangled and Lightfoot entered, holding a batch of papers. After a quick glance around the room, the solemn deputy whispered in Wallace's ear. A resigned look fell over the sheriff's weathered countenance, and he spoke to Aunt Linda in a low voice.

"What do you mean we have to close for the day?" My aunt jumped to her feet.

I hurried over.

"Judge Hoskins gave us the okay to search the place." Wallace gestured to the papers in Lightfoot's hand.

"Fine," she nearly yelled. "Search away. We don't have anything to hide." Throwing up her hands, she tried to laugh. "How long could it take?"

"Several hours," Lightfoot offered.

Wallace thrust his thumbs into his belt and puffed out his chest. "I need to finish interviewing the staff while the fellas take a look around and dust for prints."

With a glance at my aunt's tortured face, I spoke up. "Is that absolutely necessary? Didn't she die outside?"

"We're searching the entire property." The older officer exchanged a long look with his stoic sidekick. "The killer left something behind, and we're going to find it."

I was the next subject to be interrogated. Wallace asked me the same questions, but I had nothing new to add. Afterwards, I tried to stay out of the way while surreptitiously watching the deputies dust for prints. Black dusting powder sullied the dark and light surfaces everywhere I turned: the industrial appliances, the colorful ladder-back chairs, everything from the washing machine to the jar of mints at the cash register. What a mess. How many hours would we spend wiping everything down before we could reopen? And what was happening upstairs? Were they dusting my furniture as well as my clothing? And would it wash out?

We couldn't get to the kitchen to make the requested quesadillas, so we decided to order Bubba's BBQ instead. As the staff huddled around the center tables, eating our brisket sandwiches and pickles, Lightfoot sauntered over.

"Is this everyone who works here?" he asked.

"Yes, and most of them weren't even here last night. Why did they all have to stay for questioning?"

He lifted an eyebrow as if responding to a precocious child. "Procedure."

With a bang of the swinging doors, Anthony rushed through the kitchen door. "Miss Josie, I just heard about that woman being found outside behind the trash can. Is everyone okay?" In the craziness of the last few hours, I'd forgotten all about him.

"Who are you?" Lightfoot demanded.

I gave our newest busboy and dishwasher a reassuring smile. "This is Anthony Ramirez."

Clenching his jaw, the dark-haired deputy opened his mouth to speak.

"He's an excellent employee who supports his family while he finishes his GED at West Texas."

"If he's so great, why'd you forget to mention him?"

Before I could respond, the older deputy walked in from the rear entrance. He carried a clear evidence bag in his gloved hand. Inside I could see something red, shiny, and vaguely familiar.

"Where'd you find that?" Sheriff Wallace wiped his mouth and shoved to his feet.

"Dumpster." The deputy held the bag up to the light.

My breath caught as I recognized the bow tie.

"And that ain't all. There's a near perfect shoe impression as well."

Didn't he mean boot impression? That was old news. Hadn't I, a mere civilian, seen the boot impression in the dimly lit alley? The Big Bend County Sheriff's Department didn't have anything on me.

Unaware of my reaction, the sheriff and his deputies hurried out the back.

Anthony bolted out the front door and I was right on his heels. "Wait!" With all the immigration issues throughout the state, I wasn't surprised he wanted to avoid law officers, but Broken Boot was different. He didn't need to be afraid.

As soon as it became apparent that I wasn't giving up, he stopped and slowly turned. "What do you want me to say?"

"Try telling me why you're on the run."

As if longing to leave me and my question in the dust, he glanced down the street toward the Broken Boot depot. "It's mine."

He didn't have to tell me, I already suspected. Though all of our employees wore a red bowtie, his was the only one with fringe at the bottom in the Mexican style.

"The sheriff won't assume the worst if you're straightforward with him." I waited for Anthony to say something, but he merely shook his head and kept his gaze on the sidewalk. "Just tell him how it came to be in the Dumpster." If there was ever a public official with integrity, it was Wallace.

Frustrated beyond belief at the continued delay, Aunt Linda sent our employees home. "We'll have to clean it ourselves. After losing both lunch and dinner, I'm not paying a single solitary cent for anyone to clean up after the Big Bend County Sheriff's Department."

My first impulse was to complain, but I immediately

sucked it up. If my aunt said we could do it ourselves, she actually meant we had to do it ourselves. Money was that tight.

With each of us carrying a bucket of sudsy water and a rag, we began to wash away all traces of fingerprint powder in the bar.

"It is good," Senora Mari gave me a stern nod, "to clean all fingerprints."

"Powder," I corrected. "We're washing away the finger-print powder."

"Humph," she muttered, her frown deepening. "I'm getting rid of all the germs the sheriff and his posse left behind."

Either way, we had hours of work ahead of us, but still no word as to whether or not we'd even be open for business the next day.

Boots stomped down the hall and into the entranceway. "Linda," Sheriff Wallace called out.

Something about the tone of his voice pulled us up short. We traipsed into the other room without bothering to put down our buckets.

Like a third-world leader on vacation in New York City, Anthony stood surrounded by a circle of officers on high alert. No guns were drawn, but Wallace's crew had their chests out and their hands on their holsters.

"What's going on, sheriff?" I hugged my bucket to my chest, sloshing soap on my blouse.

"Nothing to get riled up about, ladies. We're only taking Anthony in for further questioning."

With her usual swagger, Aunt Linda went nose to nose with Wallace. "Does he need a lawyer?"

The older deputy butted in. "We're about to find out."

"Keep your smart comments to yourself." The sheriff lev-eled the other man with a narrow-eyed glare. With a sigh, he met my aunt's worried gaze. "If he needs one, he'll get one."

As the entourage herded out the side door to their cruisers,

Lightfoot caught my eye. He shot a quick glance at Wallace's retreating back before giving me a level look.

I lifted a brow. What was he trying to tell me?

Under his breath he murmured, "Get the best money can buy."

By eight o'clock the next morning, my family had developed a plan of attack. Uncle Eddie would meet Carlos, our cook, at Milagro to unlock the doors. After briefing our most experienced employee, Eddie would then drive to Two Boots to unlock the dance hall for his head bartender. Finally, he would meet us at the sheriff's department to find out why Wallace was still holding Anthony for questioning. The fact that Eddie might get better results from the good ole boys down at city hall irritated my independent side, but I'd lived in Broken Boot long enough to recognize the truth: we were merely women, not former West Texas football stars.

My cell rang as we piled into Aunt Linda's truck. "Hi, Elaine," I said, rolling my eyes as I hit the speaker button.

"Oh, I'm sorry to bother you so early, but we have an emergency."

Aunt Linda hit the brakes. "What?"

Elaine's voice flooded with regret. "Oh, I'm so sorry. That poor woman. No, no, it's nothing like that grisly business, thank God."

Shooting me a look of frustration, my aunt took her foot off the brake and started to reverse once again.

"What kind of emergency?" I asked, trying to hide my frustration. Why did I always miss breakfast?

"We've had one of our talent show judges just up and quit."

Coffee. If I'd had a cup of coffee I'd understand why the committee chairwoman was sharing her woes with me so early in the morning. "Uh, are you asking for a recommendation?"

"No, I'm asking you to take her place."

"Well," I flung a desperate look at Aunt Linda, who refused

to look my way, "I'm already working the tamale-eating contest."

"Yes, honey. I know."

"Why don't you ask Ryan? He'd love to work side by side with Hillary." Though I couldn't fathom why.

"That's just the thing," the chairwoman said in a patient voice, "he's too busy judging the chili cook-off, not to mention . . . what was it he said?"

It didn't take a football fan to know Ryan's favorite excuse for avoiding anything he didn't want to do. "Scouting for players?" I offered.

"Exactly!"

By now, we were only minutes from the sheriff's department. Anthony needed our help to maneuver the justice system, and we weren't going to disappoint him.

"Did you ask Hillary? She knows lots of judges."

"She recommended you. Said you had a real talent for picking winners after living all those years in Austin."

The little witch.

Before I could protest, Aunt Linda shook her head as if to say, "You're a Callahan. Don't you dare back down."

I looked to Senora Mari for support, but she only shrugged.

"You win," I said.

"No, darling. Once this is all over, the citizens of Broken Boot will be the winners."

The pedestrian and downright ugly sand-colored, brick building housed the Big Bend County Sheriff's Department, the mayor's office, and all the city services necessary to run a town of this size. Whose bright idea was it to bring Anthony in for questioning? I led the way inside, followed by Aunt Linda, with Senora Mari trailing like a forlorn caboose.

As I studied the bowels of the circa 1970 building, I realized the upside of this whole, stinking business. During the night, I'd tossed and kicked as all my frustration came to a boil until a plausible explanation for the marks around Dixie's neck had risen to the top. This would be the perfect opportunity to present my deduction to the sheriff.

I crossed to the information counter. "Excuse me. Which way to Sheriff Wallace's office?"

Before the fresh-faced volunteer could answer, the familiar bass voice of Deputy Lightfoot answered. "Shouldn't you ladies be preparing lunch at Milagro?"

"Depends," said Senora Mari.

"Are you going to shut us down again today for no decent reason?" Aunt Linda's voice echoed down the hall, turning heads in our direction. Maybe it wasn't exactly Lightfoot's fault, but he'd searched the place all the same.

"We're heading that way as soon as we see the sheriff," I said. Our eyes met and my pulse jumped into hyperdrive, embarrassing me half to death.

Lightfoot didn't look to the left or to the right, obviously recognizing the sane one of the bunch. "You need to come with me." He was trying to communicate something with those black eyes of his, but darned if I could make it out.

"She's not going anywhere without us!" Senora Mari said, grabbing me by one arm while Aunt Linda grabbed the other.

"Shh!" I hissed. Rational behavior was slipping downhill faster than a flash flood during a spring rain. "That's what he meant." I wriggled free. "Everyone just calm down."

And like magic, they did, their paranoia disappearing into thin air.

Lightfoot waited a beat, eyeing all three of us with caution. "Why don't you come with me, and we'll find Sheriff Wallace together?"

Without waiting for an argument, I took the bull by the horns. "Sounds like the best plan yet." We followed him and his neat ponytail across the lobby and past an authentic buffalo head that hung over an enormous stone hearth. At a tall bronze sculpture of a western boot with a broken heel, he made a sharp left.

We followed him down a narrow hall and ran into Elaine
Burnett coming out of the county tax collector's office. "Oh
my, are you all right?" She grabbed Aunt Linda by the arms.
"We could have all been killed!" Over Elaine's shoulder, I
could see that my aunt was aggravated, but she managed to
untangle herself from the other woman without being rude.

Before I could maneuver away, Elaine grabbed me in her
lavender-perfumed arms, "Josie, you could have been killed."
I wasn't sure why she hadn't expressed such concern over the
phone earlier, but much to my relief, she released me after a
brief squeeze.

My eyes started to tear in spite of my command for them
not to do so. "I'm fine. I was never in any danger."

"No one's dead except Dixie." Senora Mari stiff-armed
Elaine, preventing the other woman from hugging her as well.

While Elaine uttered comforting platitudes, I caught Lightfoot's eye and delivered a silent plea for help.

"Let's get a move on, ladies."

I adopted a put-out expression. "I'm sorry Mrs. Burnett,
but we have to meet with Sheriff Wallace."

"Oh, of course you do, and I'll say a prayer for all of you."
She pulled me to one side as if Lightfoot couldn't see or hear
her. "Don't let that deputy get the better of you. You're innocent until proven guilty."

Where she had whispered, I almost shouted. "I'm not
guilty of anything."

Senora Mari chimed in, "Me neither!"

Elaine's gaze flew swiftly over my shoulder.

"Don't you stare at me," Aunt Linda cried. "I've got nothing to hide."

Elaine's jaw dropped as if she'd been sucker-punched.
Folks in Broken Boot did not raise their voice to the Wild
Wild West Festival committee chairwoman.

Before she could gather herself, Lightfoot interrupted. "For
Pete's sake, let's go." He strode off down the hall.

Insulted at Elaine's insinuations, we marched after him,

fuming but no longer frustrated with the deputy who'd helped ruin a perfectly good lunch and dinner service only the day before.

We followed him down the narrow hall, passing cubicles and county workers, until we reached a wall plaque that read *The Office of Sheriff Mack E. Wallace.*

"Have a seat," Lightfoot ordered, gesturing to a seating area composed of taupe walls and gray metal chairs with lumpy gray padding. The only way the designer, if that was the correct word, could have made this room more depressing would have been to add a huge flat screen TV that played a loop of used car commercials.

We followed his command without argument while he checked in with the middle-aged secretary behind the desk.

With a frown, Lightfoot walked over. "Wallace is out to lunch."

Aunt Linda checked her watch. "It's a bit early, don't you think?"

"So he's out to breakfast."

"Is he coming back soon?"

"She says he'll be back in about fifteen minutes." He tipped his head toward the secretary, who was glaring at us over the rim of her glasses.

Senora Mari glared right back. "We wait."

Lightfoot looked a question at me, and I shrugged. "You heard her. We'll wait."

For a few minutes, no one spoke while the three of us with smartphones checked our messages.

Senora Mari tapped me on the leg. "You tell him."

"What?"

After a dramatic exhale, she whispered, "You know."

"I don't."

Aunt Linda leaned toward me and muttered, "Tell him what Dixie said."

Immediately interested, Lightfoot sat up straight. "What'd she say to you?"

Oh, boy. This could get out of hand faster than a jackrabbit on speed. "Senora Mari," I said, with an expansive gesture, "had a dream about Dixie."

"And?"

"Well . . . in the dream . . . Dixie, um, said, um, she wanted revenge."

Silence. Like a statue, he didn't blink for a full thirty seconds.

"And what else?" he finally asked.

Senora Mari spoke up. "She didn't speak, but she told me that when she died she was cold and out of air."

Another pregnant pause. He stared at Aunt Linda and he stared at me. "Is that it?"

With Senora Mari giving me a narrow-eyed glare, I didn't dare roll my eyes. "Pretty much."

His mouth twisted for a second, and I could have sworn Mr. Silent and Stoic would laugh. Instead he blew out his breath and shook his head. "Thanks for telling me," he said, his mask firmly in place.

"Who are your parents, Indian?"

Aunt Linda and I gasped. No one I knew would have dared use the word *Indian* instead of *Native American*. If we weren't waiting for the sheriff on behalf of my favorite employee, I swear I would've run for the ladies' room. Senora Mari was many things, but politically correct wasn't one of them.

Lightfoot snapped his head toward the elderly woman, eyes narrowed. "Tuti and Eric Lightfoot from New Mexico." His lips thinned. "Why? You planning a trip to Albuquerque?"

"I've gone out West." Her remark made me smile. I wondered if she knew that for most people Broken Boot was as far west as they wanted to go. She sized him up from toe to sternum. "Have you ever been to that UFO museum in Roswell?" Uncle Eddie had taken us on a vacation to see the Grand Canyon the summer before my senior year in high school. Senora Mari had insisted on choosing one of our stops.

"Hah," he barked, which meant, I assumed, he wasn't going to put her in cuffs or read her the riot act for not being politically correct. "Once, but that place was a joke."

She leaned closer. "Oh, yeah? I bet you spend your Saturday nights in Marfa, staring at a bunch of giant fireflies."

Who would have guessed the handsome deputy and the powerhouse tamale cook would share an interest in extraterrestrials?

Twenty miles southwest of Broken Boot stood the Marfa Lights Viewing Area, the perfect diversion for tourists on their trek to Big Bend National Park on the southwest Texas border. People of all ages came to stand in the dark to watch the red, blue, and sometimes white lights appear in the night sky. The cynics said this so-called paranormal phenomenon was just the reflection of cars and campfires at night. The believers said that was hooey.

Senora Mari chuckled. "I didn't see any UFOs when I was there."

The smile he flashed her could have warmed the cold canyons of the moon. "Me neither, but I've seen the Marfa lights dance on the horizon dozens of times. We're old friends." They beamed at each other, and then just as suddenly his smile disappeared as he checked his phone again.

"Who are you dating?" This time Senora Mari's inquisition was met with silence. The air fairly quivered with anticipation as all three of us leaned toward him just a smidge.

"Is she an Indian too?"

Oh, boy. The older woman might not have meant any harm, but I was embarrassed for the both of them.

"Yes, ma'am."

"I don't blame you. Best to stick with your own kind, though my son, Eddie, never listened to me. No offense, Linda."

Next to me, Aunt Linda pulled a face. "None taken," she turned her head toward me and muttered, "Now that you live with us."

"Of course," Senora Mari continued, "if you decide you

want to try something new before you settle down and have babies, you could ask Josie. She'd give you a run for your money."

Great. Now I was a racehorse.

He glanced at me. One side of his mouth kicked up. "Hmm . . . I'll take that under advisement."

"She's not a good cook, but she's smart."

And now we were back in the 1800s. "You know I can hear you, right?"

Lowering her voice, Senora Mari continued, "She acts high and mighty, but she's not, when you know her."

He leveled a glance at me. "You sure?"

"*Por supuesto*," she said, patting my head. "I am never wrong."

I talked Aunt Linda into staying with Senora Mari in the waiting area. She readily agreed that there was no need to henpeck the sheriff with an overabundance of female advice.

Humming a lonesome tune, Sheriff Wallace looked out his office window to the cloud-shadowed Chisos Mountain ridge. In the distance, a small herd of cattle grazed in the sparse grass. The sheriff turned to me with a sad smile. "I don't see you in a month of Sundays, and now it's two days in a row."

We'd met when I was ten, freckled and reddish blond from the desert summer sun. I tried to chuckle, but his remark brought me back to Dixie's cold, pasty skin. "I wish it were for far better reasons."

"I'm glad you're home. We need more young folks like you in Broken Boot."

"Like me?"

He continued, "Educated, cool," and chuckled, "you know, Austin weird."

I grinned with pride. "Maybe just a touch."

"*Austin weird*, that's a term my niece uses. She's artistic . . .

like Dixie." He frowned as if remembering the cantankerous artist was dead. "I apologize for shutting down Milagro, but I couldn't see my way around it." He and Lightfoot exchanged pointed glances. "But I do have a few more questions."

I sensed, rather than saw, Lightfoot tense at my side. "Sure thing." If I cooperated with the sheriff, he might release Anthony sooner. "Let's get started."

"Have a seat." He gestured toward a wingback chair in front of his desk. As he lowered himself to his own massive leather armchair, he gestured for Lightfoot to stand near the door.

"How long has Anthony Ramirez been employed at Milagro?" Wallace picked up a napkin with a coffee ring on it, wadded it up, and threw it in the trash.

I tapped my fingers on the arm of the chair. "Three months or so."

"Why'd you hire him?" Wallace picked up a file from the corner of his desk and flipped it open.

"Business started picking up, and we needed the extra hands."

Before I could test my ability to read upside down, the sheriff closed the file. "Why him?"

"You've met him. He's cute and personable, and he works hard. Our customers love him."

He leaned his head back. "And your family, they love him?"

"Sure, he's sweet." I realized what I was saying when Wallace leaned forward. "No, I don't *love him* love him. Come on, he's a kid."

"Any problems with him?"

"None. Seriously, it's like I said yesterday. He provides for his brothers and sisters. He's taking classes at West Texas, working two jobs. He can't afford to get into trouble."

Wallace taped his pencil on the table. "He was arrested last year for a felony. Did you know that?"

I swallowed a huge lump in my throat. "No," I said in a small voice.

"Afraid so."

I swiveled in my chair to look at Lightfoot. He gave a slow nod.

"But why would he kill Dixie? He doesn't even know her."

Removing a pack of mint gum from his pocket, Wallace asked, "Was he there last night?"

I could tell that he already knew the answer. "Yes, but only for a few minutes. He stopped by to pick up his paycheck."

As Wallace opened his gum, he tossed another question my way. "He didn't help out in the kitchen?"

"No." My gut was telling me the sheriff's questions weren't as casual as he wanted me to believe.

"Didn't take out the trash? Sit outside? Smoke a cigarette?"

I racked my brain. "No. He wanted more hours, and Aunt Linda told him not yet."

"He was angry about that?"

Talk about a fishing expedition. "No. He was frustrated because he's working two jobs and still not making ends meet, but he wasn't angry."

Wallace rolled the wrapper into a tiny ball and aimed it at the trash can as if shooting a three-pointer. "So he didn't come back later to help clean up?"

"No, sir." Whatever the sheriff thought he had on Anthony was wrong. I knew that boy, and he would never have hurt Dixie . . . or anyone else for that matter.

I leaned forward, grabbing the desk. "He wouldn't do this, sheriff. If you don't have any evidence, you know you need to charge him or release him." I had watched my share of crime dramas, and that's what the lawyers always said.

"That's the thing. We do have evidence, and we charged him this morning."

Outrage hit me hard upside the head. "You charged that nineteen-year-old kid with murder?"

"Afraid so."

"On what evidence?" What had they found that incriminated one of the best teenagers in the whole county?

The sheriff's face had closed down tighter than our to-go window on a Sunday night. "Now, Josie, you're not family or his lawyer," he said, pushing back his chair and rising to his feet.

I sprang out of my chair. "Does he have one?"

"The public defender is no slouch. You don't need to worry yourself over it."

After a quick glance at Lightfoot, I threw back my shoulders and locked eyes with Wallace. "I'm going to prove you wrong."

The sheriff came around his walnut desk and herded me to the door. "I apologize, Josie. I do have to make some calls before the day gets too far along."

"What if I find evidence indicating that someone else murdered Dixie?" With the sheriff's department out of the way, I would find what they had missed. If I, a former reporter with the *Austin Gazette*, couldn't do it, then who could?

Popping the cuffs of his white dress shirt, Wallace ushered me into the hall. "If you find anything we missed, pass it along to Lightfoot," he said, gesturing to his deputy. "He'll share it with me, and we'll figure out the best way to proceed."

"Yes, sir," Lightfoot chimed in.

They exchanged a quick glance, and I could tell that there was something they weren't telling me.

With a quick glance at the Texas-shaped red, white, and blue clock on the wall, the sheriff cleared his throat. "Don't go getting folks all riled up."

"What does that mean?"

Wallace blew out a breath. "Eddie told me all about that alleged robbery you called in while at the *Gazette*."

My cheeks flushed with heat. "That was years ago, sheriff. It was an honest mistake." All I could remember about that embarrassing night was that I'd clearly overheard two men whispering the words, *robbery*, *steal*, *heist*, and *diamonds*. My desperate yearning to find an exciting crime story had filled in the blanks I needed to hear.

"You've got to trust us," he nodded to his deputy. "We can handle the investigation."

"Alright."

"I'm guessing you want to see him?"

"Yes, I want to see him." I said, raising my chin. "We all want to see him."

"Let me make a call to the jail. Lightfoot will take you out to the visiting area while I find out what's what." Wallace tipped his hat. "Good day, Josie."

"Thanks, sheriff."

I snuck a glance at Lightfoot. Maybe the deputy would give me some information away from the watchful eyes of his boss.

The deputy's eyes met mine. "Don't ask."

So much for inside information.

Chapter 6

Back in the waiting room, I found my uncle and aunt in a tight embrace.

"They arrested Anthony," I said.

"What?" my aunt cried.

I felt sick to my stomach, but I uttered the truth. "They think he murdered Dixie."

"That's loco," Senora Mari muttered. "That boy wouldn't kill her. He's too sweet, like sugar."

"Don't worry, honey." Uncle Eddie released Aunt Linda with a peck on her cheek. "I'll talk to the sheriff and find out what's going on." One look at my face, and he grabbed me in a bear hug as well.

I guess I was still shaky from the night before—Uncle Eddie's warm affection made me want to weep.

"It's going to be okay, Jo Jo." His pet name for me did the trick and I laughed.

"Eddie, you talk to the sheriff, but we have to go back to Milagro." Senora Mari rocked forward onto her white Keds and pushed to her feet. "We must open on time."

"Mamá, the staff can handle it. You trained them, remember?" Uncle Eddie placed an arm around her slight shoulders.

"She's right. We need to be there." Aunt Linda grabbed her purse from her chair. "Our customers need to know we're okay, that nothing's changed."

"Why don't you and Senora Mari go on?" The two experienced women would have things well in hand at Milagro. "Uncle Eddie can bring me home after we find out what's going on with Anthony."

My aunt threw her bag over her shoulder. "Mitzi's been calling every five minutes, Eddie. You've got to get back to the repairman before he'll agree to do the job."

After a bit more convincing, Aunt Linda and Senora Mari headed out, debating the best choice for the day's lunch special. My aunt wanted the ever popular tilapia tacos while Senora Mari remained adamant that chile rellenos would prove the staff was undaunted by the murder.

Uncle Eddie moseyed over to prop against the counter that separated the sheriff's secretary from the rest of the waiting room. "How's it going? Is your daughter enjoying running Monday night bingo?"

"She sure is, Mr. Martinez," the secretary answered with a smile that brightened her somber countenance, "and I can't thank you enough. I guess you know it's her first job."

"I would've never known." He leaned closer. "I need to speak to Mack a minute."

After a cursory glance at her computer screen, she shook her head. "I'm afraid his schedule is full this morning."

"He and I go way back." Uncle Eddie tipped his hat. "Played football together, back in the day."

The sheriff's secretary turned pink beneath her pale foundation. "Oh, I can still picture you two in your uniforms, like it was yesterday." She called Wallace on the intercom, nodded quickly three or four times, and hung up. "He says that's fine." She bit her bottom lip. "I'm sorry, Mr. Martinez. That's how he prefers me to handle his visitors."

"No harm, no foul," my uncle said and loped off in search of his former tackle.

The phone rang. As the secretary answered it, two deputies walked down the hall talking in low voices.

I tried to appear nonchalant as I turned on my heel and hurried after them. As a journalist I'd developed the habit of listening to other people's conversations, especially if those people were in law enforcement. And in this case, there was every chance they were discussing Dixie's untimely death.

They stopped in the vending machine area. "He's going to inherit her money, every cent," said a short deputy who sported long sideburns, a full red mustache, and a shiny bald head.

Bingo. Didn't Ty stand to inherit all of Dixie's money? If she had any other relatives, none of us had ever heard her mention them.

In a high voice at odds with his height, the other law officer said, "He owes everyone and their mother money. You'd have to be half stupid and the other half crazy to play cards with him."

"Stupid hick needs to stick to guitar playing."

"Not too good at that either," the bald guy said as his candy slammed to the bottom of the machine. When he picked up his chocolate, he noticed me and froze.

Assuming a frustrated expression, I thrust my hand into the pocket of my jeans. "Dang it," I said, snapping my fingers for good measure, "I must have left my money in my purse." The bald one's eyes narrowed as if trying to decipher what I'd heard. Before he could question me, I shrugged and headed back the way I had come, a ditzy smile plastered to my face.

Back in the waiting area, I wandered over to the secretary's desk. "Is the sheriff keeping you busy?"

She shook her head in disgust. "No, but ever since that woman was found dead, it's picked up a bit."

I smiled to commiserate. "Is the phone ringing off the hook?"

"Not exactly, but the JP's called a couple of times this morning."

Ellis. Last night, Wallace had said his name was Ellis. In Texas, a justice of the peace could issue warrants, conduct preliminary hearings, administer oaths, conduct inquests, *and* perform the usual weddings. He could also serve as medical examiner in counties without a coroner. Now that Wallace believed that Dixie had been murdered, he and Ellis would be sending the body to El Paso for an autopsy. That could take weeks, even in a case of murder.

"I bet he's in a panic, huh?" I was shooting from the hip. Most JPs or MEs would never be in a panic unless their office caught fire. When I'd worked at the *Gazette*, I'd heard reporters complain that the MEs were so backlogged they refused to rush anything.

Amidst a chorus of guffaws, Lightfoot and Uncle Eddie walked out of the sheriff's office.

"Hello, again." The middle-aged secretary's face lit up like a birthday cake.

Not realizing her smile was for the former football star, Lightfoot gifted her with a dazzling smile and me with a short wave of his right hand. Perhaps he'd worked as a traffic cop prior to driving a cruiser to murder scenes. They probably put him in the road because he stopped traffic with that whole chiseled profile thing he had going on.

But I refused to be treated as a pedestrian. "Are you waving at me?"

"Who else? Come on." Before I could come up with something witty, he left me to follow him on my own.

"Such a sense of humor," I muttered to no one in particular.

"What'd you find out?" I asked as Uncle Eddie and I made our way back to the lobby.

"First off, Lightfoot says we'll have to wait until tomorrow to see Anthony because he's meeting with his lawyer."

"Do you know her?" I didn't actually think the Broken Boot public defender was a woman, but I tossed the idea out there to keep my uncle from getting too comfortable in his cave.

He gave me a sharp look. "No, but Mack says he's a fine lawyer, played tight end for UT back in the eighties."

"Since when does that matter?"

Uncle Eddie stopped in his tracks. "Of course it matters. He played football for a Big 12 team and passed the bar. That man has drive and determination."

"What about Anthony's bail?"

"I don't know," he screwed up his mouth in thought. "Why don't you call when you get back to Milagro?"

I opened my mouth to argue. "He needs—"

"I've got to get back to Two Boots or we won't be able to open tonight." His ready smile died.

If our dance hall didn't open, we'd miss payroll at both of our businesses. It had never happened, and my uncle swore on his father's grave that it never would.

As we crossed the lobby at a fast clip, I noticed Lightfoot conversing with the young, female volunteer at the information booth. I was so intent on ignoring the way she smiled at him that I almost ran over Patti Perez, who was leaving the building right in front of me.

Three months had passed since I'd crawled home. I'd hidden the first six weeks from everyone but the customers at Milagro, spending my days and nights waiting tables, hosting, or being a couch potato upstairs in my loft apartment. Gradually, I'd added trips to Casa Martinez on Monday nights. I'd reached out to Patti only a couple of weeks ago, and she'd greeted me as if we were still summertime friends of twelve.

My unemotional Goth friend surprised me by squeezing both of my hands. "I heard you found Dixie's body. Are you okay?"

"Shaken, but not stirred."

She didn't crack a smile.

"I'm okay . . . or at least I will be."

Uncle Eddie cleared his throat. "Uh, Patti, would you mind taking Josie to the restaurant? I need to run over to Two Boots to avert a crisis."

"No problemo," she said, giving him a slow, emphatic nod.

After a brief word of thanks for her and a back-cracking hug for me, my uncle broke into a trot toward the parking lot.

"Get a load of that," Patti murmured.

I glanced over my shoulder to see what had my blasé friend so in awe. Lightfoot was heading down the sidewalk, wearing dark aviator shades and his usual somber expression.

"What you see is all you get," I whispered.

"That's enough."

As he passed us, he tipped his hat. "Ladies."

"Uh, hello, again." I didn't dare look at Patti.

"You know him, don't you?"

"Not really."

She elbowed me in the side. "Introduce us."

"No."

"Hey, officer," Patti called.

Lightfoot swung around.

Without hesitation, she walked closer. "Do you think it's okay for Josie to stay at Milagro on her own tonight?"

His head turned in my direction and he frowned. "Are you sure you're feeling up to it?"

Had I given him the impression I was frail? Or was he asking because I was a mere female? "Definitely." Either way, I had to set him straight.

Patti piped up. "She has a watchdog."

His frown deepened. "That's not a dog. That's a shrimp cocktail."

"Hey!" Lightfoot had better watch it or he would get a bite from Lenny's bad side.

He shook his head and removed a small notepad and pen from his pocket. "Is your plan to stay there alone?"

You couldn't pay me to sleep there, but that didn't mean I

wanted him to tell me what I could and couldn't do. "I don't know yet."

The strong, silent deputy jotted a few lines.

"Why?" Patti smiled. "Does that sound suspicious?" She pointed a tattooed finger at what he'd written.

In the silence that followed, Lightfoot and Patti made serious eye contact. Or at least Patti tried to get something going. Nothing on the deputy's face changed, but he lifted one eyebrow.

My longtime friend shot me an exasperated look.

With a sigh of resignation, I gave in to her romantic aspirations, no matter how useless love had proven to be to me. "Uh," I began, "this is my good friend Patti Perez."

"Dude," Patti said.

At least she hadn't giggled. I turned to the silent and watchful deputy. "Lightfoot . . . what's your first name?"

"Quint."

Patti, in my humble opinion, was the only intelligent, talented, and independent woman left in Broken Boot; but due to his dark sunglasses, I had no idea whether or not the stoic deputy was interested. That hacked me off. "Like squint?"

Even behind the shades, I could feel the foul look he gave me. "Yeah," he muttered.

"Well, we've got to be going. Milagro's going to be crowded today." I grabbed Patti by the arm and herded her down the sidewalk toward the parking lot.

"See you around," she called over her shoulder.

As I spotted her jeep, I increased our speed and she laughed. "Is he yours?"

"Definitely not," I said a bit too emphatically.

She retrieved her key from her shoulder bag and unlocked the doors. "You sure?"

"I'm on the wagon." I slid into the passenger seat and stared resolutely out the window.

Backing out of her parking space, she threw me a quick glance. "I didn't know you were addicted."

"He's a man, isn't he?" What did it matter if Lightfoot was attractive or not? Brooks, the slime bucket, had proven that looks and love could be deceiving.

"And?"

"I'm taking a break from all of them."

She made a cheering sound under her breath and slammed the jeep into drive. "Perfect timing."

On the way home, I poured out all the details of the past two days including my plan to free Anthony as soon as possible.

"Let me make some calls about his bail this afternoon." Patti was on the highway, but barely going the speed limit. "That's the least I can do while you help your family get the restaurant back on its feet."

I realized something was up when an old lady driving a Taurus passed us. "Why are you driving slower than a turtle in a mud bath?"

"I'm trying to prevent global warning." She shot me a superior look. "You didn't ask me why I was at city hall."

"You wanted to take a picture of the largest brass boot in the state of Texas?"

She stuck out her tongue piercing. "Remember how you forced me to take pictures of the committee?"

"Last week?"

"Right. I emailed them the next day to the mayor so he could have his wife add them to the festival website, like he asked."

"That should have made him happier than a rooster in a henhouse."

"Since when do you go in for cornpone metaphors?"

I sighed. "Can I help it if the festival committee's necks are a bit red?"

"Red or not, the mayor asked me to help his wife upload the pictures."

"And did you?"

"I uploaded my pictures and some others Dixie had sent. Felicia Cogburn was so confused they ended up paying me for my time."

"Didn't I tell you they'd always remember you?"

"Well, I'm not about to forget the photos I saw of Cogburn and his wife for a long time to come."

I wrinkled my nose in disgust. "Gross."

"Ha," she cried. "Nothing like that."

I cringed, both anticipating and dreading the details.

With an evil grin, Patti continued. "I opened one of Dixie's emails and the attachment, just as I had the others. Instead of finding another photo of her jewelry, I discovered a candid shot of Mayor Cogburn and his wife coming out of a doctor's office."

I sighed with relief, glad to remain ignorant of any intimate details about Broken Boot's first couple. "One was probably just giving the other one a ride from an appointment."

After a glance at a passing motorcycle, Patti shot me an exasperated look. "It wasn't any building from this area. It was twelve stories at least."

Despite Patti's slow progress, we were approaching Main Street. "Why do you think it was a medical building?"

"Whoever took the picture caught the Cogburns in front of a bronze plaque, bearing a list of doctors' names."

My conscience slammed into my stomach. "What if something is seriously wrong with one of them? That's not our business."

Pulling into Milagro's parking lot, Patti turned off the engine. "*MD* wasn't one of the degrees following any of the names on that plaque."

"What do you think it means?"

"I don't know. When Felicia realized I'd seen the photo, she turned as red as a tomato and nearly knocked me out of her chair, insisting I take a break."

I gathered my purse from the floor. "That's a bit odd, but not as strange as the sheriff arresting Anthony for Dixie's murder."

Narrowing her eyes, she slowly nodded her head. "I think Mayor Cogburn and his wife were visiting a place that would compromise their reputation if word got out. I bet you Dixie was blackmailing them."

"Why would she do that?" I opened the door and stepped out.

"You know how much she hated them. She loved to take folks down a peg, especially the Cogburns. She didn't make any secret of the fact she was sick of their criticism."

I slammed the door and walked around the car, anxious to get inside to help out with lunch service. "If she felt that way, why make the jewelry for the annual fundraiser again this year?"

"To help others?" Patti called out the window and threw the jeep into reverse. She backed up, drove to the street, and backed up again until we were face-to-face. "Would you tell Elaine to replace me with someone else? What do I know about judging an art contest?"

"More than me. Besides, I thought Melanie was judging the art contest and you were judging the photos." In order to build attendance from the surrounding counties, the Wild Wild West Festival committee lassoed a number of us to judge a dozen creative arts competitions. Thank God, Elaine hadn't aspired to the more than 1100 categories offered by the State Fair of Texas.

Patti's mouth twisted. "Technically, we're judging both contests as a team."

I understood her dilemma. No one in their right mind would call Melanie Burnett Pratt a team player.

"Look," I said, glancing at my watch, "you're going to have to handle Elaine on your own. I rolled over like a wet dog."

I scurried through Milagro's back door, resisting the urge to stare at the Dumpster where I'd found the cantankerous jewelry designer's body. Inside the kitchen, Carlos was grilling savory strips of chicken and beef along with peppers and onions for mouthwatering fajitas. One of the twins was spraying dirty dishes with hot water, and Aunt Linda was expediting food service by calling out the orders as she placed them in the kitchen service window.

"About time," Senora Mari said as I greeted her at the hostess stand.

"Why are we so busy?" Even though the Wild Wild West Festival started the next day, these folks were locals, not tourists. Every booth and wooden table was occupied with familiar faces.

She rolled her eyes. "All they want to talk about is Dixie. 'Did you see the body?' 'Did Anthony kill her?'"

I wasn't surprised. Folks in this town were so thirsty for gossip they'd die of boredom if they didn't get out of bed and go to church on Sundays.

Hurrying over, Aunt Linda grabbed some menus from the counter and thrust them into my hands. "At least they're ordering and not just taking up space." She pointed to a corner booth, where a four top waited without menus.

With her usual uncanny ability to second-guess our customers, my aunt had brought in the full staff. Even with me taking a few orders and delivering chips and salsa, this would have been a perfect day to give Anthony a couple of tables of his own. How would he make bail without working? I didn't get the impression his sisters and brothers had much between them.

An hour later, the rush was behind us, but two-thirds of our tables remained occupied. We'd sold out of pecan and cherry pie, but thanks to a quick delivery from Elaine's Pies customers made do with chocolate and coconut cream. Folks lingered over their coffee and sweet tea, finding excuses for calling me over to their tables.

As I filled Fred Mueller's water glass, he leaned in close. "How do you sleep at night?" The owner of Fredericksburg

Antiques blinked rapidly at me from behind his bottle-thick glasses.

"Excuse me?"

Color flew into his faded cheeks. "Oh, dear, I didn't mean that the way it sounded. I only meant if it were me who'd found a dead body, I'd be having nightmares."

It wasn't during the night that Dixie's smiling corpse appeared in my mind but in the quiet moments of the day, when I tried to fathom who wanted her dead.

"Will there be anything else?"

From behind me a familiar voice rang out. "I'd like two El Presidenté Platters, *por favor.*"

His voice wrapped around me like a warm Mexican blanket. "Ryan?" I spun around, sloshing ice water on my shirt.

Though he wore a playful grin, his eyes held concern. "How you holding up, Josie?" Seeing Ryan, who'd comforted me on many occasions, made my knees buckle. It was as if my body could finally admit how much the tragic events of the past few days had rattled my mind.

His gaze traveled across the room to where Hillary was disappearing behind the door marked *Niñas.* "Come on." He placed a strong hand on my shoulder, led me into the kitchen, and found me a stool in the corner near the phone. "Tell me you're not staying here by yourself?" he asked, relieving me of the water pitcher.

I took a deep breath to calm myself and tried to smile. "No. I'm at Aunt Linda's." His expression was one of deep concern, and I suddenly realized how weak and fragile I must have appeared. I plastered on a grin. "I'm in my old bedroom. Remember?"

After a searching glance, he gave me a slow smile. "How could I forget? That time I stayed with you over the Christmas break Eddie made me sleep on that old couch in the garage. The one time I tried to sneak inside Senora Mari caught me and made me help her clean the oven—"

"In the middle of the night," we said at the same time. I

burst out laughing. Good old Ryan. He understood too well my need to remain strong and in control. We'd broken up for that very reason. If two strong-minded people were in a relationship, only one could take the lead.

And second fiddle wasn't an instrument I enjoyed playing.

Nearby Carlos was dishing out sour cream enchiladas onto a fiesta red plate. He followed up by adding a generous helping of rice and refried beans, and then he hit the bell and slid the savory deliciousness into the window for pickup.

Carmen, whose eldest played defensive lineman at West Texas, appeared within seconds to claim it. "*Hola*, Coach Ryan."

"*Hola*, senora. Where's Juan today?" Ryan asked.

She beamed with pride. "He's babysitting his little sisters and playing Xbox."

With exaggerated disgust, Ryan shook his head. "Tell him I said he needs to run at least two miles every day before he sits down to play video games."

She giggled at the handsome coach's antics. "Okay, I will tell him," she hesitated, "but he won't listen."

As she hurried away, Ryan and I laughed. It was good to have an old friend like him by my side. I didn't know where Hillary was, but I knew this time alone with him would be brief. "Are you eating tamales in tomorrow's contest?"

"Wouldn't miss it. Of course, Elaine has me helping Bubba judge the chili cook-off immediately afterwards." He moaned in fake agony and rubbed his stomach. "I'm going to be out of commission for a good twenty-four hours."

"You could tell her no."

"Okay." He raised an eyebrow. "And what did you say no to?"

I huffed. "I'm surprised Hillary didn't tell you."

"Tell him what?" I spied Hillary observing us closely from the kitchen door. She wore a smile, but her hostile stare said *hands off!*

I stood up, refusing to be intimidated. "The talent show. Elaine called me this morning."

"What about the talent? I'm judging it," Hillary said.

"Someone dropped out, right?"

"And I told her that Ryan," she walked over to her man and lightly touched his arm, "would be my partner in crime."

Ryan didn't look too pleased at Hillary's tone. A vein had appeared at his temple. "You didn't mention it to me."

She shrugged one shoulder and tossed her mane. "I was about to, over lunch."

This was the out I was looking for. "No problem with me. Maybe Elaine misunderstood."

"Why do you say that?" Ryan asked. By the look of things, he was trying to get out of judging Broken Boot's aspiring artists just like me.

"Because she asked me to, uh, be Hillary's co-judge this morning."

Ryan grinned. "You'd be perfect."

"That's ridiculous." Hillary thrust her hands on her hips. "Why would Elaine do that?"

I was offended, but I sucked it up. If Ryan wanted to be with her, he deserved to be her co-judge. "Look. Just call her and tell her you and I talked it over and we agreed that Ryan would make a better judge for the talent contest."

The football coach was having none of it. He stood between us, his jaw clenching and unclenching. "Hey, I'm already eating tamales and judging the chili cook-off. Don't you think that's enough heartburn for one day?"

Senora Mari came out of the office, her eyes widening. "Why are you standing here not eating?"

Ryan placed a quick kiss on her cheek. "I came to check on my best girl."

"Hey, watch it!" Senora Mari warned, flushing an attractive shade of pink.

He placed an arm around her shoulders and squeezed. "How are you holding up, senora?"

"I'm not the one that's dead." Wriggling away from him, she made a big deal of wiping his kiss from her cheek. She gestured to Ryan and then Hillary. "Aren't you hungry?" Without waiting for an answer, she swung the kitchen door wide and held it open. "Come with me."

Hillary and I stared at each other in silence. "You can cross the talent show off your list. After I call Elaine, you'll be free to enjoy all the tamales you want." She stared pointedly at my hips. Her glare swung to Ryan. "Let's eat." Without a backward glance, she sashayed after Senora Mari toward an empty corner booth.

I was angry, I was mortified, and I wanted to tell the wait-staff to refuse to take her order.

Ryan cleared his throat. "Josie, I'm sorry." He sighed. "She gets jealous, and then she says things . . . she doesn't mean."

What would it take to knock some sense into his brain? "Is that what you want?" I asked, waving in Hillary's direction.

He looked at her; he looked at me. "The hell if I know."

Chapter 7

"What's today?" Uncle Eddie cried, popping his head through the bedroom door like a deranged jack-in-the-box.

I threw the covers over my head. "Your day to go downstairs and cook biscuits and bacon?"

"Nope," he cried, ripping my comforter out of my hands. He backed away and drew two imaginary guns from their holsters. "It's the first day of the Wild Wild West Festival, pardner."

Every year, the festival kicked off with our tamale-eating contest. I'd prepped, cooked, frozen, defrosted, and dreamed tamales until I was red in the face from the fumes. I wasn't thrilled to watch adults toss back the Tex-Mex morsels until they wanted to puke, but if it brought in money, I was all for it.

Last night, I caught myself about to pray that a certain beauty queen would eat so many tamales she'd blow up like the Hindenburg, but I resisted. I am not that mean.

With any luck, it might come to pass anyway, and all for a good cause.

We loaded up Uncle Eddie's and Aunt Linda's trucks with the signs and decorations we'd created for the event and barreled over to Milagro. The Wild Wild West Festival would take place down Main Street, which thankfully meant we could set up on the sidewalk right outside our front door.

When we arrived, we found our employees waiting. Gone was the excitement of years past, and in its place were long faces and worried looks. I thought of our young employee Anthony, his warm smile and big heart. How terrified and afraid he must be, not only for his future but for his brothers and sisters who struggled to make ends meet without him.

All of us needed a successful contest today, to brighten our spirits and give us confidence.

I needn't have worried. Uncle Eddie hopped out of the truck and waded into their misgivings with two feet.

"Howdy, folks. Welcome to the Fifth Annual Tamale Eating Contest. We're glad you're here, and we hope you're hungry. This year we dedicate our contest to our friend Dixie Honeycutt. She loved to eat our tamales more than anything else in the world." The crowd chuckled quietly.

"Truth is," he continued with a smile, "if you don't help me get rid of these tamales, I'm gonna be eating 'em for a month of Sundays. So come on and sign up. It's not too late.

"Now it's time to move on. I know you're worried about Anthony, but don't be. We're going to make sure he gets the best lawyer, but we're going to need help. You can donate or you can ask your friends and customers to donate to help pay for his defense."

He smiled a kind, understanding smile. "But now it's time to make this the best contest and festival we've ever had. The more money we make, the more we can donate. The more positive energy we give to our customers, the more they'll return the favor by donating to Anthony's cause."

Our staff responded with nods and murmurs.

"How's that sound to everybody?" Uncle Eddie squared his shoulders and threw his arms wide.

A few smiles and more nods.

"Good," Senora Mari cried. "Let's do it."

He made a point to shake every man's hand and to pat each woman on the back as they made their way inside.

"Can we afford to help Anthony?" I murmured to Aunt Linda.

"We have no choice." The sharp look of disappointment she gave me made me squirm.

I resolved to visit him as soon as I could get away, tomorrow or the next day at the latest.

With each of us pulling our weight in coolers, chairs, and warming pans, we unloaded the truck and set up a long row of tables with red-checked tablecloths on the sidewalk out front. We made sure to tape down the sides so they wouldn't blow away in the West Texas winds. Hanging signs was a bit trickier, but we used fishing line and red duct tape to secure everything. With an hour to spare before the big tamale event, we stopped to drink a cup of coffee and enjoy the tasty egg, potato, and cheese tacos Senora Mari had made for us at the crack of dawn.

"Gracias, Mamá." Uncle Eddie smacked his lips. "Delicious as always," he said, planting a kiss on Senora Mari's cheek.

"What else was I going to do?" The older woman shook her head. "I couldn't sleep for thinking about Anthony."

"Don't worry." Uncle Eddie stood and stretched his arms wide. "We'll figure out a way to help him. Now, let's get these cattle on the trail."

"I feel as if we've forgotten something," my aunt said from her perch on the lid of a large drink cooler filled with bottled water. "Oh, shoot!" She shot to her feet. "Who's in charge of the sound system?"

Uncle Eddie reacted like a coyote caught in the headlights of a minivan on its way to the national park. His wide-eyed innocent expression made it clear he thought the answer was him. All the same, he remained mum and took another swig of coffee from his West Texas travel mug.

"Eddie," my aunt said in a singsong voice, "did you forget to remind the grounds committee we needed a microphone and a set of speakers today?" She stared him down like a rattler eyeing a field mouse.

"Huh, what—" he began, determined to appear above suspicion.

Aunt Linda pierced his facade with a narrow-eyed glare.

"I'll do it," I said. No need to start a war today. Too much was riding on everyone keeping a cool head.

"Thanks, Josie," my aunt said, tossing a look of disdain at her husband. "Run up to the registration booth and find Mayor Cogburn—no, not the mayor. Find out from one of the volunteers who to talk to about the sound system."

I was glad to stretch my legs. It was a gorgeous day, even as the wind blew our hair into our eyes and tossed our hats into the bushes. People on the street smiled and laughed, clearly looking forward to a tremendous event. Only three days had passed since Dixie's death, but Broken Boot's citizens and her visitors were focusing on the positive.

Yesterday, I'd seen the sheriff and his deputies traipsing up and down Main Street, entering the other businesses, but they had yet to stop in with more questions for us. Last night, Suellen Burnett delivered more pies and stayed to give us a blow-by-blow reenactment of both the questions they'd asked and the responses she'd given.

Sheriff Wallace was a fair man. If Anthony remained in jail after two days, then Wallace had something concrete on the kid. Questions without answers had percolated in my brain all night, and I was no longer going to wait for law enforcement to kick it in to a higher gear. I had better get on with it and uncover what the sheriff knew if I was going to clear the boy's name.

Lost in thought, I nearly collided with two dozen kids and their bikes. They formed a haphazard line along the sidewalk. Judging by the streamers in their spokes and the tinsel on their handlebars, they were waiting for the bicycle decorating contest to begin.

"Howdy," I said with a smile to the young couple at the front of the line, manning the registration table. I wasn't really a "howdy" kind of girl except for festival time each year. I had met the red-haired man and his pretty wife at a chamber of commerce meeting, where I'd politely taken a business card for their auto shop on Tenth Street. I had to give it to Elaine. The chairwoman certainly had a knack for matching her volunteers to the perfect event.

Too busy to reply, they gave me a quick smile and continued helping two very small children fill out their forms.

The dark-haired boy and girl couldn't have been more than five and six. Behind them stood an older girl around eleven years old, perhaps a cousin or sister. When she turned her head, my breath caught. With her long dark hair and high cheekbones, she was the spitting image of her brother . . . Anthony.

"Excuse me," I said, walking around a nine-year-old boy who sported a short haircut combed into a point near his forehead.

"Don't worry," I whispered in what I hoped was a soothing voice. "It's alright."

The couple at the table had gone on to help another child, but the man was listening intently. Was he wondering if he needed to protect them from me?

I forced myself to calm the heck down and appear as nonthreatening as possible. "Anthony was my friend," I said as she helped the smaller children move their bikes out of line. "He works for my family at Milagro. Has he mentioned the Martinez family to you?"

She nodded, but she glanced down the alley as if longing for escape.

"My name is Josefina Callahan." I added the Spanish pronunciation of my name, hoping to make her feel more at ease. "Is Anthony your brother?"

She glanced around and gave a barely perceptible nod.

"I like your brother very much. He's kind and smart."

With wide eyes, she tipped her head to one side as if trying to determine what I wanted.

"I don't believe he's guilty."

Her eyes darted from me to the couple at the table and back.

"What is your name?" I asked.

"Dayssy," she murmured.

"Listen, Dayssy," I said in a soft voice. "Why don't we go somewhere we can talk in private?" When she didn't respond, I continued. "Somewhere no one can hear us."

She nodded and her eyes darted down the alleyway again.

Across the street, the Kandy Kitchen had set up a booth outside with old-fashioned hard candies: licorice, cinnamon, root beer, and the like. I hurried over to the stand and bought a striped stick of each flavor. When I made it back across the street, she and her siblings were waiting with their bikes at the alley entrance.

We walked their bicycles, festooned with bright green, white, and red streamers, down the alley to the back of the local thrift store, Wear It Again, Sam. I helped them park their bikes, and after she translated the flavors into Spanish, gave each child their two favorite flavors, one for each hand.

Once they started eating, I offered her a stick of candy as well. "Are they your brother and sister?"

She reached eagerly for a blue-and-red striped stick. "*Sí*, yes."

I waited until she'd taken her first lick. "Who's taking care of all of you?"

"My older sister, Lily, is seventeen. She takes care of us now that Anthony is gone." The girl's face fell. It was clear she thought her older brother was gone forever.

"Dayssy." I paused to form my question carefully. "Why does the sheriff think Anthony is guilty of murder?" She shook her head several times.

"I want to free him." I placed a hand on her shoulder. "Please help me."

"I don't know." She bit her lip. "He would never do such a bad thing." Her gaze dropped to the gravel.

She was hiding something. What was she too afraid to say?

Aunt Linda did the hiring and firing. We'd never discussed it outright, but I didn't have any reason to believe she spent money on running criminal background checks on our employees. She either got along with them, or she didn't.

"Does he have a record, is that it?"

Her soulful eyes suddenly burned with emotion. "He wasn't guilty, but they arrested him anyway."

I checked my watch. Aunt Linda would have my hide if I was gone much longer. "What do they think he did?"

She hesitated, watching her younger brother skip stones down the alley. "Our cousin, Miguel, asked Anthony for a ride from Terlingua to Fort Davis."

"That's not illegal."

My question was met with silence. She bit the candy and chewed, delaying her response. Her gaze landed only as far as my neckline. "My cousin is an illegal." She sniffed. "The Terlingua deputy arrested Anthony for transporting an illegal into the country."

A very serious offense. "Is that what happened?"

"No," her gaze flew to mine, "I promise. He picked him up in Terlingua, not the border." With the back of her hand, she wiped her eyes. "Our cousin told us his papers were in order and that he had a job in Fort Davis. He said he just needed a ride to get there."

My heart broke for this family and their sad story. "Didn't Anthony try to explain?"

She began to cry. "They wouldn't listen." Her voice rose. "They never listen. They've arrested him again, but he's done nothing." Tears ran down her face, scarring her cheeks with sorrow.

"I believe you." With great care, I put one arm around her

and drew her close. "I'll speak to the sheriff and tell him what you've told me. Perhaps he will change his mind once he knows the truth."

I had my doubts that Wallace would change his mind so easily, but what if the sheriff believed that having a record meant Anthony was a hardened criminal? And, if he realized the young man wasn't a criminal, wouldn't Wallace be more inclined to believe that Anthony was incapable of committing murder?

Inside my heart, hope flared. Even though there was only a slim chance I could change the sheriff's mind, it was well worth an immediate discussion between him and Anthony.

The boy and girl, now finished with their candy, kicked a plastic soda bottle back and forth. The boy wore shorts and a T-shirt, clean but well-worn. His hair was short, but growing out over the ears. His sister sported a bright pink cotton shirt and matching shorts, her hair in two braids down her back.

Dayssy stepped away and wiped her eyes again. "We have to go." She whistled, and immediately her siblings stopped their game and ran for their bikes.

"Do you have money for groceries?" I asked as we exited the alley, heading for the street.

She nodded, but kept her eyes averted.

"Who is helping you? Family? Friends?"

Stroking her sister's hair, she shook her head.

"Is Lily working?"

With a sudden grin, Dayssy answered. "She goes to school and takes care of us."

We reached the street to find the red-haired man from the registration table handing out numbers. Several of the entrants had already tied them to their handlebars.

With a quick hug from their sister, the two young children ran forward to receive their numbers.

If I didn't leave now, the tamale-eating contest would be delayed and my neck would be on Aunt Linda's cutting board.

"You tell Lily to come see me at the restaurant," I said. "We're shorthanded without Anthony, and she can work in his place."

Dayssy's eyes brightened. "I will tell her, but now we must go." She pointed to where the children stood in line, proudly displaying their bicycles.

"Good luck," I cried, waving madly to her sister and brother.

I'd neglected to ask them their names, but it would have to wait until next time. Tamales were calling my name.

I hurried to the registration booth, but after a lengthy discussion with the elderly volunteers there, I wasn't convinced help was on its way. I tried to be gracious, but the more I talked, the more flustered they became. It took at least five minutes for the head volunteer to find the right channel for the maintenance crew on the walkie-talkie, and another five to communicate what I needed.

Chiding myself for taking the whole tamale-eating contest way too seriously, I marched back to Milagro past a collection of antique cars festooned in red, white, and blue streamers only to find, much to my surprise, almost the entire festival committee seated around our long tables. Melanie and her husband, rancher P.J. Pratt, were smiling and waving at everybody as if they hadn't seen them in a month of Sundays. Mayor Cogburn walked up right behind me, hung his sport coat across the back of his white folding chair, and reached over to buss his wife's cheek. The only two committee members not in attendance ran their businesses with very little staff. Even Elaine of Elaine's Pies couldn't fault Bubba's BBQ and Fredericksburg Antiques for choosing to man their forts on one of the busiest days of the year.

"Wait for us!" Ryan and Hillary ran down the sidewalk hand in hand, trying not to take out a mother pushing a twin stroller. My handsome ex was laughing at Hillary, trying to make her move more quickly. Though not exactly dragging her five-inch heels, the beauty queen was moving in a much slower gear, her lips pursed tight as if holding in a string of curses.

With a big smile, Uncle Eddie made his way down the tables of contestants, shaking hands and greeting each one. He raised the microphone to begin the proceedings, and everyone winced in pain as the speakers squealed at an ear-splitting decibel. Offering an apologetic grin, he stepped farther away from the amplifier and tried again.

"Ladies and gentlemen," he said with a sweeping gesture to the crowd, "thank you for joining us for Milagro's Fifth Annual Tamale Eating Contest, benefitting the Big Bend County Children's Home. We would like to thank the Wild Wild West Festival committee, many of whom are sitting right here before you, for stepping up, or should I say sitting down, to raise money for a good cause." The crowd chuckled with good humor. Again, his arm swung wide. "Let's get this party started." The crowd applauded with enthusiasm as the waitstaff delivered the plates of tamales in front of each contestant. Uncle Eddie raised a hand, fingers spread wide. "Five . . . four . . . three . . ." he cried, lowering a finger with each number, "two . . . eat!"

Now that the contest was underway, Hillary and the other female participants were taking noticeably smaller and smaller bites of the tamales set before them. The men continued on with gusto even as they turned gray around the gills. The only one who looked like he was having a grand ole time, like Father Allen on his way to bingo, was Ty Honeycutt.

"Why is he here?" Senora Mari demanded, not caring who overheard.

Pursing her lips, Aunt Linda answered in a lower volume. "I heard he's trying to come up with money to bury Dixie's body, once the autopsy's complete."

"But surely he knows we're not offering a cash prize," I said.

"Oh, he knows." My aunt snapped her fingers, making sure she had our full attention. "But word is he's been losing everything at the gambling tables, including money to eat on."

Maybe the gambling tables had been hard on him, so hard

he'd been tempted to eat his shoe leather. I snuck a look at his boots and found the pair on his feet new and highly polished. Someone, either Lady Luck or a lady from The Cat's Meow, had helped him buy the latest ostrich Lucchese boots or I was a native New Yorker.

One of my jobs had been to place buckets under the table for the sole purpose of giving folks something to spit in if needed. Yuck, yuck, and double yuck. So when someone began to splutter and cough, I knew we were prepared. I rushed over in time to hear Elaine make a horrible sound, somewhere between a cat upchucking a hairball and a humpback whale. She raised a napkin, delicately, to her lips, and tried to smile with her lips closed, but her expression looked more like one of those jack o' lanterns left to rot in the sun. Suddenly she spit into her napkin and turned bright red. She lifted a hand to her lips and pulled, and pulled, until something fell out of her mouth.

And it wasn't a tamale. It took me a few seconds to stifle my gag reflex, but then I recognized it. As Elaine pulled the chain, small figures began to pop out from between her teeth. Small carved horses.

The crowd, all thirty of them, gasped. "She's lost her teeth," a boy shouted.

"She's coughed up her lungs," an old geezer added.

Elaine spotted me first. "Help me, for pity's sake." Ty, sitting next to her, leaned over for a better look at the necklace. "Give me that water." He grabbed her half-full water glass and dropped the necklace into it, and then he began to rub away the tamale remains. "This belonged to my aunt. This is one of her designs."

All I could picture was the horse imprint on Dixie's neck as she lay dead behind the Dumpster of my family's restaurant. "Don't anyone move," I said, trying to sound official. "Not until the sheriff gets here."

Chapter 8

Uncle Eddie had already pressed the button on the sound system. It made a loud squeal. "Sheriff, we've found the murder weapon. Sheriff Wallace, we've found the murder weapon."

Geez, what a great way to let the cat out of the bag.

There was a loud crash, and Elaine fell backwards along with her chair, plate, and all the tamales she had left to eat.

"Is she dead?" someone shouted.

"Mom!" Suellen cried from somewhere behind me. "Someone help her!"

I jumped onto the platform and tossed Elaine's chair off the platform so I could get a good look at her. Maybe it was the time I'd spent on the phone with the 911 operator, or maybe it was the CPR training I'd received as a lifeguard in high school, but I didn't hesitate this time.

Elaine had fallen to her left, so I gently turned her on her back. Her lips were the color of the blue blotch pansies I'd grown on my balcony in Austin, and, aw, sugar snaps, she'd stopped breathing. I bent close to her nose and mouth, and confirmed that no air was coming from either.

"Someone call the ambulance!" I heard Aunt Linda yell somewhere in the background. A woman's voice called out, "Where's Silas?" and part of my brain remembered the retired EMS worker was scheduled to take the morning shift at the first aid station.

"He was headed toward the BBQ booth about ten minutes ago," Felicia said in my ear.

"Go find him!" As she slipped away, I started praying.

Elaine was bluer than before. I tilted back her chin and checked her mouth for obstructions, and my fingers brushed against something that was definitely not supposed to be there.

Aunt Linda was at my shoulder, nearly jumping up and down. "Have you lost your ever-loving mind?" Then I realized it wasn't her, but the mayor who was talking. "Remember our reputation. Stop talking about someone choking to death through the sound system."

The sound system cut out with a loud squeal, nearly blowing out my left eardrum. Though my nose wrinkled in disgust, I had to get that thing out of her throat. I got a tighter grip on whatever it was and slowly pulled it out. I was scared to death it would fall from my fingers, straight down her windpipe, and choke her for sure. But no such calamity ensued. Once the object hit my hand, I knew what it was. One of the horses from Dixie's necklace was determined to choke Elaine as well.

In spite of Uncle Eddie, Aunt Linda, and Senora Mari all side coaching me on CPR techniques, it took merely two rounds of puffing air into Elaine's mouth and pumping her chest the correct amount of times for her to cough the life back into her well-preserved body.

As she struggled to sit up, Suellen nudged me out of the way. "Momma, what happened?"

At first Elaine tried to push Suellen away, but the older woman was too weak to sit up on her own. Instead she dropped her head to her oldest daughter's shoulder.

With a cry of relief, Uncle Eddie and Aunt Linda threw their arms around me.

"Such a smart girl," Senora Mari crooned, and patted my head.

"Are you okay?" Suellen asked her mother.

Elaine coughed, closing her eyes as if in pain. "I will be . . . no thanks to them." She opened her eyes and glared at us.

Through the crowd, a beacon of steady self-assurance made his way toward us, and I sighed in relief.

Lightfoot knelt next to Elaine, where she rested weak as a child in the arms of her own offspring. "I've called the ambulance, Mrs. Burnett. They'll be here any minute."

Weakly she moved her head back and forth. "I . . . don't need an ambulance." Again, the committee chairwoman was wracked with a fit of coughing.

I hurried to the cooler and grabbed a water bottle.

"Get her some water, somebody," Lightfoot commanded, even as I unscrewed the lid and placed the bottle in Elaine's hands.

The corners of the stoic deputy's mouth lifted in an almost smile as he nodded his approval.

Slowly Elaine lifted the bottle to her lips.

"Let me help you, Momma."

"I can do it myself," Elaine argued. "And I don't need any ambulance."

As his phone buzzed, Lightfoot rose to his feet. "They're only a block away. The crowd's slowing them down."

"Where's the real sheriff?" Senora Mari demanded, by way of greeting.

The deputy responded with a smile. "Sheriff Wallace is taking care of a dispute over at the Feed and Supply."

"Is Patti okay?" My independent-minded friend ran the place on her own for long stretches at a time.

"She's fine." He turned to Mayor Cogburn and P.J. as if Patti was of no consequence. "What's all this about someone finding the murder weapon?" His tone was casual, but I noticed how his hawk-eyed gaze searched the crowd, taking in strangers and townsfolk alike.

"Elaine was nearly killed by the necklace that strangled Dixie." Felicia Cogburn twisted her own expensive charm necklace first one way and then the other.

"Who says she was murdered by a necklace?" P.J. Pratt demanded, bowing out his chest like a rooster in a hen house. "The sheriff's department hasn't released any details."

Felicia looked helplessly at her husband. "Uh, I don't rightly know."

"There it is." I pointed to the greasy necklace where it rested on the table below the warming pan of tamales.

"No one touch it." Lightfoot pulled a piece of foil from a nearby box and carefully wrapped the necklace into a neat package and placed it in his breast pocket.

"And here's the horse she choked on." I said, handing him the offending stone wrapped in a napkin.

"I'm going to be sick to my stomach," Elaine whispered. "Please let me go inside for a few minutes."

Aunt Linda and Senora Mari each took one of Elaine's hands and gently lifted her to her feet. "We'll get you out of this heat." Aunt Linda nodded at Suellen. "Let's take it slow."

Lightfoot started to ask a question, but my aunt stopped him with a glare that had made stronger men pause.

One of the bystanders who remained called out, "Who won the contest?"

P.J. shoved in his chair. "Forget about it."

"Aw," said some of the tourists, expressing their disappointment. The crowd began to murmur.

Uncle Eddie waved his hands to gain everyone's attention. "We can still sort all this out and declare a winner." He began to count the tamales that remained on each participant's plate.

"That ain't fair." P.J. had meat sauce down the front of his plaid shirt. "How do we know that no one kept eating while she distracted the judges?"

Give me a break. Who really cared at this point?

Ryan stepped forward, forcing a laugh. "We can trust Eddie not to cheat, right?"

The crowd grew quiet, watching the show.

"Ryan's right," Hillary said as she took her coach's arm. "Mr. Martinez wouldn't cheat a fly."

In a fit of pique, P.J. slapped his Stetson on the side of his jeans. "Don't matter none 'cause I won."

"Look again, boys," Ty Honeycutt called out, gesturing to his own plate.

Unbelievably, Ryan straightened his shoulders as if readying himself for a round of fisticuffs. "Eddie, come right over here and count mine if you want to see who won."

At that moment, the beauty queen winked at me. She spun toward the crowd. "Who thinks this handsome man won?" she asked, pointing to Ryan.

A few souls clapped in response. A couple of college girls in West Texas blue-and-orange jerseys called out, "Go, coach!"

With a frown at Hillary, my uncle proceeded to count all twelve contestants' remaining tamales. He counted P.J.'s last. "Congratulations," he said, wheeling toward the irate rancher. "You won." Uncle Eddie walked over to the makeshift podium and returned with an envelope. "Here's your prize." He waved it back and forth over his head with a flourish. "You've won a dozen tamales every day for the next month, courtesy of Milagro."

The crowd applauded, but their hearts weren't in it.

"Hold on a minute." Lightfoot stepped in front of the crowd. "We need everyone to stay right where you are until I take your statements."

"Deputy, what's going on here?" Sheriff Wallace appeared at the back of the crowd and started pushing his way through. "Excuse me, folks."

I tried to maneuver close to him to ask him about the dispute at the Feed and Supply, but it was impossible. He and his deputies disappeared inside for a brief face-to-face and then started interviewing witnesses. I tried to overhear their sessions, but whenever Wallace saw me sidling closer he sent for another round of Dr Peppers, sweet tea, and black coffee.

With an ear-popping squeal from the sound system, Mayor Cogburn announced, "Come one, come all. It's your turn to fall. The three-legged race for kids of all ages will be starting in the field across from the depot in three minutes. Don't miss it." Some of the spectators who had waited to share their side of the choking tale wandered off.

"But Mayor Cogburn, the deputy told them to stay put." I wanted law enforcement to have the opportunity to do their job.

"Um, well." The mayor grabbed the microphone again. "Wait now. If you or anyone with you was just at the tamale-eating contest, please return immediately." He turned off the microphone and gave us a smile. Suddenly, he panicked and turned the microphone back on. "Uh, it's, uh, no emergency, but a friendly request from the Big Bend County Sheriff's Department."

Aunt Linda and I exchanged looks. "Oh, that'll set everyone's mind at ease," she said.

Grabbing his wife's hand, Cogburn turned to go. "We've got to go preside over the three-legged race. Y'all let us know what the sheriff finds out, won't you?"

Before I could argue with his priorities, they'd hurried out into the crowd.

"He's trying to throw a wide loop with a short rope," Aunt Linda murmured.

It was past time to start clearing everything away. "Good Lord, what a mess," I said, collecting the burners and utensils.

"Don't touch anything. It's all evidence." Lightfoot stood in the open doorway, pointing to the warming pans full of spoiling food.

"What about the trash? It's starting to stink in this heat."

My aunt bristled like a porcupine. She ran a clean, tight operation. "This smell will ruin our reputation." I hated to point out that the choking incident and the murder had already tainted our name in at least three counties.

Two deputies I didn't know by name appeared. They checked in with the sheriff and came back outside. "Don't touch anything, ladies. Me and Deputy Kincaid here are going to have to go through all this . . ." He wrinkled his nose in disgust, "*stuff* before you throw it away." They disappeared long enough to retrieve their thin rubber gloves from their cruiser.

"Can we take everything away that's not food?" My aunt, bless her heart, was trying.

"No, ma'am. Sheriff Wallace wants us to dust these items for prints." The officer waved his gloved hand over the assorted warming pans, utensils, and scraps of aluminum foil. "It's just his way."

Lightfoot and the sheriff interviewed those who had returned to complete their civic duty, which, surprisingly, was a lot of folks. No one seemed to mind waiting their turn as long as they got to tell their all-important side of the story. Guess they couldn't resist helping solve a crime.

Suddenly, Sheriff Wallace appeared in the doorway. Behind him, I could just make out Lightfoot with his arms stretched wide, fighting to keep Aunt Linda and Senora Mari inside Milagro.

"What's going on?"

Wallace eyed the sidewalk and the crowd as if wishing he were fishing on the Guadalupe. "I'm sorry," he said quietly, turning away from the crowd. "She's claiming that she did it."

I grabbed his arm. "That's absurd. Aunt Linda wouldn't slap a mosquito unless it bit her."

"Keep your voice down." He pulled me farther away from the curious bystanders on the other side of the tables, eyeing me with a compassion I didn't understand.

My aunt called out from inside the restaurant. "Don't worry, honey. I've called Eddie."

Wallace shook his head. "She's going on about being a jailbird."

"But Aunt Linda's never done anything wrong."

"Not her," Wallace said under his breath.

"Sheriff, what's the meaning of this?" Ryan walked over with Hillary close behind. "Linda Martinez doesn't have a record."

"No, but she does." The beauty queen pointed at Senora Mari as if the petite tamale maven were the reincarnation of Lizzie Borden.

The remaining crowd began to whisper.

"What are you talking about?" I demanded. If Hillary said one wrong word about Senora Mari, I would smack her upside her pointed head.

The beauty queen took a step back. "She told me herself the night of the tamale party."

My petite *abuela* stuck her head out from beneath Deputy Lightfoot's arm. "It was twenty years ago, and it was only some smelly goats."

Wallace looked at me and raised an eyebrow. Senora Mari had lost one of her marbles.

With a toss of her hair, Hillary upstaged us all. "Everyone knows that nothing goes into her tamales without Senora Marisol Martinez's knowledge."

"That's enough," Ryan said, dropping her hand like a hot iron. "She didn't do this, Hillary. Why would she compromise the taste and reputation of her tamales by contaminating them with jewelry or anything else?"

"I was only trying to pay her a compliment." Hillary extended her hand to Ryan, but he stepped out of reach. Assuming an air of confused regret, she continued. "I love Senora Martinez's tamales." I could see in the beauty queen's eyes she regretted what she'd done. Too bad her attempt to save face had fallen flatter than a cold tortilla.

Sheriff Wallace pulled me aside. "She's admitted to the crime." He thrust his hands on his hips. "But I can't figure out why."

Senora Mari wriggled around Lightfoot and shot to Wallace's side. "Take me to jail. I am guilty . . . this is true."

I'd never caught her in such an outrageous lie.

Aunt Linda pushed out the door right behind her. "Tell him you're kidding."

Uncle Eddie came running around the corner from the parking lot. "*Mamá*, what are you up to?" He grabbed his mother by the shoulders and bent down to stare her in the face. "Tell me." He lowered his voice. "What are you thinking?"

Met with her son's outrage, she rolled her eyes. "Humph. Anthony should not be in jail." She turned to the sheriff and raised her fist. "Let me go, what do I care if I only eat stale bread and drink cold water? I am old and constipated anyway."

Through gritted teeth, Uncle Eddie murmured. "Standing around arguing about this in front of strangers is only making things worse." He removed my hand from his sleeve. "We'll help Anthony, don't worry."

Senora Mari glared at Wallace and Lightfoot. "How do I know he's safe and unharmed?"

A wailing siren grew closer as an ambulance crept through the crowd. When it reached our parking lot, it turned in and headed for the rear entrance.

As the siren died, Sheriff Wallace threw back his shoulders and turned to the crowd. He gestured wide to capture their attention. "Nothing to see here, folks. Why don't you go on and enjoy the three-legged race? Show's over."

The dozen or so folks who'd stayed to watch the craziness that was Senora Mari wandered away.

I placed my hand on her shoulder. "Sheriff, would it be okay if we went to see Anthony? We're worried about him."

After a brief glance at his watch, Wallace nodded. "He can have visitors today from one to three this afternoon." He gave

Senora Mari a smile. "Take a few minutes, eat something, and relax. You can see him very soon."

The older woman lifted her chin. "*Gracias, senor*," she said, and marched back into the restaurant.

As Wallace stepped inside, Lightfoot drew closer. "The stone Elaine choked on was turquoise. Some people believe it wards off the evil eye." Deliberately, he turned his obsidian gaze on me. "Others believe it warns us of our approaching death."

I refused to let him scare the bejesus out of me. "What do you think?"

"I think that was a smart idea, suggesting Senora Mari go with you to visit Anthony."

"Thanks."

He tipped his hat back with his thumb and studied me for a moment, a glint in his eye. "You know I think she's right . . . you would give a man a run for his money."

Chapter 9

There was a bit of an argument about whether or not Senora Mari and I should stay to help clean up after the contest, but I insisted we arrive at the jail by one o'clock. If I were in Anthony's shoes, I'd be stark raving mad, wondering when and if I would ever be free to see my family.

After I pointed out that we didn't have the usual cleanup after lunch since the sheriff had closed our doors until five o'clock, Aunt Linda agreed to stay behind and oversee preparations for dinner. She even went so far as to give me the keys to her beloved F150. We made our way slowly toward the highway, bogged down by festival traffic. For some reason, Senora Mari saluted any neighbors and friends we passed with a royal wave, like a high school queen in the annual homecoming parade.

At the county jail, a gaunt Anthony hugged Senora Mari and tears flowed between them. When they finally separated, I realized why he appeared so changed. His once ready smile had evaporated. In its place was now a haunted stare.

He had lost weight in the few days he'd been incarcerated,

his orange coveralls dwarfing his frame. "*Gracias*. Thank you for coming." Wiping his eyes on the sleeve of his orange coveralls, he murmured, "I don't know what to say."

"You don't get bail," Senora Mari said, jabbing me with her elbow.

"But we're taking up a collection," I said. "We're going to get you the best defense money can buy." I frowned at my gross exaggeration.

A deep furrow appeared in his forehead. "I met with the lawyer."

I gave him a smile of encouragement. "What did he say?"

Rubbing his temples with his fingers, he gathered his thoughts. "He, um, thinks that it's mostly, uh, circumstances . . ."

"Circumstantial?"

"Yes, that's it." He lunged forward. "How could it be anything else? I didn't kill her," he cried.

The guard spun toward our table.

With his palms out, Anthony slowly raised his hands to appease the guard. In a quiet voice, he continued, "There's no proof that I murdered her," He grabbed the table between us with both hands, "but that doesn't matter. They want to close this case, and I'm their only suspect." His eyes, once so warm, blazed with helpless fury. "They say there's no proof that I didn't do it."

That didn't sound right. "Who said such a thing?"

"One of the deputies." Anthony dropped his head into his hands. "I don't know his name."

"*Estúpido*," Senora Mari muttered under her breath. "Ignore him. You had nothing to do with that dead woman. You weren't even at the restaurant when she arrived."

After a quick glance at the guard, Anthony turned his sorrowful gaze on me.

My heart sank at what I saw there. "You came back that night, didn't you?" I whispered.

He lowered his eyes to study the tabletop and slowly nodded.

With alarm, I shot a glance at the guard. He was staring straight ahead, appearing to ignore us. Would he report everything we said? Maybe we were even being recorded.

"I will be right back." Senora Mari pushed back her chair.

"Where are you going?" I hissed.

"You talk while I keep him busy." She winked and slowly walked toward the door as if she'd suddenly aged twenty years in the last thirty seconds.

Whatever plan she'd hatched might blow up in our faces at any second. "Why did you come back to Milagro that night?"

He leaned forward. "I needed a cash advance."

"Why didn't you ask for it earlier in the evening in Aunt Linda's office?"

Rolling his eyes, he muttered, "I was embarrassed. I didn't want you to know."

"I remember that night. You were angry, but you didn't tell us you were desperate."

"Why should I tell you? I am the man of my family."

I didn't know what to say. "Did you see Dixie?"

He nodded. "Outside. She was sitting on a bench smoking one of those," he held his fingers about eight inches apart, "those smoking tubes."

"Electronic cigarettes."

He swallowed. "She was slurring her words and saying ugly things." Searching my eyes for my reaction, he continued, "When she called me over, I thought she needed help."

Across the room, Senora Mari was talking quietly to the guard.

"What happened?" I held my breath.

His breathing accelerated, his chest rising and falling. "She said she needed help. I thought she meant to stand." Beads of sweat formed on his forehead. "When I moved closer to help her, she tried to . . ." His face flamed.

"What, Anthony? What did she do?"

"She tried to kiss me."

Not what I expected. "Uh, was that all?"

Anthony's shoulders flew back. "That was too much. When I stepped back, she fell forward."

I was trying to picture the scene as he described it. "And then?"

"She grabbed my bow tie. When I pulled away, it ripped in two."

"What happened next?"

"I was embarrassed and angry. She should have treated me with more respect. I threw the tie away, and I left her sitting on the bench."

"Didn't you tell them all this?"

"Yes, but they don't believe she tried to touch me. They think I'm a stupid kid and I'm making it up. But I'm not. Why would I say she did that if she didn't? I hated her trying to kiss me, but I wouldn't kill her."

"That can't be all they have."

Senora Mari came back to the table, picked up her bag, and returned to the guard. From the corner of my eye, I saw her take out a few small foil packets and give one to the guard.

After opening each packet, the guard, satisfied that they contained nothing that could break Anthony out of his cell, began to eat each of the tamale offerings Senora Mari had prepared.

While he ate, she brought out more, and after a cursory inspection, the guard granted a nod of approval. She walked over at her normal vigorous pace and presented both of us with savory and aromatic treats. "Eat up," she said to Anthony with a smile.

I wasn't one to look a tamale in the mouth. We ate for a minute or two, resisting the urge to talk, sharing a small container of sauce. After we finished our meal, Anthony's cheeks had more color and his eyes held a spark of hope.

He licked his lips and the ends of his fingers. "*Gracias*, Senora Martinez."

With a kiss to the top of his head, she gathered the trash and threw it in the can in the corner.

"They must have something else on you," I said, wiping my mouth. "Do you know what it is?"

"A shoeprint near the Dumpster."

My heart dropped. "A boot print?"

"No, ma'am. It was an athletic shoe."

To say I was relieved would be putting it mildly. "Did you explain about your bow tie?"

He nodded. "Sure, but they ignored me. They say the print was found near the body."

"Was it your shoe?"

"Yes, ma'am."

By readily admitting what Dixie had done, Anthony must have turned the sheriff against him. I tried to lighten his load. "I met your sisters and little brother. I'll give Lily your job while you're in here."

He blinked rapidly and grabbed my hands.

"I hope that helps," I said, embarrassed by the tears that sprang to his eyes.

"You are too kind."

I chuckled. "You have me confused with someone else."

He blinked in confusion. "No, I don't, Miss Josie."

"Are you happy with your lawyer?" I asked, trying to change the subject.

"He is a smart man," he responded with a smile. "His name is Trout, Mr. Thomas Trout."

"Odd name."

He looked away and back again. "Yes, but he is a good man. He will help me, and he will treat me with respect."

The guard checked his watch and held up two fingers.

"Do you want me to bring Lily to see you?"

Anthony shook his head. "She's not allowed. She's too young to come without a parent."

Placing my hand on his, I stared hard into his eyes, trying

to give him all the encouragement I could muster. "Then we'll just have to prove that you're innocent and get you out of here."

Shoving to his feet, he said, "If you could do that—"

"Visitation is over," the guard called out.

"*Bebé*, she can do anything."

Anthony laughed at Senora Mari as we headed for the door. Before we departed, she gave the guard another packet of tamales and a wink.

When we arrived at Milagro, I made a beeline for the office. Aunt Linda was no slouch in the commonsense department, and I needed to process what Anthony had told me.

"Hey, honey," my aunt said as I dropped into a chair. "How's the poor kid doing?"

"He was here that night, talking to Dixie."

"What?"

"Yeah," I said, meeting her wide-eyed stare. "He says he needed a cash advance, but didn't want me to know." I wasn't in the mood to tell her the unsavory details.

My aunt pulled off her reading glasses and rubbed the bridge of her nose. "That's very likely."

"Then he's done that before?"

With a sigh, she slowly lowered her glasses to the desktop. "Once or twice."

A metal pan crashed to the floor in the kitchen, making me wince. "Have you heard of an attorney named Trout?"

"You're kidding," she said, her eyes widening.

"I wish."

"I'll ask Eddie if he's heard of . . ."

"Thomas Trout." I grimaced. Hopefully the guy's legal skills matched his parents' love of alliteration.

"Have any donations come in to pay a private defense attorney?" I burrowed beneath the invoices on the corner of her desk until I found her armadillo-shaped candy dish. An old, soft butterscotch was all I found.

"I put a hundred in the jar at the register, and Eddie said he'd do the same at Two Boots."

Using my thumbnails, I slowly pried off the plastic wrapper. "Did it work?"

With a shrug, she replaced her glasses. "We've raised another hundred so far."

Hopefully, this Tommy Trout was a real badass defense attorney. And maybe pigs were canoeing down the Pecos River.

"Josie," she said, turning her attention back to the spreadsheet on her computer screen. "I know you just got here, but Eddie's in a tizzy, says he needs some walnuts."

I chuckled. "So he's going nontraditional this year?"

"Oh yeah, he's convinced that new recipe of his is the best thing since God created jalapeño poppers. He swears by it." After losing soundly to Bubba and two sisters from Moss Creek in the Texas chili category last year, Uncle Eddie was hoping to win the big prize this year in the nontraditional category. His newest creation was a venison chili replete with heaps of beans and peppers and lots of toppings, including coconut and walnuts.

I blamed it on the cooking shows. He just didn't have it in him to go simple anymore.

"This is his year," I said, mimicking what my uncle repeated like a mantra at this time each year.

"Humph."

"Are you sure all he needs is walnuts?"

"So he says." She rolled her eyes. "He wants you to meet him at Bubba's. The cook-off's supposed to start in twenty minutes."

I drove to Van Zandt's Thriftway and found walnuts, already chopped. Only one checkout lane was open. If I'd had my druthers I'd have walked the aisles for exercise rather than stand behind the customer chatting with the lone cashier.

Stepping up as quiet as a mouse, I tried to stay in her blind spot.

"Josie," Hillary cried at full volume. "What are you doing back there?"

I shook the bag of walnuts at her. "Uncle Eddie's in the chili cook-off."

She glanced at the walnuts and laughed. "Are you sure he's not in the bake-off instead?"

I lifted the corners of my mouth in response, which appeared to satisfy her.

The cashier handed Hillary a small item, which she dropped into her recycled grocery bag.

I cocked my head to one side, evaluating what I'd seen. I didn't know Van Zandt's sold what Hillary was buying.

Her eyes widened in feigned innocence. "What?"

"Nothing," I said, rolling my eyes toward the ceiling. "I didn't know you were a smoker." If Ryan Prentice knew that Hillary smoked e-cigarettes, then I was a monkey's uncle.

With an exaggerated glance at her bag, she sighed. "Oh, that. Those cartridges aren't for me." She made an expansive gesture to the female cashier, who was all of sixteen. "I don't smoke. Smoking gives you wrinkles."

"I would think most people worry that smoking gives you cancer."

"I don't care if it gives you a handlebar mustache. It's not mine."

A little demon on my shoulder pricked me in the ear, and I couldn't resist. "Have you talked Elaine into replacing me as a judge for the talent show?"

With a shake of her wrist, Hillary rattled her gold bracelets. "No. She said it was too late to make more changes. I was going to have to man up." She clicked her teeth. "As if."

I bit the inside of my cheek to keep from laughing as I imagined Hillary with a buzz cut and no makeup.

"Don't worry," she said, giving me the once-over. "I'm a pro." And with that, she spun on her turquoise boots and sashayed out the door.

The cashier with the pink braces gave me a knowing look. "She is too."

"Believe me, I have no doubt."

Before I left the parking lot of the grocery store, I called to double-check that my uncle hadn't thought of something else.

"No, that's it. Get over here, Jo Jo. I have to be set up in twelve minutes."

"I'll meet you there. Bring a dish for the walnuts. They're already chopped."

"Great idea. *Vamos, chica.*"

Wishing I had one more tamale in my belly, I drove to the old historic train depot that Bubba had bought and converted into a lip-smacking BBQ joint. The high ceilings were made of tin and painted gold, a color that transformed the interior into a light, airy place to enjoy succulent meats with finger-licking sauces.

Parking was at a minimum due to the influx of tourists, but as I drove up Bubba appeared at the back door and waved. "Pull in," he said, gesturing to the no parking zone. "No deliveries today."

Bubba was tall, and to describe him as brown would be missing the mark. He was dark as fresh asphalt. He hailed from Chad and had come to Broken Boot by way of a local pastor and his wife.

Though born in Africa, his speech was Texas twang. "Can I hep ya?"

"No, thanks, but you're going to be amazed. Uncle Eddie's outdone himself this year."

As one of the cook-off judges, Bubba wasn't supposed to have any inside information. He covered his ears. "Don't tell me, but he'd better hurry, we're fixin' to start. Everyone else is already here."

"How many entries this year?"

"Fifty."

"Is that a record?"

"Yep. And once we become sanctioned by the International Chili Society, that number will bump up even more. I swear." He placed one hand over his heart. "Eight entries are from tourists out of state."

I cruised inside to find the restaurant had taken on the appearance of a ride at Fiesta Texas. They'd set up rope lines to control the traffic flow so that it would wind through the door, past the competing chili samples, regular BBQ menu items, drinks, and desserts, and back out the side entrance. My mouth started to water from the heat of chile peppers in the air.

Good thing I didn't have that extra tamale. Chili was my second favorite food in the world. Sweets had their place, but savory was my go-to food group.

"I didn't know committee members were allowed to participate." Ryan smiled as he wandered over from the jukebox.

"No one ever said. And it is a blind contest, right?"

"If you say so."

I glanced around. "Where's your other half?" I didn't say *better half* 'cause I try not to lie.

"She's around somewhere. I think she had some errands to run. Dry cleaning, tailoring, something like that." His eyes glazed over.

We laughed together. Ryan was such a dude. Again, I wondered if he knew that Hillary smoked e-cigarettes. How would he react when he found out? Ryan, the ultimate health nut, would not approve.

"So where's your chili?" he asked.

"Uh-uh," I said, wagging a finger. "It's blind judging, or did you forget already?" I hadn't entered, but I didn't want him to figure out which chili recipe belonged to my uncle.

He smacked his lips. "I only wanted to taste the miracle."

I didn't cook much. Senora Mari had that right. But I did cook a mean chili I liked to call Austin chili. I made my own delicious concoction with organically grown peppers and onions, free-range turkey, and pine nuts. A recipe I created myself, it caught people by surprise, or so they said, which probably meant they didn't like it. Ryan loved it, and it had kept us together as a couple far longer than was healthy for either of us.

"What chili is Hillary famous for?" Sometimes I'm a bit passive-aggressive.

He frowned. "I have to go to the judges' meeting."

"Aren't you and Bubba the judges?"

"Yeah, but we have to disappear while the candidates put out their entries so we don't see who's who."

"Who are the guest judges?"

"Uh-uh. It's a blind tasting," he said with a grin and walked away.

My phone buzzed with a text from Uncle Eddie even as he scurried in the back door. My phone was smart, but unreliable. Like some men I'd known.

"'Bout time."

"Quit your yammering and help me set up."

My uncle had brought three large crockpots of chili with heaping dishes of lettuce, tomatoes, cheddar cheese, red onions, salsa, and sour cream, plus the shredded coconut and walnuts.

I grabbed a bowl.

"Nope. Don't you do it." He handed me a small paper sample cup. "Got to keep the crockery for the paying customers, gal."

"Okay, fine." After the first bite, I died and finished the rest in chili heaven.

I tried to stick around to give him some support.

"Jo Jo, don't sit so close, folks will figure out which one is mine."

"Is that a bad thing?"

"I'm not sure, what with the murder and Anthony being arrested. Folks might be prejudiced against us."

"Or they might be rooting for us."

"True." He frowned. "Lord, I hope that's the case."

"Smile." I took several pictures with my phone of Uncle Eddie and his chili, one with his entry number in the foreground and one of him standing in front of the blue ribbon. Then we both skedaddled and found a seat outside.

"Howdy," my uncle said to Fred Mueller, the owner of Fredericksburg Antiques, who sat at a nearby table drinking a cup of hot tea. If I'd seen anyone else besides Mueller drinking a steaming beverage on a blazingly hot day, I'd have sworn they were one card shy of a full deck. In fact, I had no idea Bubba's sold anything other than iced tea so sweet you could stand a fork in it.

As we found a seat, Mueller stood. "Good luck," he said and gave Uncle Eddie a formal handshake before hurrying on his way. Had he hired someone to help him run his store while he enjoyed a festive lunch? Or had he closed his doors in order to deliver his own chili entry? Mueller might be German Texan, but the man could cook. His chili was usually found in the burn-your-taste-buds-off category.

He could keep it. I didn't want my meals to bite me in the butt.

While my uncle chatted with some of the other entrants from out of state, I thumbed through the pictures I'd taken and shared the best ones with Aunt Linda and Patti. My phone gallery was almost full, so I began to delete several pictures of Lenny.

I missed my silky-haired friend. Now that we were sleeping at Casa Martinez, Aunt Linda's place, I couldn't run upstairs to throw his rubber ball or play tug-of-war with his blanket. Some of the photos I could have deleted were kept, and I vowed to bring him a doggie treat when I returned.

That would give me a great excuse to see Patti's place. The Broken Boot Feed and Supply store sold a plethora of doggie treats and toys, and for that matter, I would take him with me when I went. The thought of parading him down the sidewalk during the festival lifted my spirits.

I stopped, riveted by a photo on my phone, a picture of a boot print with a coin next to it. I shook my head at my own pretentiousness. I'd seen the coin trick on a western detective series. It was supposed to indicate the size of the shoe once you compared it to the size of the coin, in this case a quarter.

A child wailed at the next table, and I struggled not to lose my train of thought. The sheriff's department had found an athletic shoe print they claimed matched Anthony's. If that was the case, whose print was this? Certainly not mine. I had worn boots with a much smaller heel that night. The shape of this boot heel looked like a traditional roper.

Why hadn't Sheriff Wallace or Lightfoot pursued this second print? Why would they have arrested Anthony if there was proof that someone else was standing near the body on the night of the murder?

Chapter 10

When I first saw the boot print the night of the murder in the pool of kitchen grease, I'd thought it was one of the busboys' prints because they were the ones who emptied the grease trap. This could have belonged to one of our guests, one of the twins, one of the family, or the murderer.

Anger pulsed in my temples. Why in the heck had they arrested Anthony when this other print existed? I'd found it next to the Dumpster just like his.

I forced myself to slow my breathing. Maybe the sheriff's department had already ruled out the owner of the mysterious boot print. Would they tell me who it belonged to if I asked them? I gave myself a mental slap. In spite of his kind bearing, Sheriff Wallace wasn't going to bend the rules. Lightfoot's serious countenance came to mind. He wasn't about to give me any information either.

Who then?

I glanced around at the tourists and familiar faces. I didn't see anyone who could help, so I decided to find the answer in my car.

From my days at the newspaper, I kept a portable office in the Prius. It was handy keeping things in one place, and right then I needed desperately to put my hand on a ruler.

Uncle Eddie was talking to a family of strangers, making them laugh with true stories about the celebrities who'd passed through Two Boots. He was doing his thing, bringing in curious customers. And he did it well.

In the car, I dug out the bendable ruler and measured the quarter in the picture. Then I measured the boot print. As that revealed next to nothing, I slapped my steering wheel with the ruler a good six or seven times. I took a deep breath and started using my smartphone to search for anything that had to do with using a quarter as a standard of measurement. Within seconds, I discovered that a quarter is approximately an inch in diameter. I am by no means a math wizard, but I found a conversion chart and calculated that the boot in the picture was approximately ten and a half inches long. After a minute or two of more searching, I discovered that a ten and a half inch boot print was either a women's size ten and a half or a men's size nine and a half. It didn't sound kosher to me, but I double-checked and found that the numbers were correct when it came to cowboy boots.

Hmm. Whoever had made that print was either a tall woman or a short man. Or someone whose feet were in disproportion to their height.

But who made the print? A man or a woman? That was like asking: Who wears boots to a tamale party? The answer: Everyone and their mother.

My uncle wouldn't miss me, and I had an idea. I would traipse over to the Boot and Bag. I'd noticed something of note in the photo and I wanted a second opinion.

The leather goods repair shop stood on Davis Road. Though only two blocks off Main, it was like living on the back side of the moon. The concrete streets were old and in poor condition. The lampposts were county issued and not the decorative faux antiques along the main drag. The shop itself had aluminum siding and a big plate-glass window.

Inside, the owner, Mr. Cho, was hard at work. Longtime residents of Broken Boot, he and his wife were the only game in town. They made a living, and some said a killing, repairing our boots, buckles, and bags because they had no other employees and low overhead. Now that their kids had gone off to college, one always found the diminutive owner in the back, his bespectacled face close to a boot or a leather pair of shoes, while his outgoing wife helped the customers in the front.

No one was inside when I arrived, not even Mrs. Cho. "Hello?" I called.

Mr. Cho came out of the back, his eyes darting back and forth as if startled by actually having to wait on a customer.

He knew me, of course, from Monday night bingo at our dance hall. Mr. Cho was a big supporter of Father Allen's fundraiser.

"Can I help you, miss?"

I enlarged the photo on my phone. "I have a quick question, if you don't mind."

His eyes widened. "Me?"

I went to the end of the counter and he eventually joined me. "See this boot print?" I pointed to the impression in the photo. "What's wrong with it? Why isn't the full print showing?"

He looked at me for a few seconds and then pushed his glasses up his nose. "The heel is broken here." He pointed to the bottom right corner of the impression. "This person walks on the outside of their feet, so no full pressure along here." He ran his finger along the inside of the print.

We stared at each other. "Do you work on a lot of shoes that belong to people who walk like that?"

"Sometimes."

"What about the broken heel?"

Shaking his head, he crossed his arms. "You have shoes that need fixing or what?"

I ran out to my car and dug out the stilettos I'd buried in the trunk on my way out of Austin. They were the special pumps I'd bought to wear to my bachelorette party, but since that had never happened, and I'd lost the receipt, I was stuck with a pair of shoes I would never wear unless hell froze over.

If Mr. Cho would answer my question for a twelve dollar repair, who was I to quibble?

"The heel's coming off." The five-inch heel had separated from the sole when I'd used it as a knocker on my ex-fiancé's door. Only after I broke the heel did I find out he'd moved to Australia without telling me.

"Expensive shoe," he said, nodding his head. "Too bad it was not made with true craftsmanship."

He wrote up the ticket, and I gave him Milagro's address. I fished out my debit card and paid him, all the while pulsing with excitement. This could be pivotal. If he identified the owner of this boot, I was one step closer to bringing Anthony home.

"So?"

"So," he said, closing the register as if we hadn't studied the photo only minutes earlier.

"How many broken heels have you seen lately like the one in the photo?"

"Lately? A dozen."

What did that mean? Since January first? Since last June?

I swallowed back my frustration and found there was a glint in his eye. Someone was having a good time at my expense.

I laughed. "Yes, well played. How about this month?"

"None," he said and one side of his mouth kicked up.

Shoot. This was only the first week of the month. "How about in the last two weeks?"

He scratched the end of his nose. "Two." He turned to walk away.

"Two broken heels?"

"Yes," he said over his shoulder.

"With outside wear like this one?"

"No." He entered the back workshop and picked up a pair of well-worn men's dress shoes.

"You mean no broken heels."

"No." He placed the shoes on the worktable and began to inspect them.

I wanted to scream. "You mean no outside wear?"

"No, not what I mean." With slow precision, he ran his fingers along the soles and around the heels.

I started to count to ten, but only made it to three. "What then?" I cried.

Turning slowly to face me, he said. "No *cowboy* boot like this one came in in the past two weeks that had a broken heel *and* outside wear like the one in the picture."

"Oh."

He shook his head with a devilish smile. "Check back in a few weeks. Boots come and boots go," he said in a singsong voice.

Clanging the bell over the door, Mrs. Cho entered. "Hello, Josie. How are you?"

"Uh, great." I caught the door before it closed. "I've got to be going."

She glanced toward the workroom with a worried expression. "Mr. Cho, he took good care of you?"

"Yes, ma'am." I gave her a jaunty wave. "See you later."

I hurried back to the chili cook-off. The line now snaked out the door, past the building and the next two businesses on the street. My chili feast would have to wait.

Uncle Eddie was wearing a new path along the side of the depot, he was so nervous.

"Are they still judging?"

"Nearly finished." He plucked his hat from his head and nervously straightened the band between his fingers.

Glancing at the tables, I studied the offerings on their

plates, but one chili could pass for another at ten feet. "Which ones are the most popular?"

He frowned with disgust. "The Texas ones."

Bubba left the line and stepped to one side, marking his judge's form on his clipboard. He started circling scores and I started praying. Uncle Eddie needed a win.

Ryan left the line next, and I saw him in the full light of day. You know those moments when you see someone you've known for years, but suddenly you see them the same way a stranger would see them? He was a handsome man, not perfect. His nose was bent from playing football and he walked a tad bowlegged. But his face told the story. It was an open, honest face. There was intelligence in his eyes without a mean bone in his body.

A good friend.

"So what do you think?" I asked him as he handed Bubba his clipboard.

"I think I'm hungry."

"You goober, you just ate twenty-four servings of chili."

"And not one helping of peach cobbler."

I laughed. Running kept him thin, but one day that belly would appear and he'd understand how the rest of us, namely me, struggled.

"Come on, coach." Bubba handed off the clipboards to the committee members tallying the votes. "You've earned your pie."

Ryan rubbed his belly and gave me a wink. "And a scoop of ice cream?"

"That'll be fifty cents." Bubba didn't crack a smile.

Ryan's brow furrowed, and the BBQ owner laughed. "Nah, it's on the house."

"Want some?" Ryan asked, lifting a brow. This week we'd spent more one-on-one time than we had in years, but all I could think of in that moment was, *Where is Hillary?* And, *It should be illegal for my former college sweetheart to still be so darned cute.*

I didn't hesitate. "No, thanks."

With a wave, the two judges traipsed back into the fray to forage for ice cream.

Uncle Eddie scurried over. "Did he give a hint as to how I did?"

"No, that would be dishonest." Ryan had never tried Eddie's nontraditional chili before, so it would indeed be judged fairly.

A third and fourth judge came out of the line with a clipboard in hand. Elaine had done things right. Now no one could accuse Bubba of choosing a friend's chili, even if they had been able to guess which entry belonged to whom.

My uncle pulled off his Stetson and wiped his brow. "I'm hungry, but I don't want to wait in that line."

"Come on, I'll wait with you. Maybe by the time we make our way up there, the winners will be posted."

We waited in line for twenty minutes, briefly discussing Dixie and Anthony and mostly gabbing about the festival lineup at Two Boots.

"Did you say Ty Honeycutt's still on the schedule to play?"

Uncle Eddie's voice rose. "Yeah, I told him he could postpone until next month if he wanted, and he threatened me with a lawsuit for breaking his contract."

"You're kidding?"

"Nope."

"Has he always been so . . . ornery?"

"Well, yeah, but he's been strange since Dixie was murdered."

"How horrible to wait, day after day, before he can lay her to rest."

A young mother, holding on to two wailing toddlers, trudged by on her way to the car park. "Jessica," my uncle called after her good-naturedly, "you should've given those girls some of my chili if you didn't want any complaints."

Jessica answered with a glare powerful enough to pierce an armadillo's armor.

"Dixie's funeral arrangements won't be cheap," I said. I'd heard tell of people being buried in a sheet when the family didn't have any money to do otherwise. It made me mad to think that Dixie might have that kind of send-off.

Ty was a reprobate, no-good gambler who shouldn't have lost all his money playing cards.

"How can he be that desperate?" I sighed. In all likelihood, Dixie hadn't left a formal will, and even if she had, Ty wouldn't be able to touch her money until the case was closed.

"Desperate or not, he better put on a good show. He's kicking things off tonight."

Then it hit me. Ty wasn't short, nor was he tall. He could easily wear size nine and a half boots.

There was only one way of finding out. I could handle his brazenness on my own, but it would be amusing to see Patti go head to head with him. She had a healthy animosity for pigheaded rednecks, so if he turned out to be one of those, we'd be covered. On the other hand, if he was merely a handsome, misunderstood musician down on his luck, she'd help me to steer clear once he'd answered our questions.

Uncle Eddie and I made our way through the line, and as we sat down to share a table with some folks from Monroe, Louisiana, the festival committee brought the ribbons forward. I didn't know the person about to make the announcements, but it was one of the guest judges, an elderly fellow with wire-rimmed glasses and a Santa beard.

Santa announced the winners of the traditional, the hotter than hell, the vegetarian, and finally the nontraditional chili categories.

Uncle Eddie gripped my hand.

"In third place, Number Twelve."

Uncle Eddie whooped, grabbed my hands, and lifted both of us to our feet. "That's me!" Holding on tight, he led me in an improvised two-step around the center tables.

"Come and get your ribbon, Number Twelve."

With pride, my uncle preened his way to the microphone,

pinned the white ribbon to his suede vest, and proceeded to shake the man's hand off.

When he returned to the table, I gave him a big hug.

"You did it!"

"Wait until Linda hears! She said the coconut was too fruity!"

He pulled out his phone and started walking, pointing out his ribbon to folks as he passed by them. He stopped at least eight or nine people on the way to the parking lot to brag. They took it with good humor, as he intended, and laughingly congratulated him. One couple, a bit too buttoned up for a Wild Wild West Festival, merely stared, and refrained from shaking his hand.

"She's not answering."

"Her loss," I said.

"I'm going to go home and surprise her," he said, sliding into the seat of his pickup. "Tell her I told you so." With a toot of his horn, he slammed the door and drove away.

I couldn't wait to walk over to the Feed and Supply to get Patti's opinion on my boot print. I tried Aunt Linda on my cell, and she answered on the first ring. Hmm, funny how she always picked up for me. Resisting the urge to tell her about her husband's win, I stuck to my plan. "Are you covered for dinner?"

"Yeah, I really am. Everyone's here today, hoping I'll use them since they missed some shifts on Tuesday."

"So you wouldn't mind if I took the night off?"

"No, sugar. You go and relax, you've worked hard."

"So have you."

She sighed with resignation. "True, but I'm going to sit here in this office with my feet up until another crisis arises."

Before I could hang up, she called out with a sudden thought. "Hold up! There's someone here dying to see you."

"Yip."

My heart soared. "You tell him I'm on my way." My plans could wait.

* * *

Brazos Road was a parking lot, filled with cars coming and going from the festival, and though Patti's store was a mere half mile around the corner on Miller's Brook Road, I chose instead to pop in on my four-legged friend. Needing the exercise, I decided to walk to Main Street and fill my lungs with the cool, clean air. I might not miss Austin's traffic and exhaust fumes, but I longed for a dozen other things. Nowhere else had I found the same cornucopia of live music, a dozen local coffee shops without the symbol of a mermaid, and people from all over the country with different views of the world.

I needed an Austin fix, and as soon as I had some maintenance done on the Prius, I'd be headed that way. Funny how I hadn't thought about my ex-fiancé, only the city itself. Well, obviously I was thinking about how I wasn't thinking about Brooks, but I hadn't thought about him since the murder, at least not where I wanted to roll into a fetal ball, the way I had only months ago.

Folks were parking up and down both sides of the streets as I passed one small business and adobe house after another. Our yards were mostly dirt with natural grasses and wild flowers, succulents and cacti, live oaks and mesquites. Many of the houses close to downtown were adobe casitas built around 1900, their pale colors as beautiful as the wildflowers that grew in the desert. My heart filled with pride for the people of my adopted town, for the grit that helped them thrive amidst the rough elements that surrounded them.

When I opened the front door of Milagro, I was met with tired glances from our staff. And though it was three o'clock, two tables were still occupied.

I found Aunt Linda, as promised, with her feet on her desk and her head resting on her chest.

"Hello," I whispered.

"What?" she cried, jerking upright. "Oh, it's you."

"Looks like you had a busy lunch. That's great!"

Wearing a wide smile, she nodded. "Oh, yeah."

"Sorry to interrupt. I'll see you later." The sooner I left, the less likely she'd think of something for me to do.

She swiveled her chair back toward her computer screen. "He'll be excited to see you."

Lenny. I ran up the steps to our apartment, but there was no sign of him.

I popped my head back into my aunt's lair. "Did someone take him out for a walk?"

Her eyebrows rose above her reading glasses. "He's had his lunch, but I thought he could wait for you."

We scrambled from her office as if our hair was on fire. Lenny in the restaurant for the customers to see was a great way to violate the health code and lose our license. Once, he'd escaped from our upstairs apartment and hid under a table. We'd almost lost our license after a customer reported we had giant rats instead of one small, but feisty, Chihuahua.

No sign of him upstairs, even after we both searched. No sign of him in the kitchen, the bar, or the pantry. I even checked the bathroom.

Lenny was gone.

I left a message for Aunt Linda's neighbors just in case he made it all the way back to her house. Before I could find the number of the nearest animal shelter, a hipster couple covered in colorful tattoos walked in. As the door started to swing closed, I spotted him. I rushed outside and found my darling boy tied to a lamppost out front, where I'd checked only minutes ago.

"What are you doing down there, Lenster?" Stepping onto the sidewalk, I glanced up, down, and across the street, but no one appeared to be acting out of the ordinary. I untied the makeshift piece of rope that someone had attached to his collar and snuggled him under my chin. "How did you get out?" He was trembling more than usual. "What if Jesse Sweetwater had hit you with his new car, hmm?" Jesse was sweet sixteen, and his new Camaro was at least that old.

Apparently, one of the staff had inadvertently let Lenny out the back when they'd stepped into the alley for a break. I cradled him close and carried him upstairs.

As we entered my living room, Aunt Linda ran up the stairs behind us. "Where did you—" Her smile morphed into a mask of horror. "Oh, my sweet Jesus," she cried, pointing to Lenny. I turned and caught a glimpse of him in my arms in the mirror. Someone had shaved his side and written on it in bright red lipstick:

MAN'S DEAD FRIEND

Chapter 11

I began to shake. Who would have dared do such a thing, and had the nerve to deliver him to the door? I wanted to believe this was just a prank, but what if the killer somehow knew I was asking questions. Had this message come from him?

"Yip," Lenny complained, making me aware I was squeezing his frail body. "Sorry, Lenster." What if they'd hurt him and left him for dead on the doorstep . . . or on Uncle Eddie and Aunt Linda's front porch?

"Oh, my goodness," my aunt said as she bounced on her toes. "Oh, my goodness."

My mind was racing. "Here, take him, but don't smear it." I handed him to her and raced for the bathroom. Under the cabinet I found a pair of plastic gloves left over from the last time I'd highlighted my hair. I ran back into the living room and slipped them on. "Aha," I cried, remembering what might help. This time I located the hairspray in the basket near the sink and strode back into the living room. "Cover his eyes, nose, and mouth."

Aunt Linda quickly complied.

Careful not to smear the ghastly message, I coated the lipstick with a layer of mist, again and again.

"What's all that about?"

"It works when I use nail polish on my pantyhose," I said, returning the hairspray to the bathroom. "Once it dries we'll take some pictures."

"You could've taken the pictures while you were running around like a chicken with your head cut off."

Lenny sneezed on her arm.

"Whatever," I said, dialing the sheriff's department.

After a quick transfer by the switchboard operator, Wallace's receptionist answered. "Sheriff Mack Wallace is not in the office at this time," she said in a brisk tone. "May I take a message or would you prefer to call again?"

"I need to talk to your boss. It's urgent."

"Uh-huh." She heaved a deep sigh. "Please hold."

After a few seconds, the sheriff came on the line. He listened while I gave him the details about what had happened to my poor baby.

"Now, Josie, I'm sorry about what happened to your dog, but you know the person who did this didn't kill Dixie. This was some delinquent's idea of a sick joke."

"A joke!" My heart started pumping like a steam locomotive. "Someone other than Anthony was behind the restaurant on the night of the murder," I cried. "I have vital evidence."

There was a long pause. "Why didn't you come forward sooner?"

I swallowed and calmed myself. "I was going to once I proved it meant something."

He sighed. "Why don't you tell me what you think you've got?"

"I have a picture of a boot print near the body."

"We already have Anthony's print, which I'm sure he told you." I hadn't discussed my visit to the jail with anyone. The tamale-loving guard must have spilled the beans.

"Yes, sir, he did. I have a boot print, not an impression of an athletic shoe."

"Which could belong to anyone."

"Or the killer."

"Why are you so sure Anthony isn't the murderer?"

Even an amateur could figure that out.

"He had no motive." I lowered my voice. "And he wouldn't want to create any more hardships for his family. They've struggled enough."

"What if I were to tell you that we have a solid case?" he asked, with a touch of pity.

I bit the inside of my cheek in an attempt to hold my temper. Finally I managed, "Please don't stop looking for another suspect, sheriff. That boy isn't the one you want."

"Listen," Wallace said, back to business as usual. "Bring us what you've got after the festival is over. Right now, our department is stretched so thin you could pick your teeth with it."

"Alright, I will." My gaze fell to where Aunt Linda scratched behind Lenny's ears. Wallace might bury his head in the yucca bushes, but I was going to treat this travesty like the crime it was.

A phone rang in the background, and I heard the sheriff say something on another line about a security meeting.

"Does that meet with your approval?" I said, sarcasm slipping out.

Aunt Linda pulled a face and mouthed, *Hush.*

"Sounds good. Drop off your pictures whenever you're out this way." The line went dead.

I kept right on talking. "I'll be sure and do that. Thanks for your *help*, sheriff." I lifted my hand, one impulse away from throwing the phone against the wall. "He said to bring by my pictures after the festival. No rush."

"Oh, honey," Aunt Linda said, wrapping one arm around my shoulders.

Now wasn't the time for sympathy. I strode to the kitchen door, spun around, and strode back to the far window. "What if they'd killed him?"

Lenny whimpered.

"What if they'd spray-painted the restaurant or our house? Would Wallace pay attention then?"

"Lord, help us." Gently, my aunt reached out to pet the small dog's head.

"Someone doesn't want us asking questions."

She turned worried eyes to me. "Then let's give them what they want."

I wanted to rip their head off. "None of us will let Dixie's name pass our lips in front of the customers." I marched to the window and back.

"We won't talk about her murder on the street or at church," Aunt Linda added.

"And you can't let Senora Mari breathe a word about her dream and Dixie's need for revenge," I said.

Aunt Linda's eyes filled with fear. "It's for the best, sweetie. It really is."

I returned to the window, spun on my heel, and paced back. "I'll act is if I've forgotten all about it." I threw a hand up in frustration. "But what else can I do to make this . . ." I pointed to Lenny's temporary tattoo. ". . . this criminal think I'm suddenly too busy to ask questions? Everyone in this town knows I'm an out-of-work journalist."

Tapping her chin, my aunt thought for a minute. "You need a cover. How about that article on Hillary the *Bugle* offered you?"

I gave her my blackest look. "Even if I did decide to waste my time writing such drivel it would only give me an excuse to question the blond bimbo."

Shaking her head, my aunt said, "Girl, you know what the good book says about judging other people."

Dang it, she was right.

"What about a cookbook? It would give you an excellent reason to ask everyone for their favorite recipes."

Not my cup of queso. "I don't think so, not unless I'm desperate."

She frowned. "We'd help you with it."

All of a sudden, Lenny growled and jumped into the chair under the window. A gecko was sunning itself on the ledge, and the small dog was having none of it. "Yip, yip, yip," he warned. The silver gecko didn't move. Lenny jumped onto the end table, planted his front paws on the screen, and barked.

In slow motion, I turned to Aunt Linda, a smile creeping across my face. "Not a cookbook . . . a blog."

"Oh, sure," a frown creased her forehead. "Lots of people turn their blogs into full-time jobs."

My mind was racing with possibilities. "There would be anecdotes about our neighbors." I gestured expansively with both hands. "And there would be everyone's favorite recipes."

"You could get sponsors. Bloggers do that, right?"

"Oh, I'm not going to write it."

Her look of confusion was priceless.

"Lenny will."

She dropped to the bed. "Go ahead. Hit me with it."

"If the sheriff isn't going to take Anthony's plight seriously, I'm going to prove to Wallace he's innocent."

Lenny whimpered.

I walked over to the window and disengaged his toenails from the window screen.

"How are you going to do that?" she asked, shaking her head.

"If we can't get any support, Lenny's going to write a blog," I said, lifting him up for a kiss on the nose. "I'll give him a little help, but it'll be under his byline." Even though reading blogs and writing one were two different things, I could do it. I looked her square in the eyes. "This new project will make whoever did this think I've given up, but I'll con-

tinue to investigate under the guise of interviewing folks for
Lenny's blog." I made a gesture that included both of us.

"You leave the investigating to Sheriff Wallace and his
deputies."

Lenny jumped onto the bed and into my aunt's arms. "He's
dry." She rubbed a finger across the message on his side. "No
smudging."

"Yip," he agreed.

Casting a worried glance my way, Aunt Linda sighed.
"Josie, what if something happens to you?"

"Don't baby her." Senora Mari walked into the room.
"She's a Martinez."

Had she heard our entire conversation? And since when
had she referred to me as a Martinez?

"I am?" I already thought of myself as part Martinez, but
there was always a rushing river of distance between her
family tree and mine that I couldn't ford.

"*Sí*, of course."

I bit my lip, overwhelmed by her answer.

"You listen to me. I'm going to teach you something you
don't know." The older woman thrust her finger close to my
face, issuing me a challenge. She leaned so close I could smell
her Chanel lotion. "I am a tough customer."

I kicked off my shoes and joined Aunt Linda on the bed,
crossing my legs in what we used to call Indian-style. Lenny
jumped into my lap and I held him tight.

"Arp!"

Too tightly. "Sorry," I whispered.

Senora Mari frowned in his direction, "Ssh!"

"Go ahead," Aunt Linda urged.

My mind was spinning. What yarn was she about to spin
now?

Before I could ask, she shook off whatever dark memories
she was about to share. She spread her lips into a grim smile.
"First we find Dixie's killer." She raised her index finger to
the sky. "And then Dixie will have her revenge."

* * *

"Lenny, you're getting a good soaking." I'd already taken pictures of the nasty message and erased the lipstick with an oil-based remover, but an oily Chihuahua was a stinky Chihuahua. I ran a bath, added his doggie bubbles, and studied his ragged appearance. I didn't see any nicks in his skin. Whoever the culprit was, they'd been careful. "I'm sorry, my friend. There's nothing for it, but to shave off the rest of your hair."

"Yip." He trembled and whined as I scrubbed him gently with a bath mitt, but whether it was because of the bath or the idea of the groomer shaving his hair, I couldn't guess.

After drying Lenny with a loving hand, I wrapped him in a towel and placed him on the bed to rest. All of the lipstick had come off, and other than looking like a mangled shag carpet, he was good to go. I hung out my living room window, and it did my heart good to watch the couples strolling down Main Street in the late afternoon sun. I grinned as kids dragged their older siblings and parents into Barnum and Hailey's, an emporium filled with toys, magic tricks, and college team novelty gifts.

One week after the death of my parents, Aunt Linda and Uncle Eddie had walked me down the street below and pointed out every shop, restaurant, eatery, and nail salon. We'd stopped at Barnum and Hailey's, and Mr. Hailey had taken great care to point out all of his wonders and jokes as if I were visiting royalty. The crème de la crème was a flea circus, which he presented with great fanfare as a gift for being Broken Boot's newest citizen. Perhaps he sensed, even then, how many fleas I'd have to contend with once Lenny came along.

I called Furever Chic, the pet boutique on Second Street, but they couldn't get him in for the much needed haircut until the next day. Anger at Lenny's attacker still rippled under my skin. I had to get out.

"Buck up, Lenster, we're off to the feed store." I clipped his purple leash to his matching collar and ventured out to join the tourists. Lenny was in a dapper mood, holding his head high, wagging his tail briskly, and greeting each gecko and cat he spotted on the street with a friendly yip.

If anyone noticed the cute long-haired Chihuahua with half of his hair missing, I didn't see their reaction. I'm afraid I was too busy remembering Senora Mari's dramatic revelation.

No wonder she was as tough as week-old tortillas.

Would she ever get around to telling the whole story? I found it a bit suspicious she'd never mentioned her stay in prison until Anthony was thrown in jail, and from what I'd witnessed of her past maneuverings, it'd be just like her to embellish her story for dramatic effect.

After walking five long blocks, we'd passed the businesses that catered to the tourists. In the distance, I could just make out the Broken Boot Feed and Supply. Two cars drove by, tooting their horns. I smiled and waved only to realize that they were waving at each other. Their tags read *Arkansas Razorbacks*, which explained why the young men hanging out the windows wore camouflage caps and red jerseys.

Anthony wasn't an average teen like those knuckleheads. For reasons I didn't understand, he had assumed the role of father and breadwinner. His main concern wasn't joyriding or drinking beer, but how to provide a better life for his siblings. He would never place his family in jeopardy by hurting Dixie. It was a ridiculous idea.

And yet, it didn't surprise me that Sheriff Wallace would find it hard to believe that Dixie would have flirted with a boy his age.

I stumbled over a cobblestone in my everyday Tony Llamas. As I paused to regain my balance, I noticed in my peripheral vision that someone was about a half block behind us.

I hadn't noticed the population thinning around me, but the block was nearly deserted except for a middle-aged couple window-shopping across the street. I had no cause to feel nervous, but then the image of Dixie's final smile swam into my mind. I was only one and a half blocks away, but I lengthened my strides.

Whoever walked behind us did the same.

It was ridiculous to feel afraid, but I wanted to make sure we weren't in any danger. Pretending interest in a window filled with garden hoses, I stopped long enough to steal a glance at my pursuer.

The teen heading toward us wore skinny jeans with holes, a chain on his belt, and a black hoodie over his head. If he was pursuing us, he was nonchalant about it. He wore black earbuds and held his cell phone as if watching a video.

Would this kid who weighed all of ninety pounds really steal my wallet or something worse? I needed to take a serious chill pill. Broken Boot wasn't Austin or Dallas.

I waited for the kid in the hoodie to pass me before Lenny and I continued toward Patti's. How did he like it now that we were following him? I laughed at myself. He was totally unaware of me and my fears.

Suddenly, he spun around and walked straight up to me. "You Josefina Callahan?" The youth's features resembled one of the angels in the painting of the nativity that hung in Uncle Eddie's office.

Except that his eyes flamed with rage.

I was shaking so much I could barely speak. "Y-yes. That's me."

"You gave my sister a message?"

I'd never seen the teen or his sister, nor did I want to from the expression on his face. Quickly, I shook my head. "No."

"I knew it," the boy cried and tossed back his hood. "She's always trying to push me." With his last plaintiff word, his vocal quality changed to a distinctive female cadence.

Wait a minute. "Are you Lily?"

When she nodded in agreement, it all fell into place. Her hair was short, but with delicate bangs that accented her large eyes, and like her other siblings, she had ultra-thick lashes. It had been easy to mistake her for a boy because her unisex clothes hid her slight figure.

I gave her a warm smile. "You must give your brother a pounding headache on a regular basis." I could just imagine macho, traditional Anthony trying to play the role of father with his modern teen sister. Forget about Saturday night wrestling; those two must have had knock-down, drag-outs.

She searched my face for signs of criticism. "Sometimes," she said and grinned.

"I'm glad you found me."

Lenny placed two paws on her legs. "Yip."

"Lenny, down."

Lily backed away as if afraid the small dog would nip at her ankles.

"That just means he likes you," I said warmly.

She frowned. "I didn't want anyone to see you talking to me, in case my sister got it wrong."

Had other people in town shunned them?

"I don't mind. You can talk to me anytime. I know Anthony's not guilty."

"How do you know?" she demanded.

"Because I know your brother. We've worked side by side for months."

Lenny licked her combat boot.

Nibbling her bottom lip, she studied him for a moment. "I want the job. What do I have to do?"

I paused. "Stay in school."

She backed away. "I knew it. You never intended to give me a job," she cried, her volume soaring. "You're just some do-gooder who feels sorry for us because our brother's in trouble."

Slowly I reached out, palms down, to calm her. "I will give you a job, if, and only if, you promise to stay in school. You can work with us until Anthony gets back, but in the fall you can only work after school and on weekends."

"I won't make enough."

"You will. I'll help you."

She flipped up the hoodie and once again transformed into her masculine counterpart. "Can I start today?"

"No."

With a frown, she turned away.

"Come by tomorrow morning," I called after her, "and we'll start your paperwork."

She spun toward me. "Tomorrow?"

"Ten o'clock," I agreed.

"Yes," she cried. "I'll be there." Wearing a wide grin, she spun back around and broke into a trot, pumping the air with her fist.

I allowed myself to breathe.

"She's tough." I bent down and stroked Lenny's head. "But you were never scared, were you, boy?"

Now that Lily had found me, I was more determined than ever to help Anthony. Waiting around for Dixie's killer to misstep wasn't a quick solution, but for now it was all I had.

Chapter 12

Outside Patti's family store, a middle-aged man came out with a length of new rope over one shoulder. He tipped his cowboy hat at the both of us, threw the rope into the back, and drove off in his mud-spattered long-bed truck. The original Broken Boot Feed and Supply store sign hung from the white plank siding above the front door, the familiar red-and-white checks forming the backdrop to the red block letters. Patti had added more signs on either side of the entrance. They were kitschy gems of homey brands that had aged gracefully, Coca-Cola, Wheaties, and Phillips 66.

We cruised inside, the cowbell above the door clanging a melody. To one side were the usual shelves of tonics, tools for cleaning horse hooves, moisturizers for cow teats, and fox urine to keep the feral animals from the pastures.

I waited a few seconds to see if anyone would appear. "Patti?" I called, walking toward the back of the store. Behind the main counter, two metal doors stood open, revealing bags of feed and cedar chips stacked five feet high. A terrible crash, like two cherubs banging pots in a heavenly kitchen, rang

from the loading dock beyond. We hurried over, Lenny barking a greeting. A long screeching sound of metal on concrete
came next, causing both of us to cringe.

"Sorry about that," Patti hollered as she came into sight.
She wore a clean black T-shirt, which revealed tattoos up and
down her arms. Multiple piercings on each ear were in place,
but she'd kept her makeup simple with cat-eye liner and crim-
son lipstick.

After dusting off her hands on her jeans, she gave me a
quick hug. "Did you see any tourists outside trying to find
their way in?" She studied the mirrors that hung high on the
walls at the end of each aisle and checked for unseen guests.

"Afraid not. Hasn't business picked up any?"

She shrugged. "Not yet, but there's still hope." She scooped
up Lenny and gave him a kiss on the top of his head. "When
is mommy going to tattoo your name over her heart?"

"Someone almost tattooed him for real this afternoon." I
pointed to his shaved left side and showed her a picture on
my phone of his twisted lipstick tattoo.

"People in this town are sick."

While she wiped down a counter with glass cleaner, I told
her all about the creepy message, how I'd found Lenny tied
to a lamppost, and how the sheriff had virtually ignored my
plea for action.

"You know he's very punk rock this way." She ran a hand
down his shaved side. "I think you should leave his coat like
it is, it suits him."

I laughed. "Don't hold your breath."

She waggled her eyebrows, lifting the silver ball of her
brow piercing. "Is that why you came by? You want me to
shave him for you?"

"Uh, no thanks. We came to see what you've done to the
place . . . and to talk about the murder. I have loads to tell you."

Patti and I had hung out at the YMCA when we were kids,
before my parents' accident, finding each other during my
summer breaks away from big D. We hadn't had much in

common except the fact neither one of us were boy-crazy, aspiring pop stars, or wannabe cheerleaders. As a result, we mostly talked about movies, books, and how stupid the other girlie-girl conversations were.

"Just wait until you hear what happened to me," Patti said.

"You first."

"This morning was the art show, right? Elaine didn't let me out of judging so I show up at the library, as ordered. I might as well have been invisible. Melanie was large and in charge from the get-go."

"But I thought you were judging the photography division?"

"That was the plan according to Elaine, but not the reality."

"What happened?"

"We began by organizing the entries according to medium and age. Elaine had made it sound as if I would judge photography and printing, but Melanie couldn't stand to hand over any of the divisions outright so she had a hand in all of them."

"Even in your categories?"

Patti nodded. "I helped her pick out the finalists, and she chose the winners."

"That's downright tyrannical."

"And a waste of my time." Patti whistled and Lenny came running. "Let me show you something I know you'll love." Scooping her new punk friend into the crook of her arm, she led us to three glass display cases on the far side of the store full of Southwestern style jewelry. On closer inspection, a small placard announced that all of the jewelry on display was made by Texas artisans.

There were earrings, rings, necklaces, brooches, trinkets, and some large silver rings for the earlobes known as gauges. I snuck a glance at Patti's earlobes and was secretly glad she hadn't added them to her personal list of body hardware.

"Wow, these are gorgeous," I said pointing to a display of necklaces. "But how many people in Broken Boot can afford these?"

"Check the prices."

They were extremely reasonable. "Fakes?"

"Imported stones from China," she said, waggling her eyebrows.

I chuckled. "I don't want to know."

Lenny sniffed the rings, and she pulled him back before he licked a man's ring set with a large colored stone in the Hopi tradition.

"Don't worry. They're authentic." She strolled away after casting a quick glance at the door, and I followed. "Want some tea?"

With a smile, I retrieved Lenny. "No, thanks." The conversation stalled while she plugged in the electric kettle. "It's good to see you."

"You too." Not one for pleasantries, she grimaced. "Now that that's behind us. Did you find something to free that kid . . . what's his name?"

"Anthony." I pulled out my phone and shared the photo of the boot print.

"Where'd you find it?"

"By the Dumpster on the night of the murder."

She studied the photo from every angle, running the tip of her tongue inside her lower lip.

"Are you chewing tobacco?"

Her extreme look of disgust made me laugh. "No." Her face cleared. "I was licking my lip, wasn't I?"

I nodded.

"I might get a new tattoo. What do you think?"

"Inside your lip?"

She shrugged. "Why not?"

With so many tattoos on her arms, I was already having trouble distinguishing where one ended and another began. "Don't you think your canvas is full?"

"Nope."

"I'm worried, Patti. There's no way Anthony could have killed Dixie. But he told the sheriff she tried to kiss him behind Milagro that night, and now Wallace is convinced he's lying to cover his tracks."

"That ain't good."

I dropped Lenny's leash and lowered him to the floor so he could explore. Without being too obvious, I changed the subject. "Guess who's writing a blog?"

"Senora Mari?"

"Close. I'll give you a hint. The blogger is here with us today."

Patti's brow furrowed, and then cleared, her eyes dancing with glee. "No?"

Holding a ball of twine in his mouth, Lenny trotted around the corner of the middle aisle, leaving a trail of twine in his wake.

I hurried to retrieve the wet ball from his mouth. "I hope this isn't your way of saying you're not much of a writer, buddy."

"Great idea. You can write what you want and blame it on your dog."

"You got it." I held the wet mass between two fingers. "How much do I owe you?"

"Don't worry, it'll dry." She bent down, pulled the twine up the aisle, and wrapped it carefully back into a ball. "Believe me, he's not the first."

"Once we solve Dixie's murder and things settle down, Lenny's going to write about everyone in town: their family history, their work, and their reaction to Dixie's death."

The kettle's whistle rang out, and Patti hurried to turn it off. She called from the other room, "Aren't you two the sneaky investigators?"

"Anthony's not guilty, and it burns my beans that someone in this town is laying low, hoping he'll get life in prison. Or worse."

"Light a fire under that holier-than-thou festival committee. They're meaner than a skillet full of rattlesnakes."

We both laughed at her Texas turn of phrase. She might

have multiple piercings and shoe-black hair, but she was a country girl underneath.

"You're hilarious," I said. "Why would they want to kill her? She donated some of her most expensive pieces to the auction. They needed Dixie."

Returning with a handmade ceramic mug in the shape of a longhorn steer, Patti leaned a hip against the counter. "I'm telling you. Some committee woman and Melanie got into it at the library while she and I were waiting for the last of the art contest entries to be brought over." She fluttered her eyelashes. "And it wasn't very ladylike."

"About what?"

"From where I was sitting, it sounded as if Dixie never delivered the silent auction necklace."

I gasped. "Oh, no. That's terrible."

"In the grand scheme of things, is that really such a big deal?" Patti wasn't selfish. She just wasn't into serving on committees with people twice her age.

"It's a huge deal to the children's home. It's their one major fundraiser every year."

Distracted by a couple walking by the plate-glass window, she didn't answer immediately. "You're right. The kids need the money." She watched as they walked to the door, paused to peer, and then continued on their way. "That's the way it's been all day," she said with a sigh. "None of the tourists believe there's more to this place than alfalfa and barbed wire."

"Show me around, but skip the barbed wire. I've been hearing great things about your place."

In the past year, Patti's parents had died. Instead of moving away, she'd renovated the old place. We took our time, cruising up one aisle and down the other. She'd added rustic and unusual home accessories, jewelry, and clothing. "This place is beautiful. You've done a super job of holding onto your roots and expressing your artistic side. Folks are going to love it." I gave her a quick one-armed squeeze around her shoulders. "I'm so proud of you."

Her grin was as wide as the store's center aisle. "About time you made it over here to see it for yourself."

As we toured the store, I continued to mull over why the auction was so important to the festival committee. "You don't know Elaine and her cronies," I said. "If they don't raise more money with the auction each consecutive year, they consider the event a fiasco and their reputations tarnished."

We made our way to the front corner of the store, closest to the window displays of antique furniture and whatnots, and lowered ourselves into a couple of gently worn wingback chairs. "Which I gather must be a fate worse than death," Patti said. "After that argument about the auction, Melanie was distressed. Told me a couple of things that I bet she wished she hadn't."

"Like?"

She leaned forward for dramatic effect. "Melanie doesn't know what to do with all of Dixie's jewelry that's still at the studio."

"She should call Ty. He is Dixie's only living relative." I was surprised that the deceased jewelry maker had left any of her trinkets on consignment at Melanie's studio. On the night of her murder, she'd made it sound as if she'd already packed up her goods and wiped the dust of the place from her feet.

"Ah, but she doesn't want to do that until the committee goes through all of it and decides what to put in the auction."

"They don't have a choice."

Patti chuckled. "You should have heard Melanie going on and on about how she was afraid to call Ty, acting as if his lifestyle would rub off on her over the phone."

"I'd be worried that he'd sell it all to settle his gambling debts."

Distracted for a moment, Patti straightened a decorative stack of journals on a nearby end table. She picked one up and handed it to me.

On the cover of the beautifully bound book was a picture

of a herd of longhorns, their faces thoughtful and wise. "Why, this is one of yours!" The image was from a series of photographs she had on display at Milagro. On closer inspection, the bookmarks bore her images as well.

"I like them." She shrugged and changed the subject. "Melanie mentioned that Dixie's pieces might double or triple in value now that she's dead."

My spirits sank. "I wonder what the sheriff would say about who has the rights to Dixie's jewelry."

"I was wondering the same thing," she paused, "because I still have some of her pieces in my display cases."

Bolting upright, I demanded, "What did you say?"

"Don't get all riled up. I bought them from her outright. They're not here on consignment."

"What are you going to do with them?"

"Double the prices?" An idea flashed across her face. "I have to run over to Melanie's gallery tomorrow morning. You should go with me."

"How early? I have the talent show at ten."

"I told her I'd drop off my photographs at eight thirty. That way I can open up here at nine o'clock."

"Sounds good. Is she showing your work?"

Patti gave me a warm smile. "She offered to sell my work on consignment. I think she felt guilty for running over me at the contest." She clapped her hands together with glee. "We could snoop around and look for Dixie's jewelry."

"You've been watching too many cop shows," I teased.

"Speaking of snooping, let's get back to the boot print in your picture. Did you find something important?"

"Not yet, but Mr. Cho assures me it's distinctive."

She gave me an assessing glance. "Mr. Cho? From the Boot and Bag? What did he have to say?"

"Not much except that the wearer walks on the outside of their foot and needs a heel repair."

"Huh," she chortled. "Sounds like you've found your killer." She flung back her hair and drank a long sip of her tea. At the base of her neck, under her ear, I spied a long, nasty scratch.

"What happened to you?"

Following my gaze, she touched the place gingerly. "What, this? Someone just needed a lesson in fair play."

"Sheriff Wallace mentioned you had a dispute when he arrived at the contest. A dispute with what? Looks like a bobcat took at a swipe at you."

She set down her teacup, lifted her legs into the chair, and wound her arms around her knees. "You should see the other guy. No one's going to shoplift from me without me chasing them down and tearing a strip out of their hide."

"It looks like they tore a strip out of your neck." Her skin didn't appear to be swollen, but the scratch started at her collarbone and disappeared behind her hair. "Is it painful?"

She lifted a pierced eyebrow. "What happened at your place? I heard someone nearly croaked."

"Not quite." I told her all about the necklace in Elaine's tamale and my successful attempt at CPR.

"Tell me about the necklace," she said, wearing a thoughtful expression.

"Ty said it was one of Dixie's."

I heard the jingle of bells as Lenny trotted down the center aisle, carrying a cat toy in his mouth.

"Come," Patti ordered.

Obediently, Lenny trotted over and placed the fake mouse in her outstretched hand.

"Sit." Patti pointed to the floor at her feet, and Lenny sat. "You're not going to believe what someone tried to steal today from one of my display cases."

Nothing had appeared to be missing. "Earrings?"

"One of Dixie's necklaces."

My eyes widened like saucers. "Who was it?" I asked in disbelief.

Shaking her head, she got up and returned her cup to her office. "Beats me."

"What? You didn't get a good like at them?"

She returned with a small leather purse that she flung over her head and one shoulder. "Oh, I got close enough." She pointed to her neck. "I've just never seen the punk around town."

I sighed in frustration. "What did he look like?"

"I don't know, really." She checked her watch. "Would you do me a huge favor?"

"Give me something."

Still avoiding the question, she unzipped her purse, smeared on some lip gloss, and headed for the door. "Young, skinny, Hispanic. That's all I got."

"Weren't you face-to-face?"

"Listen, I need to run, uh, go do this thing. I won't be gone long."

Unless I was mistaken, my friend was about to leave me in charge of her livelihood without any preparation. "Hey, you're not abandoning me here. What if you get customers?"

"That's why I need you to stay. I can't afford to miss a sale."

"I don't know how to run your register."

She thrust her hands on the hips of her low-ride jeans. "Come over here." She led me to the back counter. "Look familiar?"

We had the exact same cash register.

Maybe she needed a break. Lord knows, I couldn't have made it as a one-woman proprietress. "Okay, fine, but what are the codes?"

She slid open a drawer under the counter. "They're all right here," she said, handing me a laminated set of step-by-step instructions.

I opened my mouth to argue.

Taking my hands, she caught my attention. "Please, Jos. I wouldn't ask if I didn't think you could handle it. I really have to do, uh, run this errand before it's too late. You know I never have time to do the smallest things for myself."

"Okay. If you're sure I can handle it."

"It's almost painless," she said, releasing my hands, "and I won't take long."

"Okay, but don't be gone longer than twenty minutes or Lenny might have an accident." Realistically, I knew I could manage to stay forty, but I wasn't about to admit that.

She lifted her hands in a helpless gesture. "It's not as if you're going to be swamped with customers."

"You win."

Before I knew what hit me, she grabbed me into a bear hug. "You're the best friend ever!" Just as quickly, she released me and headed for the door. She gave the store a final glance, nodding in satisfaction.

A suspicion was growing in my mind. "Please, a guy or a girl?"

Her cheeks turned pink. "Do you have to ask?"

"The shoplifter? Do you think it was a he or a she?"

Taking her keys from her bag, she screwed up her face for a moment. "It could have been either."

"Wait a minute." I hadn't missed her obvious reaction to my gender question. "I'm not staying if you don't tell me where you're going."

She laughed. "Oh, fine. I'm going to file a police report with a certain sexy deputy over at city hall." Her eyes glittered with excitement.

"Oh." Now the pieces fell into place. "Why didn't you file one when Sheriff Wallace was here earlier?"

"He told me to stop by later." With one glance at my face, her smile evaporated. "You said you weren't interested, right?"

"Absolutely." I had no business standing in her way. I was not free to pursue love, and I didn't know how long it would take before I trusted someone to get that close again. "What makes you think Lightfoot will be there? Wallace told me the whole department is out working the festival." I didn't want to discourage her interest in love, but I wasn't sure Lightfoot was her soul match.

"One: I'm optimistic. Two: He told me he would be writing his reports after his shift. Three: He told me exactly when his shift ended."

"Are you sure? He's so . . . dry." More like moody, arrogant, and downright expressionless.

"Oh, I'm sure. You know what they say—"

"Still waters run deep," I interrupted.

"No. The drier the hay, the hotter the fire."

"Ew. I could have done without that."

"You're welcome. See you soon!" She gave me a broad smile and hurried off down the sidewalk.

"Shouldn't you leave me a key in case of an emergency?" I called after her.

Brushing my ankles, Lenny raced out the door, intent on following his tattooed friend.

Patti stepped on his leash. "No thanks, shrimp. You stay here and help your mom."

While I bent down to pick up his leash, she removed a large gold key from her ring and handed it to me. I must have looked as panicked as I felt.

With a shake of her head, she said, "Don't worry, you'll be fine. You want me to talk to Lightfoot about Dixie's jewelry, don't you?"

As soon as she left, I toured each aisle and wall display and then made my way to her office. The tiny room still bore the personality of her parents, with brown wood paneling from the sixties above the chair rail and beaten tin below. I absorbed the neat stacks on her desk, which on closer inspection turned out to be packing lists, invoices, and photo prints.

I didn't think she'd mind me being in this room if I didn't touch anything. Behind the desk, I found a narrow fifties bookcase. Calling me from the top shelf was a small album covered in ripped denim, bulging with whatnots. I swore to only open it long enough to find out what was bending the cover and that I wouldn't read any private entries.

I bit my lip. "Here goes nothing." Inside I found a handful

of stark black and white photos in her usual style. There were also several photographs of jewelry, and if I wasn't mistaken they were the same pieces displayed in her cases. At the bottom of the pile, I found a photo of Dixie's auction necklace, without the matching bracelet and earrings. It wasn't too hard to figure out as Patti had labeled the photo of the turquoise squash blossom necklace in neat letters. I didn't betray our friendship by reading Patti's journal entry, but one glance at the date told me the photo was taken one week to the day before Dixie was murdered. In letters too big to ignore, Patti had written a note, and then underlined it and added three black question marks.

Too good to be real???

Was she referring to the auction necklace? Would an artist as well known as Dixie put her reputation at risk by using low-end gems to make high-end jewelry?

That didn't hold water. Dixie had sold plenty of jewelry pieces at all price levels. Everyone in the area understood that all of the local turquoise had been over-harvested years ago. That's why they bought their expensive gems from traders from Arizona and Nevada.

I started to move a pile of bills to see what Patti had written on her desk blotter, other than skulls and crosses, when the cowbell at the front door clanged and my heart jumped into my throat.

Chapter 13

My diminutive defender ran for the door, barking all the way, only to circle back as if to say, "Let's go!"

"Lenny," I commanded. When he obeyed by running closer, I grabbed his leash.

We marched into the next room only to find a befuddled P.J. Pratt peering into one of the glass display cases, like a cowboy come to town and looking for a trinket for his best girl. In all fairness, P.J. would have looked at home in the ranch supply portion of the store, but standing over the ladies' jewelry, he made me think of the proverbial bull in a china shop.

If I had any doubts that Melanie Pratt's husband worked his own ranch, his muddy boots and sweat-stained hat laid them all to rest. "Howdy," I called out, trying on the cowboy greeting for size. "Can I help you?"

He gave me a cool once-over. "Where's what's-her-name?"

"Out," I responded without my trademark smile. I didn't care for his lack of good manners.

He glanced around the empty store as if trying to catch me in a lie. "When'll she be back?"

"Yip," Lenny said.

P.J. gave Lenny a narrow-eyed glare.

The way he asked, like he had a right to Patti's time, ir-ritated me to no end. "I don't know," I fibbed. "Why don't you come back tomorrow?" I could tell by his reaction that my disapproval was obvious. I couldn't see what had at-tracted a creative type like Melanie to this aggressive, macho, turnip head.

"Well, dad gum," he said, slapping his hat against his leg. He gathered himself and smiled. "Tomorrow's too late." He brushed back his wavy, salt-and-pepper hair with his fingers. "I bought my wife some expensive earrings here last week." He hesitated. "She said something about a matching necklace and bracelets." A deep furrow appeared across his forehead as he turned to study the wares inside the display case once again.

Something was off in his delivery. It wasn't what he said, but what was floating right below the surface. "If you're pos-itive you don't want to come back," I offered, "you can try to find them without her." I gestured to the three separate display cases.

He grimaced. "My wife, Melanie, usually picks out her own jewelry."

I just bet she did. "Why don't you come back and bring her with you?"

I could see his mental cogs turning as if sorting through the possible responses. "Well, now, you see," He ran a finger between his neck and the collar of this plaid western shirt, "this here's what you might call a get-out-of-jail present."

His mention of incarceration brought Anthony to mind. "Melanie's in jail?" I asked. Like I said, I can be a tad passive-aggressive when the need arises.

He chuckled. "Nah, nothing like that. I meant we had a dust up."

After a few seconds of flipping through my mental list of country-fried colloquialisms, I got it. "You had a fight?"

Again, he paused as if choosing the right answer. "Yeah, and it was ugly."

He wore a smile that didn't sit right somehow. Why did he feel the need to lie? I didn't know him from Tom's house-cat other than the fact he was married to Elaine's youngest daughter.

Why did Patti have to file her report now? She would've found the matching pieces and had him out the door in two shakes of a lamb's tail. And the fact I was adding more home-spun quips to my inner thoughts proved I was rattled.

I waited a couple of minutes, listening to him mumble to himself as he peered through the glass at each individual piece. "You still don't see them?"

He slammed his hand on the glass top. "No! I don't know why she couldn't do this herself."

Before I reminded him of his need to appease his wife, Lenny zipped under the counter and started to lick P.J.'s boots.

"Hey, get out of here you mangy—" His face suffused with anger, he drew back his boot as if to kick my dog. At the last second, he shot a quick glance at my outraged face and stepped away. "I'm real sorry." He squared his shoulders. "I'm not used to scrawny dogs." He tried a laugh. "Shoot, I thought he was a rat."

And I thought P.J. was a gentleman. Guess we were both wrong. "You're okay, Lenster." I scooped him up and gave him an ear rubbing and a kiss on top of his pointy head. Forget giving this guy the benefit of the doubt, he'd jumped to number one on my list of idiots. "You need to go, now."

"Listen." He put his hands out as if trying to calm an agitated filly. "I feel dumber than a doorknob. If I could just remember, I'd make a purchase and get out of your hair."

"What color was the setting? Gold or silver?"

"I'm not sure."

I'd had enough of P.J. and his foolishness. "I can't help you if you don't even remember what kind of necklace you bought her."

"All I remember is green."

"Green like emeralds?"

He ran a finger beneath his collar. "That doesn't sound right."

I studied the pieces with green stones in the first case. I was pretty sure none of them were precious stones. "How about jasper, agate, or malachite?" There was a slim chance I might be able to identify those stones from my earth science class in college.

Smiling apologetically, he said, "It'd be great if I could remember something."

His story smelled fishier by the second. "Do you recognize the setting?"

Clenching his jaw, he proceeded to have me bring out all the trays filled with green, blue, or greenish blue stones until he was visibly starting to sweat, shaking his head in confusion. "What do you call that one?" he asked, pointing to a long necklace of greenish blue rocks. I lifted the necklace from the tray and found the tag with the name of the stones written in a fine hand.

"Turquoise." I wanted to kick myself. Of course they were turquoise. Every other item was probably labeled the same way. Why hadn't I thought of that?

"Yeah, yeah, that's more like it." Then he did something that burned itself on my retinas. He looked up, stuck his finger in the air, and snapped his fingers as if a tremendous idea had dropped from the heavens. "Of course, how could I forget? The earrings were made by Dixie Honeycutt." His eyes grew wide. "Which of these did she design?"

First someone tried to steal one of Dixie's necklaces from Patti earlier in the day, then Elaine found one of the jewelry maker's necklaces in one of our tamales, and now P.J. Pratt was performing a song and dance, hoping to score a necklace of his own.

What the heck was going on?

Slowly I ran my eyes over the trays sitting on top. What

would Patti do? Had she already removed Dixie's pieces from public view? Maybe she was waiting until she discussed the issue with Lightfoot. If that was the case, I couldn't sell them without her approval.

"Um, I'll be honest with you. I don't know."

Narrowing his sky blue eyes, P.J. frowned. "You sure?"

"Oh, I'm sure," I said as sweet as honey. Without making any sudden movements, I began to return the trays to their display cases. "If you want to buy pieces from Dixie's collection, you're going to have to come back tomorrow, no two ways about it."

He grunted like a wild hog rooting for worms. "Why?"

"I heard Sheriff Wallace needs to collect all her jewelry and give it to her next of kin." I tried not to smile, but I was pleased to thwart him.

P.J. stood very still. "Says who?"

I grasped at straws. "That's what Sheriff Wallace told Patti earlier today." Hopefully, they'd actually had that very conversation.

Melanie's rancher husband studied me for a long moment, and then he leaned over the counter. Smiling, he showed off two deep lines on either side of his mouth that someone half-blind might have called dimples. "Look right there." He pointed beyond my shoulder. "The earrings are missing from that set. Those are the ones I bought for my wife."

"Well, what do you know? You remembered after all."

He continued, "Melanie's not going to take no for an answer. If I don't bring the necklace and the bracelet home tonight there's going to be hell to pay." And then he turned down the corners of his mouth like a sad circus clown. His manipulation skills needed serious work.

Crossing quickly to the register, I found my shoulder bag and dug inside for my phone and a notepad. "Look, I'll write a note for Patti, telling her to give you first dibs." The back of my neck began to sweat.

He went to step around the end of the counter just as I

pulled my phone from my bag. "Or I can call her if you prefer, but I'm not going to sell you any of Dixie's jewelry without her permission."

"She won't mind!"

A growl broke out from behind me. I turned to find Lenny baring his teeth.

I wasn't about to be intimidated by any sweat-stained cowpoke, even if he did own ten thousand acres of pasture. "I happen to know she's at the sheriff's department right now. Why don't we call her and ask her what she wants to do?"

P.J. was going to need a trip to the dentist if he didn't stop grinding his teeth.

"And while we're at it, I'll tell the sheriff that you don't know how to take no for an answer!"

From the brick red shade of his face, I realized I'd insulted him, and I knew down in the bottom of my soul he'd never forget it. He clenched and unclenched his fists. "You're half crazy," he said, his chest bowed out like a stuffed pigeon. "Put down that phone before you make a serious mistake."

Lenny lunged for him, but I shortened the leash before he took a bite out of P.J.'s Wranglers. I let out a breath and dialed. My call was answered by an automated system, but P.J. didn't have to know that. "I'd like to talk to the sheriff, please. This is Josie Callahan. I need help immediately."

After about fifteen seconds, P.J. stalked out, slamming the front door so hard the cowbell flew off, knocking over a tower of chicken treats.

Before I could hang up, an operator came on the line.

"Big Bend County Sheriff's Department."

"I apologize for the call," I said with genuine regret.

"Ma'am, are you sure I can't help you?" The operator sounded overly concerned. Maybe she was bored. If everyone else was attending the festival, I'd be starved for company too.

"Positive," I said with a chuckle. "I thought I was going to need help with an irate customer, but he's gone."

"Are you there alone?"

"No." I realized that Lenny didn't count. "Uh, yes, but I'm fine."

A group of teenagers walked by, pretending to scuffle. Lenny pulled his leash free of my hand and ran for the door, yapping up a storm.

"Lenny!"

There was a long silence on the other end.

"Sorry about that, my dog thinks I'm in danger."

"Ma'am, I'll send someone out right away."

"Please don't, we're fine. It's just my dog, he gets a bit overprotective."

"I'll stay on the line until the officer arrives."

"No, no, please. There's no emergency. I don't need an officer."

Doing his best to protect the plate-glass windows along the front of the store, Lenny jumped into the window display.

"Get down!" I shouted, running to salvage a fragile antique spinning wheel.

I grabbed his leash. "Sit." He sat, panting from his workout.

"Hello?" I gasped into the phone, suddenly remembering the operator.

The line was dead.

Double darn it.

Where was Patti? I left two voicemail messages and a text. What if P.J. came back and brought Melanie with him? It was not in my job description to handle those two together. No doubt, I was overreacting, but the rancher's aggressive demeanor had gotten under my skin. If a certain dark-haired deputy arrived with Patti in tow, I was going to feel like an idiot. I went so far as forming witty apologies in my head.

When the cruiser pulled up to the curb fifteen interminable minutes later, I shut off the lights, locked the door, and stepped out to face the music. I was closing thirty minutes early, but Patti would have to get over it.

"Deputy Joseph Barnes," the young officer said with a grin. He pulled himself up tall. "Are you Josie Callahan?"

While I was away in Austin, the Big Bend County Sheriff's Department must have recruited recent high school graduates. As Aunt Linda would say, Deputy Barnes would have to stand up to look a rattler in the eyes. His wore his auburn hair shorn like a sheep, and the sun had beaten his fair complexion to a reddened veneer. Studying his pink skin that never tanned, I added an olive complexion to my list of blessings.

"That's me," I said, trying to figure out if and when we'd met.

I couldn't make out his cruiser's logo in the glare of the late afternoon sun. "Are you from Ringo County?" Our neighboring counties worked on call for one another. Without the added assistance, none of our three expansive, low-populated regions would have coverage in case of an emergency—or a festival.

With a glance at his cruiser, he nodded. "Yes, ma'am." He placed one hand on his firearm. "What seems to be the trouble?"

A nervous tingle started in my right foot. My heart was working double-time. I squeezed Lenny until he yipped in surprise. "Shh," I said and stroked his head with two fingers. "No trouble, officer. I tried to explain to the woman on the phone that the matter was cleared up."

"Why don't you tell me all about it while I give you a ride home? That is unless you have your vehicle present."

I checked my phone. No response from Patti. What an embarrassing fiasco this was turning out to be. Looking around at the empty street, I was tempted to accept. "I can walk. It's no big deal."

"Come on. It would be my pleasure."

"How long have you been with the sheriff's department?"

"About a month." His grin widened.

"I should wait a few minutes for Patti, I mean Miss Perez. I'm watching her store."

"We can wait out here," he said, indicating the street, "or we can wait in the cruiser."

"The cruiser's fine," I said, hoping my embarrassment didn't show. Lenny barked in agreement, and we walked around to the passenger side. Barnes reached for the rear door and held it open as we slid across the seat.

Once he'd positioned himself behind the wheel, he asked. "What was the trouble?"

It made me uneasy to sit there without starting the cruiser, but I told myself I'd rather be inside the vehicle instead of standing on the street for everyone to see. "One of her customers was getting way out of line, acting all creepy and aggressive." I exaggerated so as not to appear to be a big chicken. "He refused to leave until I called you."

"Why was he aggressive? What happened?" he asked with a chuckle, shaking his head in disbelief.

I leaned forward. "I couldn't find some items this guy wanted to buy. I told him to come back later after the owner returned and he refused. End of story." Maybe the incident had felt more threatening than it really was due to Dixie's death.

"I've never known P.J. Pratt to threaten anyone."

Surprise, surprise. I had avoided mentioning P.J.'s name over the phone for this very reason. Even this young deputy from Ringo County was a member of Broken Boot's good ole boy network.

"I didn't say he did. I told her I didn't need assistance." Should I jump out before the cruiser hit the road? Would the rear doors open from the inside? Trying not to telegraph my intentions, I grabbed the handle and pulled. Nothing happened.

"Where you going and what's your hurry?"

"Oh, uh, I was feeling a bit claustrophobic." I tried to act as if butter wouldn't melt in my mouth. "I didn't know what else to do."

He lowered the windows, admitting a breeze fragrant with mimosa. Drumming his fingers on the steering wheel, he stared out the front window and clicked his tongue against the back of his teeth. "Better?"

"How'd you know the customer was P.J.?"

"We said howdy at the light as he headed out of town." He pushed his hat back from his forehead and studied me in his rearview mirror.

"What did he say?"

"Does it matter? He's headed back out to the ranch for supper." He chortled like a chimpanzee. "You're safe."

"If you think his behavior is amusing, you can open this door and let me out. I walked here, and I can walk back." My pride gets the best of me. I blame it on spending the first twelve years of my life in Dallas, a city with a huge sense of entitlement.

"Ma'am," he said in a gentle tone, "I meant no offense."

I sighed. "Patti would've known how to handle him. How was I supposed to know whether or not I could sell Dixie's jewelry?"

"Where did Miss Perez say she was going?"

Shrugging one shoulder, I gave him a partial truth. "She said she had to run an important errand."

We waited a few more minutes, but Patti didn't arrive. I checked my text messages a dozen times, but she failed to respond.

He turned in his seat and scrutinized me from hooves to horns. "Rumor has it your friend here was dognapped?"

"Who told you that?" I had only told my tale to the sheriff.

"A little birdie in the sheriff's office."

I didn't care for this guy knowing my business, but I couldn't help myself. "Is the sheriff investigating?" I grabbed his upper arm. "Did he get a tip?"

"How about a swap?"

"What?"

"Two dozen tamales?"

"You're kidding."

"No, I'm starving."

What was a rookie deputy's salary? By the look of him, he wasn't eating enough to feed a peanut.

"One dozen?" he begged.

I kept my gaze averted. "To go."

Rolling his eyes, he huffed like a teenage girl told to spit out her gum. "Deal." He started the engine and threw it into drive. "Where to?"

"We might as well head over to Milagro and pick up your bribe."

"Hey."

"Get to talking."

Slowly he cruised down the side streets, parting the slow moving cars and trucks like Moses parting the red sea. "Some gal at Elaine's Pies called in to report a dog tied up to the lamppost outside your restaurant."

"Who was it?" And why hadn't they called us?

"Don't know. That's all I heard."

"That merits one tamale and no sauce."

He grunted. "How about this? Some Asian woman called in to complain that you were hassling her husband."

"I was not!"

"Hey, don't kill the messenger. I just want the dozen."

"Fine." The folks in this town were supposed to be my friends, or so I thought.

When we pulled into Milagro's parking lot, I hustled to the to-go window and brought him back two dozen tamales.

"Whoa," he said, unwrapping one immediately and shoving it in his mouth. "Lordy, that's good."

"You're welcome." I was hurt and ready to go inside and lick my wounds. "Thanks for the ride."

"Hey, cut P.J. some slack," he called out the window. "He only wanted to help Melanie make some quick dough on Dixie's jewelry now that she's dead."

And that was the whole truth: It was all about the money.

I gave him a jaunty wave. "I'll give him so much slack, he'll think he's floating down the Rio Grande on an inner tube." If I ever saw P.J. Pratt again, it would be too soon.

"Hey, seriously," the deputy said, rolling up alongside me. "This drought's got his head in a vise. He only made forty-six bales of hay last year and had to buy the rest at sixty-five dollars a bale."

Studying his earnest expression, I asked, "Why help Melanie spend money on a scheme that may or may not make her any money?"

Barnes grimaced and shook his head. "He always buys his princess some expensive geegaw after they've had a bust up." His gaze dropped to my ring-free hand. "He's not the first man too scared to tell his wife no."

"Okay, I get it, but tell your friend to dial back his temper a few notches."

The window raised and lowered again. "I hate to say this . . ." He cleared his throat.

He wasn't fooling me. Whatever it was, he was busting his badge to say it.

"If you don't want to be the butt of every joke, you've got to man up. Just because a guy wants his own way, doesn't mean he's out to get you."

"Man up?" I lifted my chin and squared my shoulders. "That's all you got?"

With a heavy sigh, he grabbed the steering wheel with both hands as if he wanted to shake it. "You should go back to your cappuccinos and bumper-to-bumper traffic and leave the country to those of us tough enough to handle it."

I lifted my hand for a sarcastic salute, and then all of a sudden, Lenny was flying like an arrow, pulling me toward Milagro's back door. As we ran, Deputy Barnes peeled away, spraying rocks and gravel in his wake.

was hoping if I explained to Ty how vital it was to the home's survival he would help me find it amongst her things.

Main Street still flowed with tourists checking out the local shops and restaurants. Even at this hour, couples strolled hand in hand, window-shopping in the cooler temperatures.

I decided to begin my search for Ty by heading over to Two Boots. With all the tourists in town, the best place to pick up women and a hand of Texas Hold 'Em was our dance hall. On Tuesday nights, except for the week of the festival, the Future Farmers of America met there for lively discussions on the pros and cons of fertilizing with chicken manure and other fascinating topics. During the festival we gave tourists what they wanted . . . a place to two-step to kicking music.

Texas has the largest concentration of dance halls in America. It has to do with our German and Czech ancestors, who brought their love of music and dancing to the hills and wide-open spaces of this great, if ornery, state.

Two Boots was also the best place to find a fount of juicy gossip in Tim and Mitzi, two of our bartenders. Knowing Sheriff Wallace and his deputies were busy with the festival, I decided to ferret out whatever information I could find about Ty Honeycutt on my own. First, I'd corner Uncle Eddie, and then I'd hang out with our bartending couple.

When I arrived, the crowd streaming through the door was young, old, and in between. Perfectly straight, highlighted hair and skinny jeans made me think the young ones had driven down from Dallas or Houston. As I walked in, the twang of banjo and the thump of upright bass hit me in my chest, reverberating all the way down to my toes. That night a popular band from Presidio, Trigger Finger, was playing a set of danceable, energetic country tunes. They shared funny anecdotes with the audience before each set, which I adored. I didn't know if the tourists would dig it, but in my humble opinion, that was the best part of their performance.

"ID, please, ma'am." The doorman was short and wiry and had asked me to go to the Dairy Dream during the summer after sixth grade. Not one to look a gift horse in the mouth, I figured any awkward moments between us would be smoothed out for the price of a chocolate dip cone. I'd been wrong. The fool had wanted to kiss me . . . until I pushed him so hard he landed in the dirt.

"Vince, it's me."

He squinted with his one good eye. "Josie, dang it, it sure is!" Though both eyes appeared to be in working order, Vince had served a tour in Iraq and lost the vision in his left eye from unforgiving shrapnel.

I offered him my right hand. He shook it and grabbed me with his other arm, wrapping me in a tight hug. "Good to see you, gal."

"Good to be seen." I backed away with a smile, not wanting to offend him.

"Eddie's not in the office."

"What's happened now?"

"Some of the kegs have walked off." He made a production out of cracking his knuckles. "When I find out who did it, they'll be drinking beer through their ear."

Trying hard not to laugh at the image his threat conjured, I smiled. "Guess I'll check out the band."

"Since when did you become a kicker?"

"Depends on who's playing. Crazy, huh?" In high school, I'd never really listened to country music. I'd banged my head with the best of 'em and had had a permanent crush on the two older, hotter gods of rock music, Steven Tyler and Steve Perry. I'd vowed to marry a man with long hair and the name Steve.

Over the whine of the steel guitar, I made my way down the narrow hall to the saloon. I had to turn sideways and lower my head to avoid the press of girls leaning against one wall and the young men trying to engage them in conversation on the opposite. Farther along, I nearly ended up sandwiched between a couple about to dive in for a kiss, but I managed to hold them apart long enough to squeeze through.

The stage stood on the back wall, three feet off the ground. A pool of women flanked the stage. Colored lights reflected in their eyes, making them appear as if caught in the spell of the music and the young, virile musicians. I understood their pain. Music could do that to you, mix you up, make you think the man playing the fiddle or that Gibson was sweet and sympathetic like his song.

I envied them their naive dreams, but I couldn't help but feel superior at the same time. Thanks to Brooks, I'd drunk the Kool-Aid, and my ideas about love had barely survived.

Looking around, I breathed in the fragrance of money. We were jam-packed, which meant we would be able to pay our bills for at least another few months. I kept my chin high so as not to meet the gaze of any love-hungry singles on the nearby stools, and sauntered behind the bar. I was off the market and not in the mood to be pawed or propositioned.

"Baby girl, if you aren't a sight for sore eyes," Mitzi cried, raising her voice over the noise of the crowd. Next to her, Tim acknowledged me with a wink as he flipped bottles and mixed drinks. He was a baby-faced bruiser with a soft, squishy heart that beat for Taylor Swift and Mitzi. He didn't seem to care that his girl was fifteen years his senior as long as she dressed like a country music princess.

I laughed at Mitzi's heavy drawl, thick and sweet as peach cobbler with cinnamon ice cream. "How's it going?" I asked, hugging her around the neck.

Some impatient guy at the bar leaned in to give her his drink order, but she pointed one finger, cocked her thumb, and narrowed her eyes at him as if taking aim. He raised both hands, in mock surrender, and backed away.

She grabbed me in a one-armed hug as she continued to pour what looked like a dirty martini, heavy on the vermouth. "How you holding up?" she asked, giving me a quick once-over before handing the drink to a waitress at the end of the bar. Mitzi wore the Two Boots uniform: plaid shirt tied at the waist, denim skirt with leather fringe around the bottom, and brown leather vest festooned with rhinestones. Only I didn't think Uncle Eddie intended for her to wear it a size too small.

"Can't complain," I said, projecting my voice over the applause as the band finished their number.

She raised an eyebrow.

"I could . . ."

"But I won't," she said, finishing a quip I'd learned from her many moons before. "So, what brings you out this way?"

"Ty Honeycutt."

Grabbing me by the shoulders, she spun me toward her. "Tell me you're not mixed up with that horndog."

I laughed and pulled away. "Not if he was the last cowboy in Texas."

"Good thing." She patted me on the shoulder. "That man'll chew you up, spit you out, and make you curse your momma." Even though she delivered the line with a chuckle, I could see an old heartache in her eyes.

Leaning close, I asked, "How's he doing since Dixie died?"

She delivered a couple of strawberry daiquiris, and I could see she was choosing her words with care. "We didn't see him for a day or two, and then last night he was back, telling some tall tale about saving some woman's life over at Milagro."

"He's a liar!"

"I'm kidding, sugar. I heard how you saved the day." She grinned and jabbed me in the side with her elbow.

For a moment, there were no drinks to make or orders to fill. "Do you think Dixie left everything to Ty?" I asked.

"Wouldn't surprise me none. She always treated him like a son."

"How did he treat her?"

"Like a dear old aunt." She glanced around to confirm that no one was listening except Tim. "When she was paying attention."

I wouldn't put it beyond Ty to have stayed with Dixie without paying his share of rent, utilities, or groceries. Would he have truly killed her for her ancient van and the rest of her worldly possessions?

I rose to my tiptoes, but it was difficult to see through the crowd around the bar stools. "He's not playing tonight?"

"Oh, he's playing alright, just not up on stage."

"So they do have a game going here? Does Uncle Eddie know?"

"Nah, they know Eddie'd blow a gasket." She turned away to grab four frosty beer glasses, and began filling them with drafts from the tap. "But Ty's so desperate he's running a game out in the parking lot in Trigger Finger's van."

"Thanks," I said and patted her on the shoulder for good-bye.

She leaned in close. "Don't go out there." Her eyes went wide. "You'll be as welcome as a rattlesnake, and I'd hate for you to get your tail stepped on."

Standing here in my own backyard, so to speak, I had no fear. Ty Honeycutt had a soft spot for women. He'd nearly cried over Dixie's death and Elaine's close call. I didn't think he'd do me any harm.

"They'll be fine." I gave her a big wink. "I'm only poisonous on Sundays."

The band went on break to thunderous applause. In its place, canned music swelled from either Tim McGraw or Brad Paisley, one of those guys with a big hat. Couples swayed onto the dance floor, looking for an excuse to hold each other close. I located the exit and tried to maneuver my way to the back parking lot through a moving sea of bobbing heads.

"Would you like to dance?"

I turned with a polite smile and found Lightfoot way too close. "What are you doing here?" He'd abandoned his uniform for jeans and a plaid cotton shirt of the skin-hugging variety.

"Trying to relax. Won't you help a guy out?" His mouth was saying one thing, but the laser intensity of his stare was saying something else. I didn't believe for one minute he was here to two-step.

"Uh, not tonight." I turned away and he followed. "Look," I said, adding what I hoped was a hint of embarrassment and frustration. "I've got to go to the little girls' room."

"Then you're headed in the wrong direction." His grin said he didn't believe me as far as he could throw me.

He was correct, but my family didn't own this place for nothing. "I'm headed to the employee bathroom. Please, I wouldn't go in the public restroom if you gave me a trip to Vegas." I wasn't lying, I hated casinos.

Placing a hand on my forearm, he prevented my escape. "You don't work here."

What happened to stoic and silent? "Listen, you should do your homework. My family owns this place." I wanted to stamp my foot.

"You should lighten up," he said, placing his hand at the small of my back and forcing me into the throng of slow dancers.

I could have dragged my heels, but I figured why not? It wouldn't hurt my reputation to be seen dancing with a handsome man, even if he was merely trying to pump me for information. I could discover his plan of attack without him being any the wiser. "Have you ever been here before?"

"Sure. Everybody's been to Two Boots at least once."

"I'd bet my money you're not here to relax." He continued to glance around the room. "You look like you're onto something, and it's not a hookup."

"Why do you say that?" He smiled a dazzling toothpaste ad smile, acknowledging he hadn't hidden his professional interest in the customers.

"Just a hunch. What's up?"

"Looking for an old friend of mine."

"Maybe I can help. What's his name?"

"You wouldn't know him."

"Let me guess," I smirked, "Ty Honeycutt."

The dazzling smile disappeared.

"If you're Ty's friend you know he's probably playing cards out in Presidio tonight," I said.

He tried to stare me down and nearly drove us into another couple, Texas two-stepping around the throng. "How about we trade information?"

"What makes you think I'm interested?" I held my breath, praying he'd give me a fresh lead.

"'Cause you think you can solve this murder."

How'd he know? "I think crime belongs in the hands of the sheriff's department." I pretended to study the dancers on either side of us until my thoughts were hidden.

We turned, which brought us closer than before. "I hear you used to work for the *Austin Gazette*. You're a big-time reporter."

I forced a laugh. "I *was* a reporter who reported on community events, not murder, not by a long shot." When would this stupid song ever end? I was tired of this dance, his questioning, and some male singer crooning over and over about how his truck was gone.

Instead of me ditching him, something or someone across the room caught his eye and he turned the tables on me. "Thanks for the dance. See you later."

"If you're lucky," I called after his retreating figure.

Where was Ty? If Mitzi was right and he was outside, I had to find him before Lightfoot, undercover deputy.

The stalwart deputy would question Ty, take notes, nod his head, and decide to question eight other people. And once he questioned Dixie's slippery nephew, I would no longer have the element of surprise. Ty would either leave town or fill the holes in his alibi.

Determined to lift the stench of this crime from Milagro, I headed outside. I searched the parking lot without any luck, checked out the picnic tables just in case Ty was stretching his legs, and ended up circling the building. The second time around, I spotted it, a red minivan with a business sign on the side that read, *Ready Cash! Don't worry. We've got your number!*

I bet they did . . . at one hundred percent interest.

After seeing Ty again at the tamale-eating contest, I wasn't afraid of him. He reminded me of those jocks in high school. Back then they'd sauntered down the halls as if they were all that and a bag of chips, but now they slaved all day digging ditches for the county or draining oil pans at the Ten Minute Quick Lube. I approached the van with caution and found that what had appeared dark from far away was actually lit up inside. Like a custom van from the seventies, a curtain separated the driver and passenger seat from the rear.

Suddenly a gunshot exploded inside the van. I squealed, hit the ground, and started to roll as if my hair was on fire.

The side door slid open, and barrels of laughter and smoke spilled out along with a curly-headed man. "Well, hello," he said, brushing off his too-tight jeans as he rose from the dirt.

"Hi," I said, feeling twelve times a fool. The dim light prevented me from identifying him, and his slur wasn't helping. Whoever he was didn't appear too surprised or concerned about my discovery of their clandestine card game. "Did I hear a gunshot?" I asked, toddling to my feet. "Does someone, uh, need medical attention?"

He laughed and I recognized him as Dixie's nephew. "Hey fellas, some gal wants to nurse the hole in the ceiling." A sea of male voices howled.

"Ty," a male voice with a Hispanic accent called out from the backseat of the van, "what's her name?"

Another fellow of indeterminate age, sitting closest to the door, stuck his head out. "You look familiar." He pulled on his long, straggly beard and smiled, revealing a few missing teeth.

"I'm Josie Callahan, from Milagro." I gave Ty my best smile, as if we were old friends. "Remember me?"

"You s-saved that woman's life." Dixie's nephew stuck out his hand, swaying back and forth as if standing on the bow of a ship.

I slipped my hand in and out of his as quickly as possible, hoping he wouldn't notice. "Eddie Martinez sent me out here to talk to you." So far, no one else had stepped out of the van. I peeked inside and saw the game was still in motion, but no one appeared too worried about my presence, quite the opposite.

The young man on the other side of Scraggly Beard straightened up and repositioned his cowboy hat. "What's Martinez want with us?"

"He heard about your poker game and wants you to know it ain't allowed on his property." I inwardly grimaced. When had I ever said *ain't*?

Through smoke as dense as a spring fog, a dark-haired guy in the back peered over the seat in front of him. "Since when?" He narrowed his gaze and I backed away.

In spite of his comment, I found it impossible to believe that Uncle Eddie knew these guys were out here. "Since Deputy Lightfoot arrived looking for Ty."

A clownish look of concern came over Honeycutt's face. He gave me a hard stare and hitched his belt. "Boys, we've got to call it quits."

On the far side of the middle seat, a wiry guy wearing a camouflage hunting cap held a deck of cards and a hungry look. "I'm in for three hundred," he complained. "I say we take our chances."

Drunk or not, Ty swung his head toward me, back to the guy in the hunting cap, and back to me again on a neck as wobbly as a newborn's. Beneath his straw Stetson, his wavy hair fell over his ears and flipped up in the back. Probably around thirty, he was a temptation gone to seed. "What do you think?" he asked me.

"I think if my aunt were found dead, I'd stay home and mourn for at least three or four days."

Their hoots of laughter hit me like a giant wave on the Gulf. Scraggly Beard said, "Yeah, why don't you go home and find her will, Ty? She might have left you a reason to celebrate."

"Shut your mouth or I'll shut it for you." Ty yanked Scraggly Beard out of the van by his flannel shirt and shot a fierce look my way as if gauging my reaction. Maybe Ty had money to gamble because he'd searched Dixie's house and found a hidden nest egg.

The van full of men fell silent. Suddenly I realized all the fellas were giving me appraising looks, and my knees started to shake.

I dipped my chin and gave Ty a coy smile. "Could you and I speak in private?"

He answered with a leer. "Sure, sweetheart."

They hooted and whistled as we walked away, and then the van door slammed and all was quiet but the faint sound of honky-tonk music drifting through the dance hall's open windows.

"Where we goin'?" he asked, trying to put an arm around me.

I slipped away. "Let's sit out over here." The patio nearby was inhabited only by the smell of stale beer and a man and woman engaged in a mouth-to-mouth discussion in a far corner.

"What's this all about?" he asked as he flipped around a chair and dropped into it backwards. He threw his hat on the table and ran his fingers through his dirty blond hair. "You don't strike me as the amorous type."

"You don't strike me as the affectionate nephew type."

"You a cop?"

"No, I'm worried about Milagro."

"The restaurant?"

"It belongs to my family."

He took his head in his hands and turned his face to one side and then the other, cracking his neck. "So?"

"Your aunt's body was found in the alley behind our

restaurant." *By me*, I could have added, but I didn't want to reveal that tidbit. In fact, my knees were still shaking as if I'd run five miles uphill.

His Mr. Nice Guy presentation slipped. "What's that got to do with me?" he demanded.

I wanted to shout, *She was your aunt!* Instead I decided to reason with him.

"I was hoping you could tell me who might have had it in for Dixie."

He studied me for a moment, narrowing his eyes. Finally he relaxed and reached for my hand with a small smile. "That's it?"

Resisting the urge to pull my hand away, I swallowed. "That's what the sheriff's wondering. That, and why you didn't come inside to find her." I gathered my courage. "If she were my aunt, I'd have at least gotten out of the El Camino."

He squeezed my hand hard and then relaxed. "How do you know so much about what the sheriff's thinking?"

"He and Uncle Eddie are old friends."

"Why do you care?"

"Dixie and I were friendly, but that doesn't mean I want the district attorney to send Anthony to prison if he didn't do it. If I help find the killer, Anthony will be released, Milagro's reputation will be restored, and things will get back to normal around here."

Blowing out his breath, he dropped my hand. "I don't know who wouldn't have it in for her. Everybody hated her." He pulled a cigarette and a lighter from his shirt pocket.

"I didn't."

"You were one of the few."

All was silent but the drone of a mosquito.

He lit the cigarette and studied me through a cloud of smoke. "When I didn't see her on the bench at the back door, I drove by the front. I didn't figure on someone just leaving her alone back there."

My stomach roiled. I needed to turn my pointing finger of judgment back on myself. "Could I ask you something else?"

"No," he said, his voice sleepy.

"The festival committee needs the necklace Dixie created for the silent auction." I slapped at a mosquito on my upper arm. "You wouldn't happen to know where it is, would you?"

"Why do you care?" He tilted his head back and blew a smoke ring into the evening sky.

The door to the dance floor swung open, delivering a gut punch of electric guitar, but no one came out and it swung closed again. "A lot of folks have worked real hard to promote the sale of that necklace. Auctioning it off for the good of those kids is what Dixie wanted."

He touched my shoulder, and then slowly drew his hand down my arm until he held my left wrist. "You sure you're not working for the cops?"

My mind was racing, and my old friend adrenaline was back. "I swear, but if you gave me that necklace I wouldn't mention where I found it."

He squeezed my left wrist until it hurt. "Why not?"

Concentrating hard on changing my expression, I fisted my free hand. "You haven't done anything wrong by taking your own aunt's necklace, but neither have those orphans. They're needs are more important."

With a tilt of his head, he ran his eyes down my body. "I don't know."

I placed my hand over my heart. "You can trust me."

In a slick move, he released my wrist and linked the fingers of his hands with both of mine. "I might know where to find it, but I ain't going to look because that's what she would have wanted. She was ornery and mean and self-centered."

"Can't you say something kind, for God's sake?"

My tone knocked his head back. "Well, let's see. She let me stay at her place, and she was an okay cook, most days." He rested our joined hands on my knee.

Would he stop talking if I dropped his hand like the proverbial hot potato and scooted away? I didn't want to chance
it. "Where do you think it is?"

"Her studio." He grunted and dropped my hand as if un-
happy with the conversation. "Or maybe that witch Melanie
Burnett has it." Ty was growing sleepier, his head falling
toward the table.

Suddenly I remembered Patti's discovery on the mayor's
computer. "Ty?" I whispered.

"Hmm?" He folded his hands on the table and perched his
chin on top.

"Was Dixie blackmailing the mayor's wife?"

With a faint smile, he lifted my wrist to his nose and
sniffed. "I don't know nothin' about that. I do know she was
hoping to sell more jewelry, but her sources dried up."

He could sniff all he wanted, but I wasn't wearing anything
but Dove. "What kind of sources?"

"Her rocks and gemstones. Somebody got to her seller,
and all of a sudden they refused to do business with her."
Keeping his eyes on mine, he turned my wrist over and kissed
the back of my hand. The collar of his shirt pulled open, and
there, resting on his collarbone, was a necklace of horses,
identical to the one Dixie had worn the day she died.

With my heart beating out a boot-stomping rhythm, I
fought to keep my voice level. "Who was her seller?" I was
okay. I could still punch him with my right hand if he got
fresh. But how had he come by Dixie's necklace? I'd seen
Lightfoot wrap it in foil and take it away after the disaster at
the contest.

"Some trader from the Four Corners Reservation who
came through town every few months or so. I don't know his
name." Most of the agate and amethyst in our area was found
on private ranches, but Dixie had always maintained a good
relationship with the owners, or so I thought.

The door must have drifted back open for I could see
through the screen door to the dance floor. Lightfoot was

talking to a waitress, his head bent forward as if asking a question. I was standing in the middle of a moral dilemma. Did I warn Ty that the deputy was about to find him, hoping he'd give me more information at a later date? Or did I help Lightfoot do his job?

He tugged my hand until his face was inches away from mine. "How about a kiss?"

Chapter 15

His breath stunk of beer and smoke. I blinked away the stench, trying to make out if the horses on his necklace were made from the same stones as the one Elaine had swallowed, but it was too dark.

I yanked my hand from his and stood up. "Maybe next time." I'd had enough of this snake in cowboy clothing, even if he had passed on priceless information.

"Suit yourself, city gal," he said, standing unsteadily. With a short bow, he replaced his hat on his head and strode off in the opposite direction of the van.

"Ty Honeycutt?"

Dixie's nephew turned at the sound of his name. "Who wants to know?"

Lightfoot strolled toward him as if he were an old friend Ty might have forgotten. Slowly, he reached into his back pocket and flashed his badge in the other man's face. "Sit down, right there," Lightfoot said, pointing to the same chair Ty had abandoned moments before, "and don't move."

Across the parking lot, two deputies in uniform stepped up to the red van. The taller of the two banged on the door and shouted, "Everybody out."

"You two need some help?" Lightfoot called out.

Before the deputies could answer, there was a loud metal screech as the sliding door on the other side of the van opened, followed by fervent cursing as the men scrambled out.

"They're getting away!" I cried. If the deputies didn't hurry, the poker players would make for the trees.

As the officers ran around the van, I heard one of them calling for backup on his radio. For a moment, all was silent until I heard what sounded like a herd of buffalo tramping through the scrub and Barnes shouting. In Austin and Dallas, the police had to concern themselves with whether or not the criminals would turn around and shoot. But the poker dudes, though they might conceal and carry, wouldn't shoot an officer of the law over an illegal poker game.

Ty tried to run, but he crashed into the table and fell to the ground. Before he could hop up, Lightfoot placed a boot on his back. "Get up real slow and I won't cuff you," he said, swinging a pair of metal bracelets into Ty's field of vision.

"I ain't done nothin'."

"I want to ask you a few questions. We can do it here or back at the station, your choice."

Slowly, Ty tried to sit up as if he'd had the wind knocked out of him. He stood slowly and made a sharp kick backwards with his boot.

While Ty and Lightfoot faced off, sizing each other up, I slipped behind the musician and picked up the object he'd hoped to hide. I held it up to the light and recognized a substantial roll of bills. "He was trying to keep you from finding this." I handed the money to the deputy.

"Give me that!" Ty tried to snatch it from my hand, but Lightfoot was faster.

Uncle Eddie flew out the side door, a white bar towel flung over his shoulder. "What's going on?"

Ty didn't respond, but he did sneak a glance in the direction of the scrub on the other side of the van where his friends had skedaddled.

With one eye on the musician, Lightfoot opened his hand.

Ty bowed out his chest. "That's my money."

"I'm missing five hundred dollars." Uncle Eddie's hands were fisted and his shoulders hunched. Any second, his hair was going to stand on end. "Did you steal it?"

"How could I have stolen it?"

"Mitzi says you were flirting with her behind the bar before she ran you off."

Uncle Eddie counted the drawer four times a night to prevent the waitresses and bartenders from pocketing money. His persistence had come in handy this time.

"I won that money, fair and square."

Barnes and another of the deputies returned, both dragging and wheezing like a leaky valve. "They're long gone, but we might catch them where the trail ends out on Presidio Road."

"When you do, let's ask them if Ty was winning tonight or if this money belongs to Two Boots," Lightfoot said.

Ty made a big show of shaking his head and thrusting his hands on his hips. "You can't prove anything."

"Nope, not unless someone spills their guts," Lightfoot said.

The other deputy butted in, "Which they might be willing to do if you cheated them out of their money tonight."

Lightfoot stepped closer. "Bubba says you told him that you'd do whatever it took to get your aunt's money."

Ty must have finally realized that Lightfoot, the deputies, and Uncle Eddie had him surrounded. He raised his hands in mock surrender. "That don't mean I killed her."

"He's wearing Dixie's necklace." I wanted Lightfoot to haul this guy in by his belt loops. If he'd steal money from a softie like my uncle, he was desperate enough to kill Dixie.

Stepping even closer, Lightfoot reached for Ty's collar. "That right?"

Ty grabbed the necklace, his eyes skirting from one deputy to another. "Yeah, but it's mine. She made it special for me."

Standing back from any fists that might start flying, I was doing a mental victory dance. They'd have to let Anthony go if they found even one jot of evidence that Ty might have been involved in Dixie's murder.

"Hey, man, I'm innocent," Ty said, no longer bowed up and defensive. In an urgent whisper he pleaded, "Take me down to the station and question me if you want, but I didn't kill Aunt Dixie."

With a nod in my direction, Lightfoot and the other deputies led Ty out to the main parking lot while Uncle Eddie followed along behind, berating the luckless gambler.

Ty was a piece of work, but I wasn't convinced he was guilty. It was too neat, too pat, and I was too keyed up to head home. I cruised around the back of the building to the other side, making my way carefully past a metal toolshed, an abandoned deep freezer, and a rusted hulk of a GTO that Uncle Eddie had bought in an auction in Waco. Of course, he'd sworn on a stack of Bibles he was going to fix her up after the tourist season, and here she waited, six years later.

As I approached the side door, I spotted a familiar figure. Mayor Cogburn was smoking a cigarette and watching my progress through my uncle's minefield. No sign of the beautiful Felicia.

"I was afraid you'd sprain an ankle out there, but you made it." His gaze landed somewhere around my shoulder.

Good night. Was the whole town on a bender? "Uncle Eddie could pay his bills if he'd sell off this junk," I said playfully, hoping to avoid a discussion of any length.

The mayor took a long draw on his cigarette. "Your uncle's a good guy." His succinct delivery confused me. Was he sober or just skilled at masking how much he'd had to drink?

I had never seen the mayor anything but calculatingly upbeat, but tonight he was talking to me in a voice full of sorrow and regret. If I was lucky, that meant he would answer my questions no matter how rude.

"And Dixie was a good woman."

He stared at me, and I knew I had gone too far. He was going to leave. Instead he leaned forward and looked me square in the eyes. "No, she worn't." I also had never heard our esteemed mayor venture into a hick dialect.

"She created beautiful things."

"She created a load of bull crap that nearly ruined my life." He wiped the back of his hand across his brow. "Meaner than a snake and twice as crafty."

I took the plunge. "What'd she do?" I asked in a sweet, and I hoped, an unthreatening voice. I held my breath.

"She threatened me and my family."

"How could she do that? You're the one in charge."

"She knew . . . things. Secrets she wanted to spread around town . . . about us." He tossed his cigarette and ground it under his expensive boot heel.

Through the emergency exit at his back, I could hear the beat of the music and over it the buzz of the crowd. I remained silent, nodding in sympathy even as I noted how isolated we were amongst the rusting castoffs. A cool breeze tickled the hair at the back of my neck and along my arms.

"We have our hard times. Lord knows, her idiosyncrasies would force any man to drive his truck off a cliff." He waited for me to respond.

I stepped back. "Well—"

Huffing out a sour breath he rolled his eyes and shook his head. "I know. I can be a real pain in the ass myself." He didn't slur his words, but his breath could peel wallpaper.

Why was he suddenly divulging his marital problems to me? And did it matter as long as it led me one step closer to figuring out who'd murdered Dixie? "What I know is that you two are still together, and there's no other couple who represents the people in Broken Boot like you two."

"You got that right." He cast a nervous glance at the darkened windows, but unless he had super powers, all he saw was swaying shadows. He propped back against the wooden siding. "Dixie saw us. Can you believe it?" After several seconds he continued. "We'd picked a place on the other side of El Paso. We walk out the door, and there she is, big as you please, getting out of her car." He hitched at his leather belt where his pants had fallen below his beer belly. "She smiled and said hello like nothing was going on, and so did we."

Where were they? What had Dixie seen and why didn't they want her to see them? I slowly let my gaze drift left and then right, praying that no one would materialize around the corner to interrupt him.

I nodded again. "But she didn't let it go, did she?"

His fingers ran under his bolero tie, pulling it loose. "We were working on the silent auction so it didn't seem strange, her calling to donate her necklace."

"Of course not, it's the perfect thing."

"But she started insinuating that I needed to buy one of her other necklaces for Felicia. I told her no, that I'd have to wait for our anniversary." He drew a handkerchief from his breast pocket and wiped the back of his neck. "That's when she threatened to tell everyone in town about seeing us at Dr. Valentine's."

I wasn't familiar with the good doctor or his establishment, but it didn't require a rocket scientist to deduce that the photos Dixie had sent to the mayor's office had most likely been taken as the couple left Dr. Valentine's office. Patti was going to flip. Why was Cogburn so secretive? Was it an addiction? Plastic surgery? Dentures? What embarrassing secret had Dixie stumbled upon?

"I bought the other necklace, and she promised me she'd never tell a soul."

"Was, um, Dixie a woman of her word?"

"I thought so, I prayed so." He grabbed his Stetson in both hands and covered his heart. "You can't say a word, understand?"

Taking a quick step out of reach, I answered with my hand over my own heart. "I'd never tell a soul. I don't have any idea who Dr. Valentine is, and I don't want to know." I should've crossed my fingers because I was already itching to find him on the internet as soon as our conversation ended.

"That's music to my ears." He patted my shoulder a few times, righted his hat, and tightened his tie. "Felicia will be wondering where I've gone." He opened the door.

"Mayor Cogburn, did you say you bought your wife one of Dixie's necklaces?"

He pierced me with a sharp glance. "You said you wouldn't mention it."

"Um, Mayor, did you know the necklace Dixie made for tomorrow night's auction is missing?"

"Say what?" he demanded, lifting his eyebrows so high he resembled a Mr. Potato Head.

"I don't think Dixie ever turned it into the committee and now they're scrambling."

He nodded. "You want me to donate the very necklace Dixie conned me into buying so that I get nothing in return for my money, not even a gift for my wife?"

I hadn't thought about it in quite those terms. "Uh, yes, sir."

"Josie Callahan, you are a pistol." With that declaration, he headed inside as the band stepped onstage for their next set.

Though my fingers itched to immediately search out Dr. Valentine on the Web, a quick glance at my cell confirmed I had no bars.

"What are you doing out here?"

I dropped my phone as Lightfoot stepped up behind me. Had he heard us? Had he seen Mayor Cogburn walk away? I jerked open the door, hoping to lose myself in the noise and crush of bodies, but he followed close. "Not much," I shouted.

"Just thinking about how tired I am, and how I need to head home."

"I'll drive you," he said in my ear.

That sounded like an excuse for him to grill me about my own conversation with Ty. "Thanks, but I've had my license a few years."

"Maybe so, but the guy at the front said you marched in on your own steam."

Before I could slip through a row of boot-scooting line dancers, he grabbed my arm and pulled me back out the door. "You need to be cautious. Some drunken idiot might follow you home." Still holding my arm, he started walking toward the parking lot.

"Go ahead and admit it. You know you arrested the wrong man." My pulse quickened. He would have to admit what I'd known all along.

"We'll see what's what after we question Ty."

"If you admit I'm right, I'll let you drive me home."

He stared at me for a good long time. "I'm not telling you a thing. That would be breaking the law."

"Shouldn't you be heading back to the jail instead of fraternizing with the public?" I understood his ethics, but I didn't have to show it. I spun toward the door. "I forgot to say goodbye to Uncle Eddie."

After twenty minutes of dragging my heels, including a pear cider at the bar, I started for home, only to find Lightfoot and his cruiser waiting for me by the door.

"You took long enough."

"You didn't have to wait."

"Yeah, I did." He reached across and pushed open my door.

I was exhausted, so I slid in and slammed the door. In the dim light of the dashboard and the moonless sky, I asked, "Do you think Ty did it?" I couldn't read his expression in the silence that followed.

"He's got motive."

"But . . . ?"

"Do I think he's capable of great stupidity? Yeah, but I don't think he's dumb enough to do something that would put him away for life."

Without a word, we drove the five minutes to Aunt Linda's. I glanced across at his expressionless face, wishing I knew what he refused to say.

I sighed and pushed open the door. "Thanks."

"Don't worry about it."

At the porch steps, I turned.

He lifted a hand in response and drove away.

Under a sky painted with stars, bright and twinkling like an ocean filled with glowing jellyfish, my skin prickled with the thought that I might not be safe in this town, my home.

My mind was full to overflowing with images of Ty Honeycutt, Lightfoot and Barnes, the stolen money, the image of a furious Ty being thrown into the back of the sheriff's cruiser. The investigation felt incomplete, and as much as I hadn't trusted our law enforcement officers to get it right, I found I'd trusted them more than I wanted to admit.

Until now. Something in my subconscious was telling me this was too easy, too predictable, too . . . wrong. I should've felt relieved the case was drawing to a close, but not this way, not this predictable way. Ty was a charmer and a gambler, which meant he had to be a great actor, but I didn't believe he could manufacture the desperate fury I'd witnessed. When they'd taken him away, he'd reacted like a trapped animal, desperate to save his life. He'd changed my mind and convinced me of his innocence.

On the library table in the hall stood a sunflower-faced cat, sculpted from railroad ties and scrap metal. Aunt Linda had stuck a Post-it on the feline's face, telling me to call Patti. I was relieved. I hadn't heard from Goth Girl except for a short text message of thanks and a promise to call me later.

Aunt Linda waited on the leather sofa in the den, reading

a romance by the light of a faux Tiffany lamp from Target. "You okay?" She opened her arms for a hug and proceeded to squeeze the life out of me.

I gently disengaged from her grasp, needing to keep my mind focused. "They took Ty Honeycutt in for questioning."

"No!" She tossed the book to the end table. Curling her legs underneath her, she settled in for a juicy story. "Well, it doesn't surprise me any, but I wish they'd done it before they arrested Anthony, willy-nilly."

Dropping down beside her, I grabbed one of the tasseled throw pillows and hugged it to my chest. "He's not guilty."

She frowned. "Have you heard him play?"

"No." I shrugged, too tired to follow her train of thought.

"He's not going to make a living at playing the guitar, no matter how cute he is. We didn't extend his contract. This week is it."

I waited for her to explain.

Seeing my lack of understanding, she huffed. "He killed her because he needs the money to pay off his gambling debts. The cowboy mafia's probably searching for him so they can break his kneecaps or make him a pair of concrete boots."

"Ugh," I groaned, pulling the pillow over my face in disbelief.

"Come on." She pulled me up and into the kitchen. "How about some sangria? Senora Mari made it fresh."

Grinning, I spun for the stairs. "I'll go up and say hi first."

"Better not, sweetie." She removed the sweet tangy beverage from the fridge. "Poor thing's plumb tuckered out."

I scooted onto a tall stool and took a sip, information buzzing through my brain. The mayor said Dixie had seen them leaving the office of someone? Oh, yeah. Dr. Valentine. With a bone-tired sigh, I reached to pull out my phone.

"Shoot. I almost forgot." Aunt Linda had started climbing the stairs, but now she descended. "Patti said it was urgent you call as soon as you came home."

"She didn't say why?"

As Aunt Linda reached the landing, she paused to catch her breath. "No, but she was beside herself. I told her she could confide in me, but she refused." My aunt shrugged and raised her hands in a helpless gesture. "You try to help someone, and they just don't get it."

"Thanks. I'll listen to her message right now and give her a call."

Aunt Linda blew me a kiss. "Good night, sweetie."

"Night, night," I said, reverting to my childhood lingo. I finished off my glass of sangria and dug in my pockets for my phone, which I found, after checking all my pockets twice, in my back pocket.

Tired beyond what was good for me, I decided to listen to Patti's message upstairs in the comfort of my bed, but when I passed Senora Mari's room I turned the handle slowly, hoping to find her sleeping soundly.

"Come in, Josefina." She lay in the bed, her hair covered with a tight kerchief, her comforter pulled up to her chin.

"I thought you'd be counting sheep by now." I grinned and plunked down on the corner of her bed. Her bedspread was made of lovely white lace that matched her curtains. I nodded to the figurine of the Virgin Mary on the nightstand. She didn't nod back, but I think she was listening to every word.

"How could I sleep with you clumping up the stairs like a herd of buffalo?"

I inched closer. "Are you okay, *abuelita*?"

Her gaze landed near the window. "As I said, I have been in prison before."

A long pause hung between us until I had to ask, "Why were you in prison?"

"You don't want to know," she said and closed her eyes.

Refusing to smile at her obvious attempt to win my sympathy, I answered in the way she expected. "*Por favor*, tell me."

"*Cabras estúpidas!*" Her eyes popped open. "Stupid goats."

The corners of my mouth were fighting not to smile. "No. What happened?"

"Humph." She sat up, revealing her Hello Kitty button-down pajamas. "They arrested me for stealing the smelly things, when I stole nothing." Her hand rested on her heart.

"Why did they think such a thing?"

"Because they found the stolen goats in my barn."

Okay, I would bite. "How did they get in there?"

"Just a minute." She reached into her mouth, contorted her face, and pulled out her bottom dentures. She crossed herself and dropped them into the cup next to the Virgin Mary. Okay.

"My gums hurt." Her speech was hard to understand, but I got the gist.

My eyelids were dropping like weights. "The goats?"

"I put them in the barn after I bought them. How was I to know the man I bought them from was a thief?"

"And they didn't believe you?"

"Why would they believe me, a Mexican?"

She slid down beneath the covers and turned away. "That's why I was in prison. You need to go to bed. You look tired."

"That's a . . . sad story."

"It's the truth."

"I believe you, but I'm confused. Why did you never mention this?"

Silence.

I reached out and touched her back. "How long were you in jail?"

"Not long. Two hours."

Trying to hide a yawn, I widened my eyes. "Why did you really confess to killing Dixie?"

"I was the bait."

"For what?"

"The killer."

On a good day with lots of rest, I might have understood her convoluted logic. "Why would Dixie's killer want you?"

She snorted softly. "He didn't. I made him think he was

in the clear." A long pause followed, and then finally a whisper. "I brought him out into the open."

"Okay. Let's," I yawned wide, "talk more tomorrow. I can barely keep my eyes open."

A gentle snore and a whistle was her only response.

I made my way to my room, dialing voicemail as I walked.

"Josie, it's me. I've got to meet you," Patti whispered on the recording, her voice full of tears. "Jos, I'm scared. I'm afraid to take this photo to the police. I need you to tell me what you think. Call me now."

Chapter 16

I dialed Patti's number, suddenly awake and alert. Lenny licked my ankle and I flew straight up into the air. "Cut it out." *Come on, Patti. Come on.*

She picked up on the third ring. "Meet me at Milagro," Patti whispered.

"I'm in my pajamas."

"Please. I can't talk here." Her voice reminded me of a heroine in a cheap horror movie. She'd almost convinced me.

"Ha, ha."

"Gotcha!" She laughed until I swore she was crying.

"You're such a bad actress." I smiled in spite of myself.

"Am not."

Removing any trace of good humor from my voice, I demanded, "Where did you go today? I thought you said you'd be back in an hour."

"No, I didn't actually state how long I'd be gone, and for that I apologize."

"You missed the show over at Two Boots tonight. They hauled Ty Honeycutt down to the jail."

"Was Lightfoot there?" she asked, breathless as a schoolgirl.

"What do you think?"

"I would've loved to have seen him in action. Was he better than Tommy Lee Jones?"

Ew. "I should hope so, he's half his age." Tommy Lee was a serious cowboy, but he had a lot of wear on him.

"Listen, Josie, we need to talk tonight."

Patti's get-up-and-go gave no sign of waning. "Is someone out to get me?" I asked in a stage whisper.

She tried to laugh. "I don't think so, but I drank way too much coffee to sleep. Can I come over? We could work on our plan of attack for tomorrow morning."

"Forget it. I've already done you one too many favors today." I yawned and scooted under the covers.

Patti didn't sound the least bit tired. "Lightfoot mentioned something about you calling the law on P.J. Pratt," she said with a snort.

"That was an accident," I huffed. "I told the operator not to send anyone out, but she ignored me. Now everyone's going to be calling me the village idiot."

"I'm sure they thought it was related to the shoplifting incident in the store earlier."

My bed was warm and cozy, my pillow soft. "Dixie's jewelry," I said on a yawn. "He wanted to buy her jewelry." I brought the covers up to my chin. "But I told him he could forget it until I spoke with you."

"Atta girl."

"Let's create our plan tomorrow on the way to Melanie's gallery," I whispered into my pillow.

"Nightie night, Jos."

"Hmm," I said as I hung up the phone, my mind filling with images of Patti chasing Lightfoot around his desk.

* * *

Saturday, the final day of the festival, had arrived. My schedule was busting at the seams, but I was ready for the challenge. Tonight, after the auction, it would all be over until the following year. Hallelujah!

Today I would help, and do my best not to hinder, Hillary as she judged the talent show. Then it was back to Milagro to help Uncle Eddie transport our frozen margarita machines, along with trays of beef flautas, cheese quesadillas, and other finger foods, to the charity dinner and silent auction. We would take care of the drinks and appetizers, while Bubba handled the brisket and fixings.

Before the two major events of the day started, I had some minor espionage that needed my attention. I jumped out of bed with delightful anticipation. First I would bring Patti up to speed on last night's adventure at Two Boots, and then she would enlighten me on her encounter with Lightfoot. We would end our gabfest by scouring Melanie's gallery, Where the Sun Sets, for any sign of Dixie's jewelry.

My heart was racing before I hit the door. We had no plan other than to visit Melanie in her lair, but with any luck she might share some tidbit that would take us to the next step in our investigation. I had a boot print and a missing auction necklace. Patti had a shoplifter and a thing for Deputy Lightfoot. It wasn't much to go on, but so far the sheriff's department had uncovered squat. We couldn't do worse than that.

I drove to the Feed and Supply, parked the Prius, and jumped into Patti's jeep.

"You look like you've been—what's that cowboy saying?" my too honest friend asked as I put on my seatbelt.

"Rode hard and put up wet?" I gave her a dirty look.

"Yep, that's it."

I lowered my sunglasses. "With friends like you . . ."

A rich, tantalizing aroma filled the cabin. "You didn't?" I asked, my body reviving at the possibility of dark roast.

"I did." She handed me a large paper cup of steaming hot coffee. "Now who's your best friend?"

"I don't recall saying you weren't." After a big sniff, I took my first deliciously bitter sip. I dug in my purse and produced two foil packages. "And now my offering to . . . what should we call ourselves?"

"Snoop goddesses."

I laughed. "That'll do until I have more coffee." I held my breakfast offerings up high. "And now my offering to the snoop goddesses, biscuits and bacon."

Squealing to a stop at the corner stop sign, she slapped the steering wheel. "Snoop goddesses don't eat pork."

"That's why I brought us turkey bacon instead." I unwrapped the top of her biscuit and handed it over.

She stared at the flaky treat with distrust and then took a bite. "Hmm, yes an offering truly worthy."

"Now tell me how it went with Lightfoot." I had misgivings about how suitable the two hardheads might be for each other, but I was going to give my support as long as I could and remain true to our friendship. After all, hadn't I already expressed my doubts to no avail?

With a slow smile, she said, "He was at his desk when I got there, like I'd planned." She frowned. "But he apparently had four reports to write and tried to pawn me off on some red-headed dude."

"That's too bad."

"Did I take no for an answer?" She gave me a wink and stopped at the railroad crossing. "No. Before he could make a break for it, I ran the whole story by him. Once he realized the thief was after Dixie's jewelry he was very keen, wanting to know how I came by her pieces, and who else in town sold them."

The eight thirty-five train blew its whistle in greeting as it passed.

"Great."

"Can you believe the sheriff hadn't told him about it?"

"Wallace said he had his hands full with the festival." In the sheriff's absence, Lightfoot had taken charge at the tamale-eating contest, calling the ambulance and interviewing the bystanders until the sheriff came along.

Lightfoot was hard to ignore.

"Um, Patti. I mean, Goth Girl, there's something you should know."

"Tell all. Did they arrest Ty Honeycutt for the murder? Or is that wishful thinking on my part?"

"When they left Two Boots, Lightfoot said they were taking him in for questioning."

"Lightfoot," she said dreamily, "great name."

"Um, that's not what I wanted to tell you."

She heard the seriousness in my tone. "He's married?" Gripping the steering wheel in a death grip, she pushed the gas pedal to the floor. We flew down the highway, passing family sedans and SUVs with license plates from New Mexico, Arizona, Alabama, and, of course, Texas.

"No, but he does have a girlfriend."

"And you didn't tell me this earlier because . . . ?"

"I forgot. I'm sorry. Senora Mari was grilling him about whether or not he had an Indian girlfriend."

A loud whoop came from Patti's side of the jeep. "Of course he'd say that to Senora Mari, if for no other reason than to get her off his back and out of his business."

I smiled at her glee. "I guess you could be right."

"Bet you twenty there's no girlfriend."

"Not a safe bet for me. You'd win." I wasn't too sure Patti was correct. Lightfoot didn't appear to be the type to lie to anyone, not even an old woman.

She slowed for the exit ramp before swinging right onto Gallery Road. "Tell me about your conversation with Mayor Cogburn."

With little fanfare, I filled her in on my conversation with the mayor, making sure to include the intensity behind his every word.

Patti slowed the jeep, pulled it over to the shoulder, and threw it into park. "He didn't say what Dixie had on them?"

I glanced behind us, but the road was empty. "No, but he was acting as if I already knew. I'll tell you the truth, I was nervous. For a minute, I thought he was going to give me all the intimate details. If he hadn't suddenly gone inside, I would have run off."

"You're exaggerating. You would've done no such thing." Her gaze followed the road to where the two-story gallery stood in the soft morning light. "So what kind of doctor is this Valentine character?"

I made a face. "I don't know. I was going to look him up last night after we talked, but I fell asleep."

She shook her head in mock disgust. "Do a search for him while I think for a minute."

I turned to the left, the right, and then front again. "Of course there's no blasted service," I muttered. I glanced up in time to spy an armadillo scurrying across the road. He made short work of crawling under a barbed wire fence, and then disappeared into a field of tall grass and pink evening primroses.

"I have a plan." Patti said. Then she paused to gather her thoughts. "We go in together. I'm bringing my photos and you're . . ."

"There to ask Melanie about displaying another one of her paintings at Milagro."

She nodded her head and grinned. "Now it's your turn. Whatcha got?"

"Um, one of us keeps her busy while the other one looks for the jewelry."

"Easier said than done." Her mouth turned down as she pondered our next step. "I don't expect we'll find it."

"And she won't tell us anything."

"Not unless we get her rattled."

I sighed. "It's pretty much a crapshoot."

She slapped me on the back and started the jeep. "Yep, but I'm great at improvising." Patti put the jeep in drive and let off the brake. As she started to accelerate, a red Porsche rocketed past us, nearly putting a quick end to our plans.

"Hey! What the—"

My heart in my throat, I reached out to calm my friend. "That was Melanie."

"She could have killed us!"

"I bet she's thinking the same thing about us."

Blowing out a heavy breath, Patti gripped the steering wheel. "Right." She took a deep breath and let her foot off the gas again. "Let's go get her."

We caught Melanie in the parking lot as she removed a painting from the Porsche's trunk. Her linen suit draped her svelte frame to perfection, while her red silk blouse brought out the red highlights in her deep brown hair. It was her jewelry that always seemed overdone. She wore three or four gold necklaces in varying lengths, several gold bangles, and long, gold hoop earrings. In addition to the wedding rings on her left hand, she sported a gold ring on each of the four fingers of her right. It made me wonder if she was diversifying her investments for a rainy day.

"Have you been drinking?" she asked me. I had tossed and turned well into the night, forming a strategy, but her comment made me feel uglier than a naked mole rat. The fact she'd dared to ask me such a thing made me notice she looked a bit hungover herself.

"Heavens, no."

She stared at me. "What are y'all doing here?"

Patti was ready. "You said you wanted to sell a few of my photographs, but if today doesn't—"

She gave Patti a beautiful smile. "Today is fine." Her smile noticeably dimmed when she turned to me. "Don't you have a talent show to judge?"

I waved my hand. "I don't have to be there for another hour."

Watching me closely, Melanie remained silent.

"Aunt Linda and I were talking, and we'd like to hang more of your beautiful paintings in the restaurant."

Melanie pulled down her designer sunglasses, the better to evaluate what I was up to. "I thought you said only last week that they weren't selling."

We hadn't planned this out too well.

"She sold one yesterday," Patti proclaimed, crossing her arms in front of her chest.

I tried hard not to react, for there's one thing Patti never did, and that was tell a lie. Or so I thought until I noticed she'd crossed two of the fingers on her left hand.

"Which one?" Melanie asked, perking up considerably.

I wasn't a fan of her work and couldn't name a single one of her paintings, so I kept mum.

Patti looked at me, and I looked at her. "You know," she said, "I can't rightly remember what your Aunt Linda said, but she did think it might help Melanie's sales to trade some of them out."

Melanie's perfectly arched brows flew skyward in disbelief, but I could see she found some merit in the idea. She needed the money, as we all did, and she couldn't take the chance of ignoring us and possibly losing our business. "Give me a sec," she muttered as she unlocked the door and began to disarm the alarm.

"Come on in," she called over her shoulder, heading off for the back room.

Elaine had inherited the oldest home in Broken Boot from her Aunt Louise and sold the lovely Texas Tudor home to Melanie after the birth of her second child for the price of one of her paintings.

As soon as we stepped inside, Patti set her photos on an antique sideboard by the door and began scoping out the place. She pointed to the gallery room on the right and headed that way. Melanie's gallery may have once belonged to her great aunt Louise, but she had lovingly blended the features of the house with her own style. She'd warmed the rooms by adding wide oak flooring. Mission-style arches drew the eye from one room to the next, and exposed wood ceiling beams brought the Southwest indoors.

"Let me check my messages," Melanie called from the back.

Patti stuck her head back into the main room. "Lightfoot needs to run a magnet over this place," she whispered. "There are built-in cabinets in this room, and their doors are all locked."

"Shh."

I picked up the closest painting, *Begonias at Twilight*, and lowered my head. "I can't imagine how you feel now that Dixie's dead," I said in a loud voice, expecting Melanie to answer from the back. Though she was no Georgia O'Keefe, she had the smarts to display talented sculptors, photographers, and jewelry makers alongside her own work. As a result, the gallery did well when the tourists hit town with a notion to spend their hard-earned money.

"What are you going on about?" she asked, waltzing in and tossing her sunglasses atop the mountain of debris on her desk.

I cringed as if embarrassed. "Didn't I hear something about you and Dixie fighting over at Bubba's only a day or two before she died?"

She gestured as if waving away the gossip. "Oh, that. You know how Dixie was. She always thought people were out to steal her ideas. Where's Patti?"

"Patti," I called, "come look." I hurried over to a painting on display on the opposite side of the room. "I'd like to take this one with the guitars."

With long graceful strides, Melanie joined me. "You must mean *Slave to Guava*," she managed through clenched teeth.

Guava slices? Hells bells, I thought they were guitars.

From behind us, Patti laughed. "Don't mind Josie. She slept through humanities."

"Obviously." Melanie reached out a hand and removed the painting from its easel. She crossed to her desk, found her glasses, and checked the price marked on the bottom edge of the frame. "I need the other one back this afternoon."

"I'll bring it over."

Again, Melanie reserved her elegant manners for my friend. "Patti, I can't wait to see the photographs you brought me."

"Do you mind if I look around?" I asked.

"Make yourself at home."

That was the plan. I decided not to start in the same room as Patti so I veered off to the left. If I were Melanie, I would hide my most valuable items in the safe. I wasn't a safecracker, so that was out. On the other hand, if I didn't want the police to find Dixie's jewelry in the safe, I might find a hidey-hole in this big house.

The gallery to the left was a bust. I continued down the hall and found a back door that led out onto a small porch. In a flash, I had an idea.

"How much longer are you going to be?" I asked, walking through the room where Patti and Melanie stood discussing one of my friend's photos.

"I apologize," Patti said. "Josie's really keyed up over the silent auction. I guess your mother told you the auction necklace is missing."

Melanie's eyes grew wide. "How did you know that?"

Patti turned to me and waited.

"Uh, well, you see . . ." I said.

"Lightfoot mentioned it in passing," Patti interrupted, proving to be a premiere liar when the occasion called for it. And to think I never knew that about her until today.

"And he's on his way over here to look for the necklace," I added.

"He's what?" Melanie hurried to the window.

With a dramatic sigh, Patti laid it on thick. "It's true. When I saw him yesterday he said the only logical place to look would be here in your gallery where she sold her work."

Melanie stamped the toe of her shoe. "That makes no sense. Why would I send P.J. to your store to buy some of Dixie's jewelry if I already had it?"

"Oh, so you do have it?" I asked, playing dumb.

"For pity's sake, I don't have the auction necklace, but Dixie did have things on consignment here." She swallowed. "There's bound to be a stray piece or two in one of the cabinets."

I glanced at Patti and she nodded. "Oh, hey," I said, glancing at my watch. "We've got to be going or I'll be late to the talent show."

Melanie's countenance cleared. "I completely understand." She handed me the painting of guavas. "Take this for now and bring me one of the others when it's convenient."

We said our good-byes and drove down the road, but only until the gallery was out of sight. "What do you think she'll do?" I asked.

Patti made a left and then another left until we could see the back of the gallery from a block away. She looked around, found a large sycamore that overhung the road, and parked underneath it. "Only one way to find out."

"One cup of coffee isn't enough for espionage."

"Stow it," Patti said as she jumped from the jeep and headed down the road on foot.

The back side of the gallery was blocked by a low fence and neatly trimmed shrubs. From our viewpoint, we couldn't see any of the windows along the back of the building, which meant she couldn't see us either. We tried the gate and found it locked. "I'm a numbskull. I should have checked the gate."

"Ssh," Patti warned. She bit her lip and stared at the lock for at least thirty seconds.

"We should go."

"Stand back," she said, waving me behind her.

Before I could stop her, she raised her combat boot and kicked not the lock, but the wooden frame that held it.

"Hey," I cried. "We're not supposed to damage the place."

Before she could kick the frame again, the rusty lock sprang open and fell to the ground.

"Strange," I said, giving it a little kick with my boot.

"Humph. She needs to beef up security around here."

"Do you think she heard us?" I whispered.

"Ssh." Patti peeked around the fence. "There's no sign of her."

I expected my friend to scurry from bush to tree, like they do in the cartoons and action movies. That's not what happened. Instead, she walked straight to the back door and peered through the window. "Come on," she hissed.

I hurried after her. "Wipe your feet," I said, keeping my voice low. It would be a dead giveaway if we tracked dirt across Melanie's pristine wooden floors.

Once that was accomplished to my satisfaction, Patti turned the knob. "Snoop goddesses reign," she whispered and stuck her head inside.

My heart was thumping so hard, it felt like a stampede of buffalo in my veins.

Patti waved me forward.

I swallowed my fear and followed her lead. We were inside the breakfast nook of the original house. In the corners of the room were stacks of stretched canvases on frames of varying sizes. Ahead of us was a kitchen, replete with old appliances, a modern microwave, and a one-cup coffeemaker.

Walking quietly, Patti made her way to a closed door on the right. With a look at me, she opened it. Inside we found a pantry filled with paint, paint thinner, cleaning supplies, and veggie chips.

I pointed to the kitchen cabinets and shrugged.

Patti shook her head.

In the background, Melanie was playing classical music, which would help cover any sounds we might make. A growing sense of extreme panic was settling in my chest. Why had we come back while she was still here? Oh, yeah. I had to go help with the confounded talent show and, more importantly, the committee needed the necklace by tonight.

Catching my attention, Patti raised a hand for me to wait. She tiptoed to the kitchen door and slowly peered around the corner. With two fingers, like an agent in an action movie full of spies, she motioned for us to leave the kitchen and go right.

I followed even though the buffalo were still stampeding through my bloodstream. Slowly we crept our way down a narrow hall. We found the bathroom, but no jewels. We found an empty bedroom with a treadmill, but no hidden safe. And finally, we stumbled into another bedroom being used to store paintings. A narrow path separated the large number of paintings leaning against the walls, fifteen and twenty paintings deep.

I glanced at my watch. "We've got to go."

With a slight hesitation, Patti nodded.

We headed for the door, and then I knocked over a painting, which knocked over a second, a third, and five or six more.

"Ladies, can I help you find something?" A furious Melanie stood in the doorway, her arms full of plastic trays.

Like rats caught in a trap, we scrambled to free ourselves. "Inventory," I offered helplessly.

"Inventory?" Melanie repeated, raising an eyebrow.

"That's right," Patti proclaimed in a loud voice. "I wanted to check out your inventory."

Melanie's gaze narrowed. "Why would you want to do that?"

"Because . . ." Nodding several times, Patti tried to answer.

"Because," I interrupted, "she wanted to decide whether or not to carry your paintings in her store without hurting your feelings."

Melanie studied us down the length of her nose. "What did you decide?"

Patti glanced at me. "I haven't. I only just now found your inventory."

I stepped closer to Melanie, hoping to see what she carried. "I felt guilty earlier for not telling you the whole truth."

With a quick glance at the trays she was holding, she hugged them to her chest. "The truth about what?"

"Uh," My mind was flipping through a file of possibilities at lightning speed, "the truth about why Deputy Lightfoot's coming to see you."

"Go on."

I prayed Patti would follow my lead. "To question you about Dixie's murder."

"He is?" she squeaked, hugging the trays even tighter to her chest. "Why?"

"The truth is I don't think you had anything to do with Dixie's death, but . . ." I glanced at Patti, hoping she'd save my bacon.

"But you sent P.J. over to the store yesterday to buy up all of Dixie's jewelry, didn't you?"

"That's not a crime," Melanie said.

"It's a crime if he tries to force the issue and scare my friend to death."

The phone rang in the other room. "Come with me," Melanie ordered.

We didn't hesitate.

I didn't think she could have us arrested for entering the gallery from the rear while it was open to the public. On the other hand, she didn't know that Patti had wrecked her fence.

As she led us through the main gallery room and into her office area, she continued, "Josie told P.J. that you can't sell

Dixie's work. It all belongs to Ty." She hurried to the phone, but it stopped ringing before she picked it up.

"But," Patti said, "the jewelry I have of hers isn't on consignment. I bought several small pieces outright. They're mine, and neither you nor your overbearing husband can force me to sell."

With a sigh, she plopped into her office chair. "P.J. has the finesse of an elephant."

I gestured to the jewelry she held. "Reorganizing?"

Melanie's face turned purple as her gaze darted around the room. She hurried behind her desk and opened drawer after drawer, but they must have been full for she held on to the trays. "Truth was Dixie was getting too big for her britches."

A poor choice of words, considering the woman who was now pushing up daisies had been on the hefty side. "Is that what you two argued about at Bubba's?"

With a toss of her sleek, dark hair, Melanie studied me for a minute, like a queen deciding whether or not to confide in a lowly, less put-together handmaiden. "All I wanted was for her to sell her turquoise jewelry somewhere else for a while. She'd still draw customers with her other pieces, and we would both make a sale." Her arms relaxed and the trays lowered, revealing silver and turquoise rings, agate necklaces, amethyst earrings, all in Dixie's distinctive style.

"Makes sense," I said softly, not wanting to jolt her from her reverie.

"Of course it does. When I invited her to display her work, I didn't anticipate that once folks spent money on her jewelry, they'd have nothing left over for my paintings."

I didn't state the obvious. If customers loved her paintings, her plan would have worked either way. "So you fought over the turquoise?"

Melanie hugged the cases to her chest once again. "We were waiting in line for ribs at Bubba's to-go window. I told her I wanted her not to sell the turquoise stuff for a few months until I sold a few paintings to make my mortgage."

"What'd she say?" I didn't dare take my notebook out of my bag, but I was taking mental notes in indelible ink.

"She said she didn't have to do anything unless she wanted, and it'd serve me right if she moved it all to another location!" Melanie's eyes narrowed. "Of course, she was a natural-born liar and a cheat, so who knows if she meant a word of it."

She turned away, opened a nearby file cabinet, and crammed the cases in the bottom drawer, and then locked it with a small key she wore at her wrist. Turning back, she checked her watch and walked to the door. "Listen, she may have threatened to take all her merchandise to the Feed and Supply, but Josie Callahan, I didn't touch a hair on her head." She pushed the door open and hesitated. "I wanted to spit in her face, but I controlled myself." Time was up. Melanie was kicking us out.

"What are you doing with her jewelry?" Patti asked, pointing to the file cabinet.

This time Melanie drew in a deep breath and smiled. "Wouldn't that be just like some clever thief to steal all her jewelry and sell it on the black market once she's famous? I'm going to hide it until this all blows over."

"What about Ty? He should have a say," I said.

"He'll have a say once her will goes to probate and the attorneys sort out her affairs. How do I know who her next of kin was? Or if she wanted them to have the proceeds from her jewelry sales?"

Liar, liar, pants on fire. Most likely, Melanie had been planning on selling it for more than a few pretty pennies.

"Holy crap," Melanie muttered, glancing out the window.

Deputy Lightfoot had arrived.

Chapter 17

Lightfoot was out of his cruiser and walking up the sidewalk like a man on a mission. I was torn, for I wanted nothing more than to stick around to hear his conversation with Melanie, but I had only fifteen minutes to get to the stage where the talent show was being held.

"Be right back," Melanie said, slamming the door at our backs.

It didn't take a mind reader to figure out she was hiding those trays of jewelry. A crystal bell rang as the front door opened.

"Good afternoon," Patti said with a big smile.

When Lightfoot saw Patti and me standing there, his mouth fell open. He looked at her, and then he looked at me. It was the first time I remembered seeing the confident deputy even slightly rattled. "What are you two doing here?"

"Well, hey," I said, interjecting a note of surprise. "What are you doing here?"

"I'm doing what Big Bend County pays me to do, which is more than I can say for you." Without taking his eyes off of me, he pulled a small spiral notebook and pen from his breast pocket. "Where's Melanie Burnett?" He walked to the doorway of the room on the left. Not seeing Melanie, he crossed the gallery to check in the room to the right.

"We were just discussing Dixie Honeycutt's jewelry."

"That right?" he asked, thumping his spiral against his palm.

"Yes, that's right." Melanie said. She was posed in the archway that led to the gallery from her office. "You must be new." She sauntered over to the deputy and extended her hand. "I don't think we've met. I'm Melanie Pratt." She extended her hand, causing her gold bangles to clink.

"Deputy Quinton Lightfoot," he said, shaking her hand briefly. "We met at Elaine's Pies the day after Ms. Honeycutt's murder."

Melanie didn't even stutter. "I was just explaining to Josie how I need to gather all of Dixie's jewelry so I can pass it along to her family, but I don't know who that would be." She smiled and tilted her head to one side.

"I believe that would be Ty Honeycutt, ma'am."

She laughed. "Of course." With a toss of her beautiful mane, she lowered her chin and smiled up at him through her lashes. "I guess I didn't get enough sleep last night." She fiddled with the key on her wrist and waited for him to make the next move.

Churning in my gut was a deep, perhaps unwarranted, suspicion that if Melanie was left to her own devices some of Dixie's jewelry might come up missing or appear on eBay with someone else's name listed as the seller. I was sorely tempted to tell on her, but I bit my tongue. I would bide my time. Everyone needed the opportunity to do the right thing, even Melanie.

With ill-concealed impatience, Lightfoot turned to me. "Don't you have somewhere else to be?"

"Yes, I do." I pointed at Patti. "But I'm with her."

He cleared his throat. "Do you have an inventory list of

the merchandise Ms. Honeycutt was selling in your establishment, ma'am?"

Melanie rolled her eyes as she twisted a wedding ring the size of Gibraltar round and round her finger. "There must be one somewhere. Last time I saw one it was on the computer, but that was so long ago."

"I suggest you turn on the computer and print out the list for me, or I serve you a warrant for your computer and all your files."

Like a tourist after a week on a dude ranch, Melanie's face flamed tomato red. The woman seriously needed to work on her game face.

Maybe a nudge from me would help her do the right thing. "What if Melanie tried to find Dixie's jewelry right now, while you're here?"

He stared at me as if trying to figure out what I was up to, and then he shrugged as if he had nothing better to do. I wanted to know he wasn't asking her about her fight with Dixie. Or had he already covered that subject over pie?

Fixing me with a glare scary enough to frighten small children on Halloween, Melanie dropped her sickeningly sweet act and thrust out her chin. "I'll wait for the warrant."

"Suit yourself." Slowly he placed the pad and pencil in his pocket, all the while shaking his head. He gave her a long stare, and when she remained silent, he pulled out his phone. "Pleasant, it's me. Yeah. Find that warrant on my desk that I worked up for Where the Sun Sets and take it over to Judge Hawkins." He listened for a moment. "Right, and then take it to Judge Hawkins. If he's not available, try Mooney." He shot a glance at Melanie, who was listening intently. "No, I'll wait for you to bring it here."

I had to give Lightfoot credit. After Ty's confession from last night and the shoplifting incident at Patti's place, the deputy had the good sense to realize that with no one else around to look after Dixie's affairs, the sheriff's department was going to have to step in and do the neighborly thing.

"I'll take it from here, Miss Callahan. You and Miss Perez can go."

I gave Melanie a big smile. "I'll bring that other painting by later on. Is tomorrow soon enough?"

"There's no hurry. It's not as if I don't trust you to do the right thing." The corners of Melanie's mouth lifted in a sketch of a smile, but the rest of her face told us in no uncertain terms where she wanted us to go.

With all the subtlety of a brick, Lightfoot walked to the door and held it open.

The door might not have hit me on the way out, but Melanie's piercing laugh made me wish it had.

"Gotta love all that confidence," Patti said as she slid behind the steering wheel.

She had a point.

Dodging pedestrians and out of state license plates, I parked in Milagro's lot then hurried to the main stage at the end of the block. Though I hadn't seen it up to that point, I'd heard it was a real humdinger, which meant a person would have to be blinder than a mole rat to miss it. The committee had rented a three-foot-high platform on wheels from an amusement company and secured the brakes on the thing so it wouldn't roll. They'd managed to add a black velvet backdrop on the back and metallic streamers in red, white, and blue on the front. All in all, the performance space was about fifteen by eight, which was plenty of room unless your talent was tumbling or twirling fire batons.

On the street in front of the platform, the committee had set up metal folding chairs and a judge's table dressed with red, white, and blue bunting from last year's Fourth of July parade.

"Over here," Hillary cried when I was still twenty yards away. She waved me over to the table and handed me a clipboard. "I already organized the entries last Saturday and emailed the contestants their place on the program."

"Uh, thanks?" I was glad someone was taking this event seriously. I had so much falling off my tortilla as of late that organizing this event hadn't made the menu.

She sighed. "Well, of course. We don't want three singers followed by three high school rock bands. People would throw a hissy fit."

I should have called Elaine personally and begged her to replace me with Ryan, no matter what the cost to my pride. Why couldn't I have been chosen to judge the pies instead? What did it matter that the Burnetts owned a prize-winning pie shop conveniently located on Main Street in the center of town?

"The order of contestants is here." Hillary pointed to the first page on the clipboard with a silver acrylic nail. "And the ballots for each contestant follow, with the performer's name at the top." Not trusting my hearing or ability to reason, she reached over and flipped through the pages.

I scanned the list of contestants: five children under the age of thirteen, eight teen acts, and seven adults unless you considered that one of the adult acts was really a dancing poodle named Hercules.

"All you have to do is fill out the ballot and write the total score at the bottom. I'll tally them up as we go."

I could have made a wisecrack about her math skills, but I refrained. If she wanted to drive the ship, I'd give her the wheel.

After the first three acts had finished, to the exuberant applause of their families and friends, I knew I was going to have to plumb the depths of my coping skills to get through the morning without grinding my teeth down to nubs. Hillary insisted on giving me her opinion of how I should score each one, at least until I moved my chair over as far as it would go and turned it so that my legs were between us.

Between an oboe solo of "The Eyes of Texas" and a cowboy that yodeled the national anthem, I was hit by a bolt of inspiration. The editor of the *Broken Boot Bugle* had been bugging me to write an article about Hillary and her new job at the college. Why not kill two birds with the proverbial stone? I could use the setup time between acts to interview the beauty queen about her job and earn brownie points with the paper.

While the volunteer stagehands cleared the stage for the poodle, I scooted over next to Hillary. "I hope you don't mind me asking, but I'd love to interview you for that piece in the *Bugle* while we're sitting here."

Hillary cast an officious glance at the program and another at the slow progress of the stage crew.

"Frank Wilson said he mentioned it to you?" I pulled out my phone and snapped a quick photo before she could complain, or brush her hair. "It was his idea."

"Hey, you have to ask my permission before you take my picture, got it?"

Wrinkling my forehead in confusion, I played dumb. "But you gave your permission for the article, right?" I resisted the urge to scratch my head. I didn't want her to catch on to my passive-aggressive dramatics. "Did you change your mind?"

She narrowed her eyes for a moment before plastering on her perfect smile. "Now is as good a time as any," she said magnanimously, straightening her golden locks with her fingers.

Scrambling for my phone, I opened up my notepad app and fired the first volley. "Tell me about your position at West Texas."

She dutifully filled me in on the minutiae of her classes and her role as mentor. "Our newspaper staff is brilliant. They challenge me as much as I challenge them."

Nodding as if she hadn't spouted yet another brand of beauty queen speak, I asked the obvious question, "What do they think of your celebrity status?"

Was she blushing? "They don't ask." She studied her hands. "And I don't tell." She shrugged one shoulder. "We pretend I'm just like them."

It was her use of the word *pretend* that egged me on. "How are you coping with us peons now that your pageant days are long gone?"

Like a lemonade Popsicle on a summer day, her smile evaporated, leaving a tight line of pink lipstick where her mouth should have been. "I'm calling Frank."

I leaned back and crossed my legs. "Go ahead. I've got time."

She started searching through the contacts on her cell phone, but before she could dial, the emcee introduced the dancing poodle and his owner. In a fit of pique, she stomped one of her expensive boots.

And that stomp started me thinking. One of our busboys had admitted to me, rather sheepishly, to spilling the grease in the alley on the night of Dixie's death, but he'd laughed when I'd asked if he wore a size nine and a half, proudly showing off his size elevens.

"Where'd you get your boots?" I asked, playing nice.

"Why? You running out of things to make fun of?"

As the poodle and his dance partner made their way to the center of the stage, I whispered, "I've been meaning to buy me a pair like those, but they're awfully expensive."

She rolled her eyes and huffed. "I'll tell you if you give me Frank's number."

We lifted our pens to our ballots only to have the poodle's accompaniment fail to play. During the emcee's impromptu stand-up routine, I continued trying to make nice with Hillary.

I thumbed to the contact and turned the screen toward her. "Here you go." I pulled it out of reach at the last minute. "Let me try on your boots and I'll give it to you."

"Are you crazy?"

"Please?" I waggled the phone back and forth. The boot

print could have been made by a man or a woman. Why not Hillary?

"Fine, but only one." She tossed her left turquoise and silver boot at me. Hillary was tall, which meant she had man hands and big feet, the better to balance her big head.

I tried it on. "Ooh, nice." I stood up and said a silent hallelujah. It was too big for me, which meant it could have left the print the night of the murder.

"Give it back, you're grossing me out. Take your foot out of my boot."

"You're an eleven, right?"

"No." She sniffed. "Sometimes I wear a nine and a half."

I slid it off, but before I handed it back I found the size. Ten and a half. Inside I was doing somersaults. Once I explained to Sheriff Wallace about the boot print I'd found at the scene of Dixie's murder, he would have grounds to bring Hillary in for questioning. True to my word, I tossed it back and gave her the editor's office number.

She left a curt message for Frank to call and turned to me with a tight smile. "Let's wrap up the questions about the university. What the *Bugle*'s readers would love to know is that I've got The Kitchen booked for a four o'clock session on Monday."

I hated to bite, but I was dying of curiosity. "What's that? A cooking class or a hair salon?"

Her response was delayed while an eight-year-old sang "Your Cheatin' Heart." Once more we listened with earmuffs of kindness and marked our ballots accordingly.

Hillary picked up the conversation right where we left off. "I'm recording a CD."

Of course she was. "Country?"

"I've sung so many country songs," she said with a groan, "I should own stock in the Grand Ole Opry." She dropped her gaze pointedly to where my hands lay idle on my phone. I typed a few random sentences, making sure to include her words: *I should own stock in the Grand Ole Opry.*

I pitched Hillary a nice, fat softball. "What kind of music then?"

"Rhythm and blues."

"Like Beyoncé?"

"Exactly."

If I gave the slightest hint of my story angle, she'd edit what she was saying. And I didn't want her to change a thing. "Are you doing Beyoncé covers?"

"One or two, but I'm also covering Lena Horne, Roberta Flack, and Gladys Knight and the Pips."

The Pips. "Huh. Who's going to sing the Pips part?"

She frowned.

"So how do you like living back in Broken Boot?"

She shrugged, her mouth twisted in disdain. "It's nice and all. The scenery's gorgeous." Beyond the stage lay the mountains and desert and the big Texas sky.

"So you like to hike, rock climb, and those kinds of things?"

Wrinkling her nose, she corrected me. "I'm more of an art connoisseur, but Ryan and I do enjoy driving to Austin regularly for live music."

Her shot bounced off my skin like a drop of water on a hot iron skillet. Ryan and I were simply friends. "Isn't he on the road a lot scouting next year's team?"

"He's hired a scout this year so he can spend more time at home." She smiled sweetly.

"Right. What would you say is the thing you like most about Broken Boot?"

She screwed up her mouth. "The people, the food . . ." Her face brightened. "And the football."

Maybe they were the perfect couple, or maybe she was full of it.

She leaned forward in her chair. "What's going on at the crime scene restaurant?" She made quotation marks in the air as she said this.

"What do you mean?"

"Oh, I don't know. Someone was murdered in your parking lot."

I played it cool. "You almost sound as if you know something worth telling." I met her eyes, pretending to be skeptical.

"Ha," she said triumphantly. "I know I saw Ty Honeycutt's black truck squeal out of the parking lot that night as we were leaving."

"You need to get your eyes checked. Ty was driving an El Camino that night." I shook my head in disgust. "What you probably saw was Bubba's Tacoma."

That shut her up for a good ten seconds. I didn't know what she'd seen, but I was secretly thankful for another bread crumb to follow. She reloaded. "What are you going to do when Elaine sues your family for nearly choking her to death?"

I shot to my feet. "That was an accident."

With a glance at her watch, she continued as if she hadn't heard. "And Sheriff Wallace told me they're going to follow every lead." If looks could kill, I would've been six feet under. "Like the fact that Senora Mari's done hard time."

"I didn't know you and the sheriff were such good friends." Why would Wallace give her the inside track unless he was enchanted by her so-called beauty?

"I know who's responsible for Dixie Honeycutt's death, and it wasn't a man."

The emcee announced a ten-minute intermission.

"Oh, give it a rest," I muttered.

"Were you or were you not trying to get Ty to pick up Dixie that night?"

"She was too drunk to drive," I continued.

"Is that why you offered her another margarita when you knew she was clearly over the limit?"

Without warning, Ryan joined us. "Have you finished— uh, hi?"

My cheeks grew hot. He'd nearly walked in on me giving his girlfriend a bloody nose. I'd never punched anyone, but the urge to try was overwhelming.

"That drink was mostly water and lime juice," I said. "I don't remember you and her speaking to each other that night."

"Oh, we did. I followed her outside, and we had quite the chat before she passed out."

"What about?"

Hillary raised her hands and gazed at Ryan with a perplexed look. "Why, about whether she was okay or not." She stood up and took Ryan's arm. "I didn't want her dying of alcohol poisoning."

"Did you see her outside?" I asked Ryan, my eyes dropping to his orange socks and blue Nikes. He might not be wearing boots now, but he'd worn them the night of the *tamalada*.

He looked away, clenching his jaw. "No. I went out front and started up the truck."

"Guess you weren't concerned enough to say *no*, were you?" Hillary asked, clobbering me with another accusation. "Or did that call for too much backbone?"

Chapter 18

"That's enough," Ryan said through clenched teeth.

"Nothing hurts worse than the truth." Hillary nodded in mock sorrow.

"You have no right to talk to Josie that way."

I placed a hand on his arm. "Don't worry. She'll get what's coming to her." I cast my eyes toward heaven. "Now that you're here, I'm going to leave the judging to the dynamic duo. I have a million things to do to get ready for tonight."

After my weak parting shot, I gathered my things and scurried away like a lizard that'd lost his tail. And as for that article for the *Bugle*, I would write that article on the beauty queen from h-e-double toothpicks when that same place froze over.

I took a quick shower, drank a banana and kale smoothie, and felt my resilient nature rise to the top. Hillary wasn't going to get my goat. I was going to solve this crime.

Discouraged, but not defeated, I arrived at Milagro and found Lily, Anthony's sister, seated in the dining room.

"That girl," Aunt Linda gestured with her chin, "says she's Anthony's sister."

"She's telling the truth."

My aunt's eyes grew round. "She also said you offered her a job."

I grabbed Aunt Linda by the arm and pulled her into her office. "I apologize for not discussing the matter with you first, but she's the only person left to take care of her three younger siblings."

"We barely have the business for our current staff."

"If this is the only way we can help Anthony, then we have to give her a job." I held up my hand to stop her protest. "She'll have to work as hard as everyone else."

"You're darn right she will."

"But if we had enough business to hire Anthony, we have enough to hire Lily."

Aunt Linda walked to the door and peered out to where the teen waited. "She's kind of rough around the edges."

"Have her fill out an application. Maybe she has experience."

With a snort, my aunt crossed to her desk and handed me Lily's application. "I already did that, of course. She does have experience, working at Elaine's Pies."

That was news to me. "Why'd she leave?"

Aunt Linda shrugged. "I'm not sure she did. I think she still cleans up after the restaurant closes."

Elaine's Pies closed at seven. Hopefully, Lily didn't return home later than ten o'clock. Even so, who was watching Anthony's younger siblings while she was out? I thought I knew the answer.

"Why not give her a chance?" I said, pleading with my eyes and tone.

"Okay, okay. How could I say no?"

"There's one last thing to do." I marched into the dining room with Lily's application and sat down across from her in one of the booths.

"What took you so long?" she asked.

I frowned. "Were you in school today?"

She looked away. "Yes, but I think school's stupid."

Leaning forward, I tapped on her hand. "We're going to give you a chance, but you stay in school. That was our deal."

"What if I'm sick?" She lifted her chin.

"You better be running a fever, or else."

With a nod, she stuck out her small, unblemished hand.

I shook it, fighting back a smile. "Deal?"

"Deal."

"Aunt Linda tells me you're working at Elaine's?"

"Yeah, I clean on Monday nights for a few hours."

"Why only one day a week?"

She rolled her eyes. "Some old woman cleans the other six nights."

"What's her name?"

"I don't know, but my little sister cleans toilets better than she does. "

"Are you sure that's the reason?"

"Why else?" Before my eyes she'd transformed again into the angry teenager.

"Who puts your brother and sisters to bed when you're gone?"

Her eyes narrowed. "Our neighbor."

"You trust her?"

With an almost imperceptible nod, she agreed.

I couldn't work miracles or raise money for a private defense attorney for her brother Anthony, but I could keep her in school, and we could help her place food on their table.

Wanting to lighten the mood, I slapped my hands to the tabletop. "Can you start today?"

Lily's eyes grew wide with excitement as if the cloud of despair that hung over her head had suddenly blown away. "Yes, oh yes!" she cried, slamming her fist to the table.

Sliding out of the booth, I grinned. "Come on, don't just

sit there. We've got a ton of work to do to get ready for the auction dinner tonight."

She bounded from her seat. "Yes, ma'am."

"Can you get someone to watch your brother and sisters this evening on short notice?"

"I'll call and fix it."

Clapping her on the back, I brought her to Aunt Linda. "Okay, sweet aunt of mine, she's all yours." My aunt and I exchanged a look full of understanding. We would make a place for this one, this teenager with the world on her narrow shoulders.

In spite of all the work before me, I made time to stop in at the Boot and Bag for my high heels. Though tomorrow my feet would pay back my foolishness with pain, today it was all about looking stylish for the silent auction. Hillary, Melanie, and every other society glamour girl that Big Bend County had to offer would not find anything lacking in my appearance at tonight's event if I had my way.

Mrs. Cho greeted me with a polite smile, took my claim ticket, and went in search of my heels. I followed only far enough to peek around the corner of the workroom door. Mr. Cho was not as his workbench, but his wife turned and caught me poking my head inside their inner sanctum.

"Please, you wait up front," she said, waving her hands as if to brush me away like so much dust and grime.

I gave her a sunny smile. I had no real expectation that he had information to pass along. It was too soon. Heck, for all I knew he might decide to keep his observations to himself. He hadn't exactly promised to join me in my search.

A moment later, she returned with my shoes, rang up my repair, and handed over the source of tomorrow's torment.

I bade her good-bye, and she watched me go as if she thought I would sneak past her to rummage through the piles of stinky, well-worn shoes in their workroom.

She wasn't far off the mark.

As I opened my door to the Prius, a champagne-colored luxury car pulled in beside me. I turned, expecting to greet another person picking up shoes for the auction dinner. Instead I came face-to-face with Mr. Cho.

I hesitated. Should I ask him? Was it too soon?

His alarm chirped as he walked around the hood of the car.

"Hello, Mr. Cho. How are you today?"

Without acknowledging my greeting, he stopped to inspect the hood ornament on his car. He took a white handkerchief from his pocket and wiped a bit of something from the metallic finish.

Had I really expected a clue to drop from his mouth like the proverbial pearl of wisdom? I sighed. Yes, I had.

I started my car, threw it into reverse, and saw Mr. Cho in my peripheral vision. He was standing outside my window, gesturing for me to roll it down.

"Yes?"

"Mrs. Callahan, there are too many boots in this town for you to find the ones you seek."

"Uh," I decided to ignore the married prefix. "I hadn't thought about it in exactly those terms." Out of three thousand citizens, at least a thousand of them owned a pair of boots, and some of them owned two or three pairs. Yikes!

If eyes truly twinkled, his shone brighter than the stars over the Chihuahuan Desert on a cloudless night in October. "Today I received two pairs of boots, one size nine and a half and one size ten."

"Men's or women's?" I demanded.

"Men's."

Even though I was no stranger to the fact that most murderers were men, especially those who killed by strangulation, I was disappointed. In the back of my mind, I had begun to consider Melanie a viable suspect.

Now I was back to square one.

"Did either pair have a broken heel?" I asked.

He threw a hurried glance over his shoulder toward the shop window. "Both pairs need new heels."

Who was I fooling? This whole boot print idea of mine was about as ridiculous as looking for a needle in a haystack.

"Thanks, anyway."

"Wait," he said, leaning closer. "One pair is worn on the outer edge, not both."

It was all I could do not to whoop and holler. "Who was it? Who dropped them off?"

"No one dropped them off." He frowned as if regretting his decision to help me in my campaign for justice.

"But—"

He held a white paper sack from a restaurant in his left hand. He held up a shopping bag in his right. It was a large to-go bag from Elaine's Pies.

"What are you doing?" Mrs. Cho called from the doorway. "I don't understand."

"When I picked up lunch, Mrs. Burnett gave me the boots to repair."

"A man's pair of boots?" Did they belong to P.J.? Could he have strangled Dixie for some unknown reason?

"Yes, yes." He turned to his wife. "Go away. I'll be there in a minute."

She responded in a high, piercing voice. "You come now or you'll be in big trouble." She went inside, but she continued to glare at us through the window.

"Did they belong to her husband?"

"I don't know. The soles were . . . grimy, slippery."

"Greasy?"

He thought for a moment. "Yes, greasy, that's the word."

A red pickup truck drove up on the other side of the Prius. An elderly woman made her way slowly to the Boot and Bag's front door.

"I tell you all I know." Mr. Cho hurried away.

I pulled out, more than ready to escape Mrs. Cho's censure.

My adrenaline was pumping. I tried telling myself to calm down, to not treat this new information as a salient fact in the investigation.

All I could think of was Melanie and P.J. Which one was more likely to wear an old worn-out boot into a dark alley?

Perhaps she had seen Mr. Cho while having lunch at her mother's restaurant and given him the boots to save herself a trip. *Or* she wanted to give them to him at Elaine's to prevent anyone seeing her dropping them off at the Boot and Bag.

My mind was racing. I told myself hundreds of people walked on the outside of their feet and hundreds more worked in environments where they wore out their heels. I swallowed. How many people in a town this size walked on the outside of their feet, broke their boot heels, *and* stepped in grease so thick it coated the soles of their shoes?

I didn't have enough to accuse Melanie and P.J. Pratt, but my gut told me one of them stepped in the grease next to Dixie's cold body. If one of them hadn't killed her, then they knew who had.

During tonight's auction dinner I could watch them unobserved during the dinner and dancing. Behind my role as caterer, I could question all the key players: Mayor Cogburn and his wife, Suellen and Elaine Burnett, Ryan and Hillary, and even Lightfoot and Sheriff Wallace. It was a tall order, and one I wasn't confident I had the finesse to pull off. Being a hostess and a community reporter had helped me hone my idle chit-chatting skills, and that would have to be enough.

"Lily, this way," I cried. The teen had made a herculean effort to serve tonight, securing the neighbor as a babysitter, rustling up black pants and a white button-down shirt, and borrowing a bow tie from Aunt Linda. Now she carried yet another tray of bite-size braised beef tacos from the truck to the kitchen.

The festival committee had secured Mars Hall to add a genuine historical feel to their main event. Once a country

church, the simple wooden structure offered wide oak flooring and arched windows with panes of clear and stained glass.
There was plenty of room inside for dining and for viewing
auction items. Outside, a bandstand and wooden dance floor
waited under a bower of live oaks festooned with twinkling
lights.

Gingerly, I took the platter from her. "There should be only
two more trays of grilled shrimp. If you prop the back door
open, you can bring them both in at the same time. She stared
as if processing what I'd said and then bolted for the door like
a scared jackrabbit. I had to smile. From the ankles up, she
wore the same outfit as the rest of our staff, but on her feet
she sported black converse.

"We're set to go, Jo Jo." Uncle Eddie raised his hand for a
high five.

I slapped his hand but had to mention a potential fiasco. "Just how melted are the margaritas?" We'd brought
two frozen margarita machines filled with traditional and
strawberry-flavored deliciousness for tonight's event. Regret-
tably, the machines were loaded into the truck first and had
to sit in the sun while the equipment, food items, and trays of
appetizers were brought out and secured.

He waved off my concern. "They're plugged in and re-
freezing as we speak. No harm, no foul."

"I could use one right about now."

Chuckling, he gave me a thump on the head. "Got to keep
your head clear tonight."

If he only knew how clear my thinking needed to be over
the next few hours.

With a cursory glance at our setup, he left me to supervise
the staff until Aunt Linda arrived. My aunt always made sure
everything was ready for our events except for herself. After
we'd loaded up the trucks, she'd raced home to shower and
throw on her only evening dress.

Uncle Eddie and Bubba struck up a conversation outside

at the BBQ smoker, where the BBQ king was finishing off his briskets. Soon he would take them out to let the meat rest. Minutes before dinner service, he and his staff would slice the beef and serve it with plates of German potato salad, black-eyed peas, pickles and onions, and gigantic dinner rolls.

As Lily added her trays to those on our serving table, I made a welcome announcement to our staff. "We have forty-five minutes until the evening begins and twenty until they open the doors to the early arrivals. Senora Mari sent some tamales, rice, and beans for your dinner and some flan if I'm not mistaken."

A whoop exploded in the air from Lily's direction. I smiled. "Enjoy, but be finished in fifteen minutes." Our youngest server easily maneuvered to the front of the line.

Now was a perfect window of opportunity to do reconnaissance over at Elaine's setup area. She and Suellen had arrived with their servers fifteen minutes earlier. Though Elaine was dressed to the nines, she was directing her staff as they plated the pies. She'd brought traditional Texas favorites that were guaranteed to please locals and visitors. There was peach and blackberry cobbler, and there were pies. She'd brought so many I couldn't imagine how she'd managed it without pulling her hair out: pecan, Dutch apple, chocolate pecan, chocolate, and coconut cream.

I wandered over to wish them well.

"Josie, how's that waiter of yours doing?" Elaine said as I opened my mouth to say hi.

"Uh, do you mean Anthony?"

She reached over and moved a dessert plate filled with pecan pie back away from the edge of the table before she spoke. "Yes, I believe that's his name, the one that killed Dixie."

"He didn't kill her."

Looking at me with sympathy, she nodded her head.

"What they have is merely circumstantial. They can't convict him without hard evidence," I said.

"You and your family must feel like you've been put through the wringer."

I studied her kind face. What could I ask her that wouldn't make it appear as if I were out to accuse Melanie or P.J.? "Thanks for hiring Anthony's sister. His family is in dire straits."

Her attention snapped to where one of her servers was slicing pie. "Make them bigger, Michele," she ordered. "We'll never live it down if folks think we're being chintzy with dessert.

"What were you saying? Oh, yes, the girl. Suellen didn't know she was that thug's sister or she wouldn't have hired her. She's . . ."

"He's not a thug," I said and bit my tongue hard to keep from sassing my elders. "Has she given you any trouble?"

Elaine's mouth pulled down. "Something happened between her and Suellen, but I never got in the middle of it."

"I'm sorry to hear it." I glanced to where the girl stood, spooning tamale sauce into her mouth. Suellen was the one I really needed to talk to. If I finessed the conversation with her, we could start talking about Lily and end up discussing Melanie and P.J.'s whereabouts on the night of the murder following the *tamalada*.

Vibrating with nervous intensity, Elaine cast a vigilant eye over the dining room filled with her handiwork: western-themed decorations, fragrant down-home catering, honky-tonk musicians, auction items, and enough volunteers to shake a stick at.

"Congratulations," I said with genuine appreciation. "You've done a wonderful job pulling everything together."

She gave me a cursory nod. "Thank you, but it's not over until we auction off the last item."

I glanced around again and saw no sign of Suellen, but I noticed our staff cleaning up after their meal. "I'm sorry Dixie never gave you the auction necklace as planned. It would have been the highlight of the evening."

Smiling like the cat that swallowed the canary, Elaine placed her hand on my arm. "May I show you the best surprise ever?"

I smiled in return at her obvious delight. "Sure."

She led me to a display of gift certificates, spa getaways, concert tickets, televisions and stereos, candles and candle-sticks, home decorating items, and other auction items until we reached the end of the last table.

"Fred Mueller donated these pieces." She pointed to a set of pearl earrings and a matching necklace.

"They're lovely."

"Oh, yes, as far as fakes go." We had reached the last display. "Here is the pièce de résistance."

My eyes widened. Before me was Dixie Honeycutt's squash blossom necklace, a twin to the one I'd seen in Patti's journal. Where the stones in that piece were greenish blue, these were blue as a tropical sea. Nestled in a velvet-lined display case, it was joined by a matching bracelet and dangle earrings.

"Where did you get this?"

"From Dixie, of course."

"I don't understand. This isn't the original. Patti heard Melanie say that one was stolen."

The committee chairwoman's mouth fell open and then snapped shut. "My daughter should learn to keep her lip but-toned." I couldn't make out if Elaine was angry or embar-rassed, but she managed to lift the corners of her mouth while clenching her jaw—which looked painful.

"I won't tell anyone," I whispered. "Believe me, the chil-dren's home comes first, but where did you find this one?"

For a few moments, she merely stared. "Mayor Cogburn called me up this morning out of the blue and said he wanted to give until it hurt." She laughed a light tinkling sound. "And he did."

"And the necklace and earrings?"

"My Melanie found those in her gallery. I didn't think Dixie would mind."

"What if she wanted Ty to have them?"

A young voice spoke from behind me, "Miss Linda needs you." I recognized the curt delivery and turned to find Lily standing behind me, glaring at Elaine.

"Lily," I said. "Let's go see what my aunt wants."

Reluctantly, she broke eye contact with Elaine and focused on my face.

"Good luck tonight," I said to the committee chairwoman as Lily and I hurried to our setup area.

I threw a final glance over my shoulder and found Elaine staring intently at Anthony's sister. When I raised my hand in farewell, the older woman turned away.

Chapter 19

An hour later, I found myself soaking in our success. My gaze lingered on the boisterous crowd. Some folks visited around the tables while others danced outside to "Boot Scootin' Boogie." Broken Boot's citizens and tourists had left Monday's deadly drama behind them and ponied up their hard-earned cash to enjoy a delicious BBQ dinner, lively music and dancing, and an auction to benefit a praiseworthy cause.

The Wild Wild West Festival committee had hit one out of the ballpark.

Soon all the hard work and frustration would be behind us and only the silent auction would remain. Once again, I walked along the tables lined with enticements. Fifty items was a hefty amount for the size of our crowd, but there were at least five signatures under each item. Under Dixie's jewelry there was a long list of interested buyers, which bode well for the finale, a live auction between the area's big guns.

I grabbed a cup of coffee and crossed to the window. Outside, folks danced in formal and casual evening attire. When a woman in a sequined formal dress and tiara waltzed by, I had to smile. I noticed several individuals that I'd never seen before. Perhaps the mayor and his wife had used some of their influence to invite the mayors and councilmen of other towns and counties nearby.

Elaine waltzed by with her head held high like a queen. She lifted her gloved hand from the shoulder of Fred Mueller's tuxedoed shoulder and gave me a royal wave. The smile on her face told me she was basking in her success.

I turned and found her daughter Suellen straightening the clipboards under the auction items.

"You look so beautiful," I said, and she did. She wore an emerald dress with a halter neck and glittering stones around the choker neckline.

"Thanks, you clean up pretty good yourself."

"Whatever," I said and laughed. I was wearing a glittery pantsuit I'd found in a resale shop in Austin. My back was bare and my halter bra was working overtime. "My feet are killing me."

Speaking of feet, Suellen was a tall woman, very tall. "What shoes are you wearing tonight?" I asked.

"High-heeled boots, but they're hidden under my dress."

"Can I see?" I stepped behind the table.

I followed her behind the table. She sat down in a chair and held up the dress to her knees. The boots were black and expensive with a dressy three-inch heel.

"I wish I was wearing what you're wearing." I showed her my own toe crunchers. "I have trouble finding my size."

"Why's that?" she asked, lowering her skirt. "What are you wearing, an eight and a half?"

"An eight."

"You should try looking for a ten and a half."

The smile on my face froze into place. I swallowed. "Uh, wow that must be terrible. How do you get by out here in the sticks? Mail order?"

"No. I usually wear men's boots. Easier to find."

I held my breath.

"Are you okay?" Suellen asked.

My heart started thumping. "Oh, I was just recalling all the times I've seen men's boots on sale. You'd think they'd show us some love once in a while."

Could I continue to talk about boots without giving away my motive? She'd obviously seen my reaction.

"Mind if I join you?" I asked, pulling up a chair. "I'm beat."

She quickly looked and found her mother on the dance floor. "I could use the help."

"Did Elaine's do a booming business this week?"

Stretching her neck first to one side and then to the other, she sighed. "Much better than we hoped. This week should carry us at least until the end of the year."

Out of the corner of my eye, I noticed our newest employee taking a load of warming pans and burners out to the truck. "I hired Lily to help out tonight."

Suellen followed my line of sight and frowned. "No kidding."

"She started today." I was thinking so fast my ears were burning. "One of the reasons I hired her was because she told us she was working for you."

A distinguished-looking old man stopped in front of us to write down a bid on a ski trip to Breckenridge. "Good luck," Suellen said.

"Thanks for supporting a worthy cause," I added.

She smiled in amusement. "You're a natural."

"Has Lily worked out for you so far?"

With a grimace, Suellen said, "We didn't realize her real age when we hired her. In fact, she outright lied about it."

"She is her family's sole source of provision until Anthony's released."

"That's not all she lied about."

"Oh?"

A young woman waddled up to the table, so pregnant I thought I'd have to interrupt the band to ask if there was a doctor in the house. "What's the item number for the day spa in Phoenix? I can't find my program."

Both Suellen and I grabbed a program and started skimming the item numbers. "Thirty-nine," Suellen blurted. I guess she wanted there to be no doubt about who was in charge while her mother made time to dance with the dignitaries in attendance.

"What else did Lily lie about?" I asked, watching the pregnant woman searching the numbers until she found the getaway of her dreams.

"I keep a pair of P.J.'s old boots at the restaurant just for mucking about outside. Last time I looked for them they were gone."

My mouth was dry. "What made you think she stole them? She's practically half your size."

"Because the next day they were back right where I left them, only shot to hell."

"Which was where?"

"In the janitorial closet."

"What day was that?"

She rolled her eyes. "So much has happened since then." She straightened. "I do remember because it was the day after Dixie was murdered."

"Are you sure?" My knees started to tremble. I was about to find out who murdered Dixie if I could hear over the sudden roaring in my ears.

She glared at me. "Of course, I'm sure. I was so scared that the next morning I made sure everything was still in place. I opened the closet door in my office and noticed they were gone."

"Surely someone else who works there could have taken them."

She shook her head. "We've never had anything stolen."

"Why would she take them? She's much shorter than you." I shrugged. "And her feet are probably tiny."

"I didn't consider that." A frown settled between Suellen's brows. "Everyone in my family has big feet."

A thrill hummed through my veins at her admission. "If you think Lily's guilty, why didn't you fire her?"

A dazzling couple made their way down the table toward us. The blonde wore a gold strapless confection, and her date sported a suit that showcased his physique.

Darn it.

"Hey, look at you," Ryan said, giving me a grin.

"Go away." I had no time for pleasantries from the she devil and her minion.

Suellen stepped on my toe.

"Ouch," I muttered.

She shot a glance of warning my way.

"Sorry. We're about to collect the bids so we don't have long to talk."

"Aren't you two a sight to behold?" Suellen chimed in. "Hillary, where did you find that dress?"

The beauty queen with attitude took her time responding. She finished reading the item description before her as if mesmerized, but she wasn't fooling me. She'd punch herself in the face before she'd ever set foot in Marcy's Cut and Curl.

"Thank you." Hillary beamed at Suellen and ignored me completely. "I found it on the clearance rack at Neiman Marcus. Can you believe it?"

Ryan was staring at me as if I'd grown a second head. I shook my head at him, trying to get him to go away.

From the bandstand, strains of "Stand by Your Man" drifted into the room.

"Oh, Ryan, that's my song." Hillary hurried to the open doorway, waving for her man to follow.

"What's wrong with you?" Ryan whispered.

"Nothing," I said for Suellen's benefit, praying my old friend would ask me again when we were alone. I needed serious backup.

Leaning forward, he whispered in my ear. "Liar." He gave me a knowing glance, and then followed Hillary outside.

"Uh, would you watch the table for a minute?" Suellen asked.

"If you'll tell me why you kept Lily on if you think she stole your boots."

"I hardly ever wear them anymore. They're too tight now that I have a bunion on my right foot." She made a face and hurried toward the ladies' room.

With five minutes until the bids were collected, I had to hurry. I had to find Sheriff Wallace, get him away from everyone else, and tell him what I'd learned.

Suddenly my phone vibrated, scaring the bejesus out of me. But it was only Aunt Linda sending me a text message. She and Uncle Eddie were leaving early with the staff, as she had the neck ache. He would supervise unloading the equipment and then drive her home. Would I please drive her truck back to the house after I picked up Lenny from Milagro?

I answered in the affirmative and quickly scanned the room for Wallace. He wasn't inside. Praying Suellen would hurry it up, I crossed to the window and peered out into the dark.

"Who are you looking for?"

I squealed and heads turned at a table nearby. "Stop doing that," I said to Lightfoot.

"What's wrong?"

"Nothing's wrong," I said in a low voice. "I need to speak to Sheriff Wallace. Have you seen him?"

Searching my face, Lightfoot nodded. He pointed to the dancers through the windowpane.

"He's not—" Sheriff Wallace was two-stepping around the dance floor with his wife, having a grand ole time if the grin on his face was anything to go by.

Lightfoot gave me a hard look. "Why don't you let him have this one night off?" Was I that easy to read?

"There's something—"

Shaking his head, Lightfoot raised his hand for me to halt. "I'm off duty. Call me tomorrow."

"But—"

"No. I was going to ask you to dance, but you look like you have a lot to say and I'm not in the mood to hear it." Turning on his boot heel, he wandered outside.

I glanced around in time to see Suellen return.

Facts like dominoes were lining up one behind the other in my brain. Soon they would fall, one by one, into a marvelous pattern of truth.

Suellen's arm went up, beckoning me over to help her circle the winners.

I ignored her and hurried outside, determined to find the sheriff. I wanted to get these fears out of my head and into the hands of someone who could tell me whether or not I was sane.

Elaine stepped up and placed a hand on my arm. "What's wrong, dear?"

I edged away. "Nothing, but I need to talk to Sheriff Wallace right now." He and his wife had disappeared in the throng of dancers.

As I struggled to find them, the auctioneer took the stage. "Howdy, folks. The time for this year's auction has come." The crowd cheered and the drummer hit the snare. "As you know, the winners of the silent auction will be announced following this here live auction of a necklace, bracelet, and earrings designed by the late Dixie Honeycutt." The crowd applauded. "Let's get this—wait a minute." A volunteer crossed the stage and handed the auctioneer a note. He cleared his throat. "Would Miss Josie Callahan please meet your party in the parking lot?" Glancing left and right, he searched for me. "Josie Callahan?"

I lifted my hand.

"Well, no wonder your party wants to meet you outside." The crowd laughed.

Confused and not amused, I hurried outside. The streetlight revealed nothing but cars, trucks, and a stray tiger cat. I wandered over to Aunt Linda's truck, thinking that perhaps someone had dinged the bumper, but there was no sign of an accident. Suddenly I noticed a note under the windshield wiper.

I read it once, and then I read it again:

the dog dies tonight

Chapter 20

Lenny!

My ears started to burn. How dare that sicko joke that way? Dear God, let it only be a joke. I unlocked the truck and squealed out of the parking lot. I hit speed dial and called the restaurant. No one picked up and a recording of my own voice came on.

I took the right onto the highway too fast and went into a skid, careening toward the shoulder. I lifted my foot off the gas and coaxed the wheel. The truck found the lane at the last second.

Breathe slowly. I forced myself to breath slowly. No one was going to kill Lenny. If anything they would merely shave his other side. My pulse was racing so hard I could hear the blood rushing in my ears.

There was barely anyone on the road. Most folks were at the auction. I hit speed dial and tried Aunt Linda. Voicemail again. I slowed just enough to take the exit without doing myself an injury. Maybe the staff would still be there. Maybe this whole thing was a fake, a ploy to upset me. If so, it had worked.

I prayed for forgiveness and ran the light at Main, spraying gravel and sand as I pulled into Milagro's parking lot. No one was around. The staff and my family were gone.

My phone buzzed and my heart flew into my mouth. This time it was a text from Patti.

Eddie let me in. Can't wait to dish the dirt.

I glanced around and noticed a familiar jeep parked on the street out front. Thank God. If Patti was here, then Lenny was here. I looked up at my apartment and saw that the light in the living room was definitely on.

As Uncle Eddie would say, I was so angry I wanted to spit. First I needed to see my Lenster and give him a big kiss, and then I would call the sheriff's department and lodge a complaint.

I picked my way through the parking lot, cursing my newly repaired heels. I inserted the key in the lock and the door swung open on its own. I forced myself to relax. Once I made it upstairs, I would have a talk with Patti about leaving doors unlocked. Then again, how was she to know that the sicko was threatening Lenny again?

The kitchen lights burned brightly.

"Patti," I called.

I looked around and everything was in order, except for a trickle of water running in the sink. On closer inspection, I found crumbs on the counter and the fridge ajar.

It made me smile. If I'd been given access to a restaurant, I'd find it hard not to sample the wares as well. Unless my eyes were deceiving me, Patti had sampled a batch of tamales left over from lunch service. I opened the industrial fridge and discovered that only a couple of tamales remained.

A beloved bark erupted from the ladies' room. "Lenny!"

What was he doing in there? I ran down the hall and yanked open the door.

"Yip, yip, yip," Lenny said.

I scooped him up and danced around the room. "Who's the sweetest dog in all Broken Boot?"

"Grrr."

I halted my spinning. "I'm sorry, boy." I placed a kiss on top of his head. "Did Patti put you in here?"

"Yip, yip," Lenny said. He wriggled, fighting to get down.

"Okay, okay." Gently, I placed him on the floor. As if chasing a mouse, he bolted for the apartment steps. The lights in the dining room were off for the night, and I walked through without turning them on.

Lenny came yipping back down the stairs, demanding my attention.

"You hungry, boy?"

"Yip, yip, yip."

"Okay, okay, so you're not hungry."

Above my head, the floor creaked. Milagro was located in an old building, built around 1906. It creaked at times with no explanation.

"She's up there?"

"Yip," he answered, placing his paws on my legs and looking up at me almost beseechingly.

"Okay, okay." I started up the stairs, but my feet hurt. "Patti," I cried from the bottom step. The door was closed to my apartment, but she should still be able to hear me.

"What's she doing?" I asked Lenny.

With a big sigh, I scooped up the waistband of my pantsuit to keep from tripping over my bell-bottoms and started up the steps. I reached the top and opened the door.

"Patti?" No answer.

"Come out, come out, you're creeping me out." I laughed at my own tired joke. I locked the door behind me and heaved a sigh. I had no reason to be afraid. Lenny was unharmed, and Elaine, Suellen, Melanie, and P.J. were in the middle of auctioning off some of Dixie Honeycutt's most valuable work. Even now, I could picture Elaine, basking in the glory of a job well done.

"Go ahead and hide. I'll come and find you in a minute. You won't believe what I have to tell you."

I pulled out my phone to call the sheriff's department. It connected for a second, but suddenly went dead. Great. My stupid phone had no bars in my own home . . . as usual.

If I was right, one of the Burnetts murdered Dixie with her own necklace. My money was on Elaine, though I couldn't explain why, at least not yet.

Lenny ran through the living room and into my bedroom like the house was on fire.

A prickly feeling came over my neck, and I shook it off. I wasn't one to believe in ghosts, other than the Holy Ghost, but the hairs were standing up on the back of my neck.

A tapping noise made me jump out of my skin. "Patti," I whispered. "Is that you?" Nothing.

Lenny ran back into the kitchen and jumped into my lap.

"Hey, watch it," I didn't want him to pick the front of my slacks. "What is it?" I crooned, trying to kiss his nose. He wriggled in my arms. I lowered him to the ground just as he jumped. He ran into my bedroom again, but this time I followed.

Tap. Tap.

OMG. The tapping was coming from the closet. If this was Patti's idea of a joke, I was going to kill her.

Lenny began scratching at the closet door.

I looked around my bedroom for a possible weapon. Even if it wasn't Elaine, there was always the possibility that a rat, squirrel, possum, raccoon, or bat had taken up lodging in my closet, not to mention my clothes.

With Lenny in one arm and a ski pole in my hand, I slowly opened the closet door. The closet was dark, but the bedroom light shone bright on Patti's head.

"Patti," I cried.

My best friend was there on the floor, duct tape on her mouth and around her wrists and ankles. Her eyes wide, she motioned wildly with her head, crying out as best she could behind the duct tape gag.

I lowered the ski pole and dropped to my knees. In her eyes, there was no sign of tears or weakness, only outrage.

Lenny whined, and I pulled the tape from her mouth.

"Ahh," she whimpered. She shook her head to clear the pain. "She's coming back. She's out there somewhere. Go and get help."

"But—"

"Put that tape back on my mouth so she won't know you found me. You don't have time for anything else."

I started to do as she said. "You do mean Elaine, right?"

She nodded and her eyes fell to the tape in my hand. "Hurry."

"I don't get it. I left her at the auction. She wouldn't leave in the middle of her big moment."

"She did this." She tried to pick up the tape with her fingers, though her wrists were tied together.

"Okay, okay, I got it." I smoothed the gray sticky tape over her mouth as best I could.

The room went black. I barely held in my scream. "Patti," I whispered, "I'm going to go get help, but I won't go far. Promise."

I could still see the whites of her eyes. I fumbled for the flashlight app on my phone. She was frantic, gesturing with her tied hands for me to go.

As I hurried into the kitchen, Elaine's voice floated up from the stairs below. "You shouldn't leave your extra set of keys where just anyone can find them." She sounded calm and in control as usual, as if advising the committee members on their festival duties.

"Yip," Lenny said.

I dialed 911, but the screen remained dark. No service.

Still holding Lenny in one arm, I fumbled through the knife drawer. In the very back, I found the old skeleton key that belonged to the closet. I hurried back, opened the door, and whispered. "I'm coming back. Hang on."

Patti struggled to speak through the duct tape.

"No." I caught her eye. "I couldn't live with myself if she were to harm you."

Wide-eyed and shaking her head as hard as she could, she tried to speak around the tape, but to no avail.

I checked my phone. No signal.

Lowering my mouth to Patti's ear, I whispered, "She's downstairs. I don't have a signal. I've got to find a way outside to call the sheriff before she breaks down the door." I backed away enough to make eye contact. "Elaine Burnett is not going to send you or me to our maker, not while I have breath in my body."

At last Patti nodded, her steady gaze riveted to mine as if transferring all of her cool self-assurance to me. I nodded in return, placed Lenny in the closet with my best friend, and then quickly locked the closet door.

In the bedroom all was quiet, no sign of Elaine.

I threw the skeleton key under the bed and suddenly remembered the knives in the drawer. I hated sharp objects, especially knives. I even looked away in a movie if a character cut themselves by accident. And forget slasher movies, I avoided them like last week's leftovers.

But if a knife was all I had against crazy Elaine, then a knife it was. I'd channel my inner horror movie heroine and pray. Those chicks might run throughout the entire movie, but they managed to kill the creeper in the end.

I was standing in the bedroom when Elaine jammed the key in the apartment door lock. Why hadn't I placed a chair under the doorknob? Horror movie heroines were dimwits. I made it only as far as the kitchen doorway when the apartment door flung wide. Elaine stood on the threshold, wearing a tiny headlight. In her right hand, she held a pistol.

In the closet, Lenny flew into a fury, barking and growling like a dog twelve times his size. "Don't worry," Elaine said. "I'll take good care of him."

I backed into the living room, grabbed the coffee table, and flung it between us, hoping to give Elaine an obstacle.

She laughed. "I haven't used a pistol in a long time, not since my husband taught me to shoot on our honeymoon. But I'm pretty sure I can figure it out in time to put a hole in you if you don't stand still."

Her words gave me a boost of confidence. Maybe the gun would jam. I ran for the bedroom and locked the door. I tried to check my phone for service, and she started firing at the doorknob. I dialed 911 just as the knob fell off.

I looked around, frantic for even a wisp of an idea. "Elaine, what did I ever do to you?"

She fired again, and a bullet plowed through the door-frame. Spotting the other ski pole, I crawled over to it and wedged it beneath the door handle.

"What didn't you do?" she demanded. "All you had to do was stay out of the way so Wallace and his deputies could bungle it."

"I couldn't let Anthony go to jail."

She banged the door and the ski pole jumped. It wasn't going to keep her out for very long.

"Nine-one-one." The female operator's voice crackled to life. "What's your emergency?"

"Elaine Burnett's trying to kill me."

"Ma'am, can you get to a place of safety?"

Gunfire hit the door and wood chips started flying.

"What's under the door handle, Josefina?" Elaine's irate, church lady voice suddenly reminded me of my seventh grade band director, Mrs. Chambers. After one band contest too many, the old drill sergeant retired early to a mental home in Corpus Christi.

My gaze soared around the room, desperate for anything that would help. If I ran into the bathroom I was a sitting duck. She'd only have to shoot off the doorknob again to reach me.

I spotted the street lamps and ran toward the light. I pried open the window and kicked out the screen. The balcony rested on the covered porch below. It was sturdy enough for me to sit outside on sunny days in my lawn chair, but not secure enough to hold two people. It was fifteen feet in the air and it was my only choice.

I climbed through the window and shut it again, hoping she wouldn't look to the windows first as I tried to get down without breaking my legs.

I knew in a flash that once I stood long enough to lift my leg over the balcony rail, I'd be a sitting duck. I could hear the operator talking on the phone, but I couldn't carry on a decent conversation in the midst of someone trying to riddle me with bullet holes. I crawled to the side of the porch, away from the window.

I heard the window start to open. My adrenaline pumping like an oil gusher, I rolled back against the wall.

"Josie," Elaine whispered in a voice now devoid of anything but motherly concern. "Are you out there, hon?" If I didn't know she was trying to kill me, I'd think she was worried I might fall of the roof. "Don't make me turn on my light."

I gave no reply, and she said nothing further. It was a Mexican standoff between two women, one desperate and the other insane.

"Have it your way. I'll just go check on Patti." Through the open window, I heard her struggle to open the door of the closet. Lenny barked as if he would rip her stockings off.

"Very clever, Jo Jo," she called. "That's what your uncle calls you, right? Jo Jo." She began to tug and bang on the closet door. "Bark away," she raged, "you little health department nightmare."

Why wasn't she shooting the handle off? Or did she think yelling at them through the door and banging on the panel would frighten them more? Maybe she was hoping to shock them into a stupor like a mistreated goldfish.

Sirens began to wail, and two sheriff cruisers zoomed down Main Street, heading straight for us. I came to my knees, convinced I could wave them down. She wouldn't dare shoot me with the deputies as witnesses.

The cruisers zoomed on past, crossed the train tracks and disappeared, heading toward Two Boots.

The deputy dogs had missed me.

I dropped to my stomach and inched my way back to the wall, determined to make it over the balcony before she spotted me.

As soon as I stood up, I heard the pistol cock.

"There you are," Elaine said sweetly. "Come on over here."

I leaned back against the wall, making a smaller target. "Why would I want to do that?"

"Dear, I wouldn't try to be clever at a time like this."

Holy cow, Elaine was trying to mother me with a gun in her hand. I peered at the ground. How much pain would I feel if I flung myself over the balcony? What if I caught my heel on the rail? Would I land on my head?

In the background, I heard the sirens, but then they disappeared on the wind.

"Say something," she demanded.

I inched closer to the railing.

"Fine. I'll teach you to ignore your elders."

I heard a thwack as if she'd hit the closet's door handle with her pistol. With any luck, the gun would go off and put her out of commission.

Without delay, I lifted one leg over the railing and froze as a heartbreaking cry from Lenny reached my ears.

"If you want me to have mercy on your friends, you'll come back inside this minute." Lenny's whining came closer. She had to be standing at the open window.

One leg over the railing and fifteen feet from either freedom or a broken leg, I wavered. "Why don't you clean out your bank account and make a run for the border? No one would ever find you."

"Why would I do that?" Elaine asked matter-of-factly. "No one else knows I killed Dixie except you two."

Patti cried out.

"I guess Miss Tattoo Queen isn't as tough as she thought."

I ignored the adrenaline racing through my brain that was telling me to jump. I faced my fear and turned my head to stare straight into Elaine's eyes. Holding the pistol like a club, she swung it by her side, and in her other arm she held Lenny close to her body.

With one leg over the railing, I lied. "I told Lightfoot the whole story only forty-five minutes ago."

"When was that, my dear? Before or after he drank three frozen margaritas?"

Chapter 21

My mouth was as dry as dirt. "After, but you'd be surprised how well that man holds his liquor." I was blabbering. Lightfoot hadn't been drinking when he was with me.

"I don't believe you, Jo Jo. Why, you hardly said two words to him all night." She could have been a disappointed parent.

But how could she have seen us without me seeing her? "That's what we wanted you to think. I told Lightfoot all about you murdering Dixie while you were on the dance floor." I was grasping at straws.

"Hmm . . . I danced with him just before I left. He didn't act suspicious. He was too worried about not tripping over his own feet." She laughed and her voice was light as a crystal bell.

She had me cold, but how had she slipped away before me? "I don't understand." Maybe I could keep her talking? Or did that only happen in the movies?

"Ow . . ." Elaine cried, dropping Lenny to the floor. "The mongrel bit me."

"Run, Lenny, run!"

"Oh, that's cute, right out of *Lassie*. How do you expect him to get out of the building?" Elaine waved me toward the window with the gun. "Get in here, Jo Jo, while I decide what to do with you."

I was a sitting duck. "You win." I lifted my leg back over the railing and crawled into my apartment under her watchful eye. I dropped into the wingback chair. My hairbrush, mascara, hair dryer, and straight iron were on the top of my dresser, close at hand. Lenny had disappeared.

"Why'd you do it, Elaine?" I reached down and she brought the gun to my face. Her eyes were overly bright, her gaze intent as if I were a snake in her garden that needed to be exterminated. "Why, Elaine? What did Dixie ever do to you that was so horrible you had to kill her?"

She shook her head. "Now, Josie, you know she was rude to me every time she saw me." She patted her perfectly curled hair the same way I'd seen her do so many times before. "I could have stood it. I mean, really. What did I care what that fat, obnoxious hippie thought?" She looked at me expectantly.

"I thought Dixie was just kidding around."

She put the safety back on. "I could have stood her kidding around if she hadn't tried to squash Melanie's chances for success."

I must have looked as confused as I felt.

"Now listen up, first she claimed that Melanie was trying to destroy her sales by asking her to sell her jewelry elsewhere, and then she claimed that Melanie was a . . . what was it she called her . . . a two-bit hack?"

"That was unkind."

Elaine still held the gun at her side, but she was glancing at herself in the mirror that hung on the closet door. I thought this was odd, especially if she was about to take my life.

I tried to lift up a few inches to pull my foot out from under me to position myself for a fast getaway.

"Unkind?" Elaine repeated as if lost in thought. "She was deluded."

My eyes grew wide before I could stop myself. The queen of delusion was holding court in my bedroom at this very moment.

"She had the nerve to tell *The Texan* that my Melanie has no talent." Elaine wiped her eyes, underneath her glasses.

"Where is Melanie?" If she were on her way to end my life, I wanted to know.

Elaine turned to the mirror again, smoothing down her hair at the crown, again and again. "With P.J., I imagine. She kept her head high in spite of all Dixie's yammering about how Melanie was trying to steal her designs." She gestured with the gun to emphasize her point, and I covered my head.

"Did I scare you?" She laughed in delight.

"Yes, ma'am," I said politely as I lowered my hands.

"I've never used one of these on another living, breathing soul." She brought the pistol close to her face. "Did you know that after Dixie's murder P.J. insisted that Melanie, Suellen, and I all learn to shoot?" She chuckled. "I was proud to tell him that I had learned to handle a gun over thirty years ago."

As she studied her weapon, I checked the window and bedroom door, evaluating which way to run.

A loud thwack hit the closet door and it swung open.

Elaine walked over and peered inside. "Patti, you need to stay quiet in there. You're going to hurt yourself."

"Where will you go?" I asked. A better question was how could I get away from this crazy woman?

"Go? Why, nowhere, honey. I'm staying here."

Where was my phone? I placed my hands on my thighs and tried to feel for my cell with my elbows. Not there. It must be on the balcony. Had the emergency operator believed my story?

"Where's her camera?" Elaine asked, pointing to Patti.

"I don't know." Had I seen it since I'd entered the apartment? Slowly, I stepped toward the closet and peered inside and met Patti's eyes. She was listening, no longer frightened out of her wits. "Elaine, you don't really mind if I take the duct tape off of Patti's mouth, do you? She sure would be able to breathe better."

The festival chairwoman from h-e-double-toothpicks gave us a narrow-eyed stare. Finally she nodded her assent.

With my back to Elaine, I bent over to remove the duct tape from Patti's mouth and whispered, "Where's your camera?"

Even though I stood between her and Elaine, she took no chances. Silently she mouthed the words, *in the oven.*

"Patti Perez?" Elaine called sweetly.

"Yes . . . ma'am?"

"You stay in there, honey."

"Uh, yes, ma'am."

I patted Patti's shoulder and left her in the closet.

Elaine's eyes were still overly bright, as if she were high on adrenaline. "You stay over there." She pointed with the pistol to my favorite piece of furniture, a handcrafted Shaker chair placed against the wall.

"Yes, ma'am."

Suddenly she slapped the arm of the loveseat. "Where's Patti's camera?" she demanded, her eyes snapping like a rattlesnake prepared to strike.

"Um . . ." Her agitation level was rising faster than a flash flood. Grasping for straws, I remembered that Texas mommas are a proud lot. "You know, Dixie was wrong. Melanie has a gift." I decided to lay it on thick. "My whole family loves her paintings. That's why we display them on our walls."

"All she wanted was to sell her work to the tourists and make a success of her gallery. She's slaved hard for her success."

"Haven't we all?"

"No, we all have not!" Elaine cried, gasping for breath. "Dixie sure as hellfire didn't. Oh, but she wanted to take everything my Melanie had worked so hard for." Elaine lowered herself to the bed. She leaned forward, the gun hanging loose in her limp hand. The older woman's voice was growing weaker by the minute.

"How'd she do that?"

"Why, she stole all the glory for herself, selling her necklaces to the tourists and keeping them from buying my Melanie's beautiful paintings."

"She didn't mean to steal, uh, the glory."

"Oh yes, she did. Mean was her first, last, and middle name. Mean, proud, and ugly, telling Melanie she was going to leave and find her own place."

Making a big show out of considering Elaine's words, I nodded my head in tacit agreement. "Wouldn't that have helped Melanie's business if Dixie had left?" I was stalling for time, rifling through my mental card file for any tidbit to distract her, but I wasn't coming up with anything useful.

Elaine's face went slack for a moment. "No, darling." The older woman made a *tsk-tsk* sound. Obviously, the good Lord hadn't given me enough sense to come in out of the rain. She leaned forward, eager to help me understand. "Melanie wanted Dixie to sell her turquoise jewelry somewhere else. You see, my daughter needed," Elaine wrinkled her nose in disgust, "that woman to keep selling her other, less popular pieces at the gallery. That way, folks coming in to buy from Dixie would be awestruck by Melanie's work and buy one of her paintings instead. She could have sold her turquoise baubles anywhere, but oh no. She wouldn't have it." Elaine jerked to an upright position, her right hand opening and closing as if grabbing onto an imaginary flashlight. "She had to grind Melanie's face in it."

"Your daughter is so talented," I soothed. "She's going to become famous."

"Of course she will, once you're out of the way. You see, I can't afford for anyone to find out that I murdered Dixie. If the world found out her mother was a murderer they'd never take Melanie's art seriously."

I wet my lips, desperately trying to formulate an argument.

"I always thought you were an intelligent girl. Unfortunately, you've proved too smart for your own good."

"Josie, you okay?" Aunt Linda's voice floated up the stairs like a ray of sanity.

From under the loveseat, Lenny sprang like a mountain lion upon Elaine's chest, growling and biting her face while the older woman screamed. "Get him off me! Get him off!"

"Lenny, heel." My tiny defender stared at me as if I'd lost my ability to command. "Now."

"Yap," he barked in Elaine's face before jumping from her chest and running to my side.

Elaine pulled up her knees, dropped her head onto her arms, and began to weep.

"We're okay, Aunt Linda!"

With a tenderness I usually reserved for Lenny, I joined Elaine on the edge of the bed, after I kicked the pistol underneath it.

"Josie, what happened to your door?" Aunt Linda called from the landing.

"Stay where you are," I cried. "I'm going to invite Aunt Linda in to sit with you. Is that all right, Elaine? You know she wouldn't harm a fly."

The weeping chairwoman lifted her head. "That's okay, I guess. Your Aunt Linda's a kind woman." She patted my hand. "I really should have killed you, but I just couldn't do it. You're the spitting image of your mother."

"Come on in."

My worried aunt nearly fell through the doorway. She wrapped her arms around Elaine and proceeded to rock her back and forth while the older woman cried.

Right on her heels was Senora Mari, and behind the Martinez women were the cavalry, Sheriff Wallace and Deputy Lightfoot.

"Yip," Lenny said. I was so consumed with showing my gratitude, I didn't mind that he licked my face and mouth. He was my hero.

When Lightfoot helped Patti remove the last vestiges of

duct tape, she smiled at him as if he were the second coming. If I hadn't been so happy to see her freed, I would have kicked her in the shins for making her attraction so obvious.

Wallace pulled me into the hall.

"What's going on here?"

"Sheriff, it's another case of the Texas cheerleading mom. Elaine wanted so badly for her dear, sweet, talented Melanie to get all the glory for being the most talented artist in Broken Boot that she convinced herself she had to get rid of Dixie."

"That sounds too crazy to be untrue." The sheriff took off his hat, which meant he was thinking deeply.

"In Dixie's upcoming interview in *The Texan* she skewers Melanie and her gallery, calling her a no-talent hack and worse. And she goes on about how Elaine bought Melanie's success."

"How would Elaine know what was in that interview?"

"Dixie didn't hide any aces up her sleeve. Knowing her, she probably threw it in Melanie's face."

Senora Mari stuck her head out into the hall. "She's coming, sheriff. You got the handcuffs ready?"

"That's not the way we treat upright, solid . . . I mean, that's not the way we do things here." By his deep frown, it was obvious he hadn't completely comprehended how deep a puddle of crazy the festival chairwoman had fallen into. Straightening his shoulders, he hitched up his belt and went to talk to Elaine himself.

With an arm around Patti, who mysteriously appeared a lot weaker than she had fifteen minutes ago, Lightfoot paused in the doorway. With a quick glance toward the couch, he whispered to the sheriff, "She's sobbing a confession all over herself in there. If you ask me, someone should hand her paper and pencil while the words are flowing."

"You okay?" I narrowed my eyes at Patti to make sure she knew how much I disapproved of her sudden display of feminine wiles.

She sighed and gave me a weak smile. "I'm fine. Guess I'm in shock," she said, looking up through her eyelashes at the deputy.

Growling was not an option, but I wanted my friend back, not this flirt with dyed black hair and facial piercings. I couldn't help but feel a tiny bit disgusted with her and with myself. Hadn't I found Lightfoot attractive? And hadn't I looked for him every time a cruiser drove by? The whole thing was sickening. I was Josie Callahan, dang it.

I was not about to jump out of the pan and into the fish fryer. She could have him.

"Lightfoot, take Patti downstairs and find her a Dr Pepper. The sugar and caffeine will make a new woman out of her." I gave her a knowing look, making sure she got the message.

"What about you?" she asked as an afterthought.

"We'll stay here." Aunt Linda and I would stay with the sheriff and Elaine. Only minutes earlier, she'd threatened me with a pistol, but I wasn't afraid. If my aunt chose to be a comfort to Elaine, the killer committee chairwoman, then I chose to be a comfort to my aunt.

I found a spiral notebook and a gel pen for Elaine. As long as Aunt Linda stayed by her side, she was content to pour out the whole confusing and sordid truth.

It turned out that Elaine had always wanted to throw pots and own her own pottery shop as a girl, but no one believed in her abilities. She'd sucked it up and married Mr. Burnett, raised her girls, and started Elaine's Pies, all the while wishing she could follow her dream.

By the time Elaine lowered her pen, Lenny was snoring in the middle of my bed, and I was wondering how rude it would be if I left Aunt Linda to chaperone the confession while I joined him for a quick snooze.

Sheriff Wallace placed his hat on his head and hiked his belt. "Time to take you down to the station, Elaine. There's no getting around it."

"If you say so, sheriff. I voted for you because you're a man of integrity." With Aunt Linda's help, Elaine rose to her feet, lifted her chin high in the air, and followed Wallace down the stairs. Aunt Linda and I watched them go in silence. With one mind, we turned to each other and hugged.

Chapter 22

On Monday night, Milagro closed its weary doors for a much needed respite after the end of a bumpy, but successful, Wild Wild West Festival. Or rather, the festival was as successful as it could be, considering the fact the festival committee chairwoman murdered Broken Boot's premier jewelry designer.

Funny, but most folks didn't think that unsavory detail affected the popularity of the festival as a whole.

Though it was our usual night off, it might as well have been a Friday night on Austin's Sixth Street. The festival committee, sans their unhinged chairwoman, gathered as planned for the annual festival postmortem. All aspects of the weekend from attendance and revenues to talent and murder would be evaluated, discussed, and raked over the coals.

No one even considered cancelling after Elaine's arrest. What did it matter that a murderess placed the meeting on the calendar? The committee would not be swayed.

Senora Mari planned on making tamales, but we talked her out of it. When I closed my eyes I could still envision Elaine Bennett choking on our most popular menu item. If I didn't see another tamale until Labor Day, that would be fine by me. Instead our tamale maven grudgingly supervised the preparation of fried ice cream, jalapeno poppers, and steamed tilapia with roasted vegetables.

I popped into the kitchen to check on the evening's fare. "*Hola*," I said, making sure to greet Carlos, our cook, and Senora Mari in a friendly, nonthreatening way. Whether she wanted to admit it or not, our executive chef was as worn out as an old leather boot.

"*Ah, Dios!* Take out more chips and salsa if they're so hungry," Senora Mari growled as she removed a tray of jalapeno poppers from the industrial oven.

I grabbed a few serving plates and hurried to her side. "Shh, no one's complaining, *abuela*." Together we gingerly plated the appetizers. "Thanks for changing the menu. I know you're disappointed."

She clutched me in her arms. After a long pause she said, "Never disappointed in you. I thank God you're alive." She backed away, her eyes bright and full of unshed tears. "Even if you are a pain in my backside."

The kitchen doors swung open and a young, dark-haired waiter stepped inside. "What can I do to help?"

"Anthony, take these out with additional napkins," I said with a warm smile. Sheriff Wallace had wasted no time in releasing our newest waiter into the arms of his family.

"Yes, ma'am." He gave Senora Mari a wink and headed into the dining room with the first course.

"Go, go," she said, shooing me out the door. "Go make margaritas or something."

Back in the dining room, Mayor Cogburn cleared his throat. "Congratulations, y'all, on the best Wild Wild West Festival ever." Everyone cheered, and Bubba and Uncle Eddie whooped. "In spite of everything," the mayor continued, "we overcame adversity and persevered to . . ." The mayor, trying to make eye contact with everyone in the room, locked eyes with his wife. They smiled at each other like two teenagers on their way to prom.

"Celebrate another day," said Mrs. Mayor, her cheeks turning a pretty shade of pink. It was the first time I could remember her ever finishing one of her husband's sentences. The room burst into applause.

"Guess what Felicia told me, not two minutes ago, outside the ladies' room?" Aunt Linda whispered from behind me.

"Do tell," I whispered back, resisting the urge to turn around.

"She and the mayor have been driving to El Paso for couples counseling for the past six months." I could hear the barely restrained laughter in her voice. "Working on intimacy issues . . . if you know what I mean."

Well, shut my mouth.

No wonder the mayor paid Dixie to stop spreading his business up and down Main Street.

After several minutes of listening to Mayor Cogburn field the same questions about the murder without any sign of discussing the festival, Aunt Linda escaped into her office, complaining of a headache. If I knew my aunt, she'd already kicked her feet up on her desk and was scanning the Internet for pictures of Chuck Norris to add to her electronic scrapbook.

I refilled several glasses of sweet tea and left the committee to wrangle it out. Unlike last week, Uncle Eddie was behind the bar mixing margaritas with loving attention to detail, though he sometimes added salt when none was wanted and vice versa. I found a booth nearby, put up my feet, and rested my head against the stucco.

The cowbell over the front door clanged. "Must be nice to be such a celebrity," Ryan said. "You think you can do as you please, don't you?" He grabbed my left boot with both hands as if he meant to pull it off.

"Hey, stop that!" He meant well, but I didn't need cheering

up. I was simply in a thoughtful mood, reflecting on the good things in my life. Elaine had tried to steal them away, but instead, my everyday blessings—my best friend, my family, and my dog—had all saved *me*.

The sheriff and his deputies ultimately rescued me from crazy Elaine, but the people I loved the most had saved me from heartbreak.

"What are you up to?" I asked, lowering my feet.

He took me up on my invitation and sat down across from me. "Looking for Eddie, of course."

I glanced at the bar and discovered Uncle Eddie had miraculously vanished.

Ryan gazed into my eyes and I gazed right back. I couldn't resist asking one last time, "What's Hell-on-Wheels up to tonight?" The former beauty queen and I shouldn't have any reason to speak until next year's festival. Watching Ryan formulate his reply, I wondered if Hillary would notice if I disappeared into thin air each time they came to dine.

Then again, why should I give her that much power over me?

"I don't know." Ryan looked away, stared at the clock, checked his watch, and then scratched his thumb with a fork.

"What did you do to hack her off?"

His jaw clenched and unclenched. "Now you mention it, I seem to remember telling her I didn't want to see her anymore."

All my thoughts evaporated like dew on a cactus in the morning heat. My pulse rushed through my veins, and suddenly I was fighting mad. "Why the heck did you do that?"

"What's wrong with you? It's not as if you liked her."

My heart was thumping with rage. "I couldn't stand her, but that doesn't mean you had to break up with her."

"You make no sense, as usual," he muttered.

Uncle Eddie wandered back in. "Hey man, what's going on? I thought you were heading out of town to Southlake to meet some prospective parents."

"Had to postpone a day," he said and glanced my way. "I thought I had some business here."

"You thought wrong." I could tolerate Ryan if he had a girlfriend. But I didn't want him, and I didn't want him to think I wanted him. And he had another think coming if he thought I was putting myself out there to get my nose lobbed off again, to be told I was a great friend, but not a girlfriend—which was what had happened last time he and I dated.

Plus, we backed different football teams.

"Jo Jo, you okay?" my uncle asked, stepping out from behind the bar.

I smiled. "I'm fine." He would be overly protective for the next few days until football drew him back into her jealous arms.

"Yip, yip," a familiar voice called.

Before I could stop him, Ryan ducked into the stockroom and came out with the Lenster. With his new buzz cut, he resembled a ferret, but he held his pointed head high. In return for saving my life, I'd given him a bath and many tasty treats.

"Hey, Lenny, how's it going?" Ryan crooned. "When do we get to read your first blog post?"

"Yip," the brave Chi answered. Elaine had merely shaved him instead of doing far worse, and for that blessing I would be eternally grateful.

"He's decided to take a sabbatical until I finish writing my follow-up articles on Elaine's arrest," I said.

Ryan tipped his head down to Lenny's mouth. "Right." He nodded his head in agreement. "She's mean to me too, meaner than a snake at a rattlesnake rodeo."

I whistled and Lenny jumped from Ryan's arms and came running. I scooped him into my lap. "Don't listen to the Neanderthal football coach, he's a bad influence."

"Tell me about Southlake," Uncle Eddie interrupted. He gave me a sharp glance, warning me, in no uncertain terms, not to treat football or his friend with disrespect.

Without the benefit of the cowbell, Lightfoot walked into

the bar area from the kitchen. "You know I could write you a ticket for having that animal in here."

I grinned. "Dream on. Last time I checked you weren't the health inspector." I bolted out of my seat and hurried toward him with my arms open wide.

His eyes widened in fear like a horse about to bolt for the pasture until my favorite Goth princess stepped out from behind him. I threw my arms around her. "Patti!"

Yesterday, for the first time in forever, she'd hung a sign on the door of the Broken Boot Feed and Supply:

CLOSED UNTIL FURTHER NOTICE.

We'd hung out at her place, baking cookies, painting our toenails, and processing our near-death adventure.

Only two nights after Elaine's pistol-packing rampage, Patti was as feisty as ever. Her eyes shone with mirth as she shot a glance at Lightfoot and back at me.

I shook my head in mock dismay. I didn't think he was a good fit for her. What did he know about artistic, intelligent women? Would he support her need to run her family business and pursue her photography? No. He'd work long hours and expect her to kowtow to his demands and work schedule.

Whoa.

Inside, I groaned. When would I stop projecting Brooks onto every man I met? I kept saying love stinks. But maybe it wasn't love, but how I acted when I was in love that stank up the joint.

"Y'all come on and join us." I gave Patti a wink when Lightfoot wasn't looking.

He tossed his hat on a table and sat down. "I don't care about your rat of a dog. I'm now officially off the clock."

"What are you two up to?" Uncle Eddie asked. "Want some dinner?"

Lightfoot's eyes widened and his brown cheeks darkened. "Uh, we're not together." I couldn't get a read on him. Why was he embarrassed? If Patti could handle him, she could have him.

"Oh, no," my best friend said, "we just happened to walk in together."

"I hope you're hungry. You can't get better tilapia in this county." Ryan pulled up a chair as well.

"That's not saying much," Patti said, pulling a face.

"Uncle Eddie, will you do the honors?" I asked.

"Sure thing."

"Hey, bring me a taco salad with grilled chicken," Patti called to his retreating back.

As I joined them, Lenny reached over and licked Lightfoot's arm.

"What was that?" He wrinkled his face in disgust.

"That was the seal of approval."

"Yip," Lenny said.

My friends all laughed in agreement.

"Something's been nagging at me," Lightfoot began, reaching into his jacket. "Why did I find Patti's camera in your oven?" He placed a familiar Nikon in the center of the table.

I shrugged. With all the excitement, I'd forgotten all about it.

"As soon as Elaine started banging on the door of Josie's apartment, she demanded my camera." Patti leaned forward. "I didn't know why she wanted it, but I sure as shootin' wasn't going to give it to her."

The intoxicating aroma of spicy fish tickled our noses seconds before Uncle Eddie entered the room with our dinner.

"Don't worry," he said to Patti. "I'll be back in two shakes of a lamb's tail with that salad."

After eating nearly half of his fish in three bites, Ryan paused. "Why do you think she wanted your camera?"

"I've been trying to figure that out since Saturday." Ryan tried to raise a bite of fish to Patti's mouth, but she batted his arm away. "All it had on it were some pictures that Dixie asked me to take of her jewelry."

"What else?"

"Nothing except a few photos from the tamale party."

I grabbed her by the arm. "Show us."

Slowly Lightfoot lowered his fork. "Right now."

With a shrug, Patti turned on the camera and started scrolling through her pictures.

"Who all did you take a picture of?" Ryan asked as he looked longingly at my untouched plate.

She adjusted her chair. "Everybody. Elaine, Bubba, Frederick, Hillary, Ryan, Melanie, Suellen, Mayor Cogburn and his wife." She rubbed the back of her hand back and forth across her forehead. "A few were posed, but most were candid shots of the committee members making tamales."

"Did you take a picture of me too?" Senora Mari asked as she joined us.

"Shh," I said to the older woman, taking my life in my hands. "Was Elaine making tamales?" I held my breath.

With sudden understanding, Patti caught my eye. "Yes. Maybe. I think so."

"When was that crazy woman making tamales in my kitchen?" Senora Mari demanded.

"Shh," we all said in unison. We crowded close to the camera as Patti quickly flew through the photos until she reached one of Elaine and her daughters.

"What's so special about that?" Ryan asked.

"Nothing, you dimwit," Patti groaned. "That's not the one."

Clenching my hands so tight that my nails bit into my palms, I urged. "Come on. Where is it?"

And then Patti stopped, her eyes glued to the camera. Wordlessly, she turned the display so we could all see the truth.

"OMG!" I cried. "Elaine hid the necklace in the tamales during the party!"

"She must have thought you caught her in the act," Lightfoot said quietly.

"I had the evidence all along."

The four of us sat for a moment in silence.

"Wasn't she afraid of someone catching her in the act?" Ryan asked.

"I wish I had her here," *Abuelita* said. "I'd pull every hair out of her head."

"Exactly," Ryan said, slapping his hand on the table and nearly toppling the salsa. "Didn't she know Senora Mari would find it?"

Senora Mari's scowl was frightening.

"Yes, but we all know how demanding Elaine Burnett can be," I said. "She probably wanted Milagro to look bad so that her own business would take up the slack."

I glanced from one to the other. "And she nearly died by her own hand."

"I thought she was going to choke to death during the tamale-eating contest, for sure," Ryan added.

"You have a keen grasp of the obvious," Patti muttered.

"Yip," Lenny said, and I put him down. He ran to the supply room and came back with his leash.

"Someone needs you," Uncle Eddie said in a singsong voice.

"And I need him," I said with a smile. "Best friend and hero rolled into one."

What else could a girl want?

Recipes

🌶 Senora Mari's Tamales

Yield: 4 to 5 dozen chicken and pork tamales

MEATS:
3½ pounds whole chicken
3½ pounds pork roast

CHILE SAUCE:
24 pods dried red chile
2 teaspoons salt

MASA:
1½ pounds lard
5 pounds masa harina
5 tablespoons baking powder
5 tablespoons salt

FILLING:
1 large onion, chopped
3 cloves garlic, chopped
2 tablespoons lard
3 cups meat broth (from cooked meats)
4 cups chile sauce

2 tablespoons salt
shredded meats

TAMALE ASSEMBLY:
2½ pounds corn husks

MEAT: Boil chicken and pork roast and cook until meat falls off bones. Remove from stove and let cool. Discard fat. Drain meat and save broth. Then shred meats.

CHILE SAUCE: Wash red chile pods and remove stems and seeds. Bring chile and water to a boil; reduce heat and steam 10 minutes or longer. Pour liquid into blender; strain sauce through colander or sieve to remove any remaining chile skins. Add two teaspoons salt. (This should yield approximately 4 cups.)

MASA: Whip lard to consistency of whipped cream. Mix with masa, adding baking powder and salt. Beat until mixture is fluffy.

FILLING: Sauté onions and garlic in 2 tablespoons of lard; add 1 cup of broth, 2 cups of chile sauce, 2 tablespoons of salt and shredded meat to make filling. Simmer 20 minutes, adding more broth if needed. Add 2 cups of chile sauce and 2 cups broth; mix well. More broth can be added if masa is too thick to spread easily.

TAMALE ASSEMBLY: Clean and dry husks. (Corn husks brush off more easily when the husk is dry.) Wash in warm water and leave to soak until ready to use. Spread husks with masa and filling by placing 1 heaping tablespoon of masa in the middle of the husk and spreading toward outside edges, top and bottom. Spread closer to top of husk than bottom.

Spread 2 tablespoons filling in the middle of the spread masa lengthwise. Overlap husks and roll. Fold bottom of husk up 1½ inches. Place on flat surface with fold underneath. Repeat until all masa and filling has been used.

STEAM TAMALES: Steam cook tamales by placing them upright on the folded end in steamer. Place husks or foil on top; cover tightly and steam 2 to 3 hours. If no steamer is available, use a large cooking vessel such as a cold-pack canner. Line bottom with foil, as the husks scorch easily. Place tamales on rack or pan inside of a cooker and put a tin can, which has had both ends opened, in the center. Stack tamales around can and pour 4 to 5 inches of water in cooker. Steam 2 to 3 hours tightly covered. Tamales are done when one can be rolled clear and free of the husk.

Hints on Making Tamales

One pound masa to 1 pound meat makes approximately 1 dozen tamales. *The yield is determined by the size of the tamale. Filling may be prepared the day before and refrigerated. Beef as well as chicken or pork may be used if desired. Masa harina may be purchased at most stores. Canned red chile sauce may be substituted for fresh chile sauce, but the same rich flavor is not obtained. Finger tamales may be made for appetizers. In making tamales, the cut end of the corn husk is used as the top and the slim, pointed end as the bottom. Dried red chile may be purchased as mild or hot, whichever you prefer.*

✒ Aunt Linda's Healthy Sweet Tamales

4 cups masa harina
4 cups water
½ cup vegetable oil
1 tablespoon cinnamon
1 cup sugar
Pinch of salt
1 tablespoon baking powder
1 cup raisins
1 cup coconut
3 apples diced with skin
1 can pineapple tidbits without syrup
2 cups mozzarella cheese
1 cup pecan quarters
48 corn husks soaked in water

Place masa harina in a large bowl, add water and mix using a mixer. Mix together oil, cinnamon, sugar, and salt until they dissolve. Add to masa and mix, using a mixer on high for 2 minutes.

Add baking powder and mix on high speed for 5 minutes. Add remaining fruits, cheese, and pecans and mix them using a large spoon. Let the masa rest for 10 to 20 minutes.

Place a quarter cup of filling in the center of each husk lengthwise. Spread the masa and fold, the same way Senora Mari does in her recipe. Place in steamer with open ends up and steam for one hour and 15 minutes.

✒ Awesome Texas Chili Pie

2 pounds ground chuck
3 cloves garlic, minced
1 (12 to 14 ounce) can tomato sauce
1 (10 ounce) can Ro-tel
½ teaspoon salt
1 teaspoon ground oregano
1 tablespoon ground cumin
2 tablespoons chili powder
1 (14 ounce) can kidney beans, drained and rinsed
1 (14 ounce) can pinto beans, drained and rinsed
¼ cup masa (corn flour) or corn meal
½ cup warm water
Corn chips
Sharp cheddar cheese, grated
Diced red onion (optional)

Brown ground chuck with garlic in a pot over medium-high heat. Add tomato sauce, Ro-tel, salt, oregano, cumin, and chili powder. Cover and reduce heat to low. Simmer for 30 minutes.

Add drained and rinsed beans. Stir to combine, then cover and simmer for another 20 minutes.

Mix masa with water, then add to the chili. Stir to combine and simmer for a final 10 to 15 minutes. Set aside.

Serve by lining bowls with corn chips, and pile in chili, cheese, and diced onions.

A crowd-pleaser!

✎ Melanie's Texas Peachy Pecan Pie

Serves 8

¾ cup sugar
3 tablespoon flour
4 cups sliced peeled peaches
1½ tablespoons lemon juice
¼ cup brown sugar
¼ cup flour
½ cup chopped pecans
3 tablespoons butter
1 (9-inch) unbaked pie shell

Combine sugar and flour in large bowl. Add peaches and lemon juice. Combine brown sugar, flour, and pecans in small bowl. Cut in butter until crumbly. Sprinkle one-third pecan mixture over bottom of pie shell, cover with peach mixture, and sprinkle remaining pecan mixture over peaches. Bake until peaches are tender (about 40 minutes).

✎ Uncle Eddie's Favorite Chile Rellenos

6 fresh ancho, pasilla, or Anaheim chiles, or 1 (27 ounce) can poblano peppers or mild whole green chiles
½ pound Oaxaca cheese, thinly sliced
1 cup corn oil

6 raw eggs (separated)
¼ cup flour
Salt or Mexican seasoning to taste
2 cups salsa verde
2 cups homestyle Mexican salsa

Rinse the chiles. Preheat your oven to broil. Place the chiles in a 9x14" baking dish and place on the top shelf of your oven. Watch and listen closely. When the skins start to make popping sounds and to char and turn black in places, take the chiles out and flip them over. Be sure and use a potholder so you don't burn your hands!

When both sides are fairly evenly charred, remove them from the oven. Wrap each chile in a moist paper towel or place in a sealed plastic bag to steam. After a few minutes, check them. Once the skin comes off easily, peel each chile.

Cut a slit almost the full length of each chile. Make a small T across the top, by the stem. Pull out fibers and seeds (this is where the heat is) and replace with a slice of cheese. You can set these aside, for a few minutes or a few hours if you put them in the refrigerator.

Heat the oil in a skillet until a drop of water sizzles when dropped into the pan.

Whip the egg whites at high speed with an electric mixer, until stiff peaks have formed. Beat the egg yolks with one tablespoon flour and salt. Mix the yolks into egg whites and stir until you have a thick paste.

Roll the chiles in the remaining flour and dip each one in the egg batter. Coat evenly. Fry, seam side down on both sides until golden brown. Place on paper towels to drain.

Meanwhile, heat the salsa in a medium saucepan (either one or some of each). Place one or two rellenos on each plate and pour salsa over them. Serve them immediately.

Tips:

Fillings can be made ahead of time and refrigerated, then brought to room temperature before stuffing chiles. Fillings should be at room temperature or slightly chilled. If fillings are hot, the juices will flow out and cause the coating to slide off. Use enough filling to stuff each chile relleno as completely as possible, but not so much that the seam won't hold together.

M2G0610

P.O. 0000359765